"I want justice for my brother,"
Beau replied.

"No, you don't," Deb answered him coolly. "It's your pride making you do this. It's my belief that you just cannot bear anyone getting the better of you."

Beau's eyes were narrow slits. "My motives, Miss O'Hara, aren't yours to question."

"But your strategy is, since I'm to play a major part in it! How can I seriously pretend to be Paulette?" Her composure appeared to be cracking at last. She got to her feet and walked to and fro.

He, too, rose and came slowly toward her, and she was utterly shaken by the lithe movement of his lean body, by the sense of his power and strength. She'd never met anyone like him, and she knew she was in deep, deep trouble.

"You *will* be Paulette," he said. "We shall make you Paulette, in every way."

* * *

The Rake's Bargain
Harlequin® Historical #1210—November 2014

Author Note

In Regency times, troupes of actors roamed the English countryside from spring to fall, presenting a variety of entertainments to the usually appreciative crowds who gathered to see them. Deb O'Hara, heroine of *The Rake's Bargain,* leads one of these traveling troupes, and it's her dream to someday find a permanent theater for them in London. But first, she has to face a rather formidable opponent—Damian Beaumaris, known as Beau, who isn't impressed in the slightest by her theatrical skills!

As ever, I've found writing about the Regency era an absolute delight, and I really hope you enjoy Deb and Beau's story.

Lucy Ashford

—

The Rake's Bargain

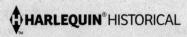
HARLEQUIN® HISTORICAL

Recycling programs
for this product may
not exist in your area.

ISBN-13: 978-0-373-29810-5

The Rake's Bargain

Copyright © 2014 by Lucy Ashford

Printed in U.S.A.

www.Harlequin.com

**Did you know that these novels are also
available as ebooks? Visit www.Harlequin.com.**

Chapter One

June 1803

Miss Deborah O'Hara pressed herself close to the ivy-covered mansion and tried not to flinch as the rain trickled off the brim of her cap and dripped steadily—coldly—down inside her jacket collar. She'd scrambled over the boundary wall and run here through the shrubbery, keeping her head low; but now she was able to look around. Now she was able to see that the acres of formal gardens stretching away on all sides were quite deserted—and as waterlogged as the overcast sky.

Hardgate Hall. The very name was enough to send shivers down her spine. Swiping fresh rain from her cheeks, she glanced up once more at the small window on the second floor that some servant must have carelessly left open. It was almost sixteen years since she'd last entered this house, a bewildered six-year-old clutching her mother's hand; though a few minutes later they were being hustled out again and Deb's mother was weeping.

'You made your choices!' Deb remembered Hugh

Palfreyman declaring harshly. 'You made your own bed, sister mine. And you can lie on it.'

Deb was twenty-two now and her mother had died long ago. But she'd never ever forgotten this place, and she always imagined it under grey skies, just as it was now.

She scanned the garden once more, trying to suppress her growing anxiety, and relaxed just a little when she saw two familiar figures hurrying towards her through the rain. 'Luke. Francis. There you are. I was beginning to think…'

'Think what, Miss Deb?' Young Luke's straggly blond hair was plastered to his face.

She was beginning to fear they might have been caught by Palfreyman's men. Deb said instead, 'You took your time. What news?'

'We looked to see if there was anyone around. Just as you told us to, Deborah.' This time it was the older one, Francis, who spoke. 'Though we were careful to keep under cover, always. And we've good news—it looks as if all the groundsmen have been ordered to spend the afternoon tidying up Palfreyman's glasshouses, on the far side of the south lawn.'

Deb nodded. 'So they'll not catch sight of us here. What about the guard dogs?'

Young Luke spoke up next. 'We heard them barking in the distance and they sound *big*.' He shivered. 'But they're kept in a yard close by the stables—though I've heard they're let loose after nightfall, when they prowl around the grounds with teeth so sharp they'd take a great lump out of your thigh, and—'

'Thank you, Luke,' Deb interrupted. 'That's enough.' *More than enough, in fact.* 'So we're safe for now?'

Francis tipped his black hat with the feather in it to gaze up at the vast house that loomed before them. 'It depends,' he said narrowly, 'on what you mean by "safe", Deborah.'

Deb sighed inwardly. Francis Calladine, almost twice Luke's age, was a stalwart friend, but he'd been dubious about Deb's plan from the start. Although it was Francis who'd spotted earlier, as they'd examined the house from the far side—the *safe* side—of the boundary wall, that the rooms to the north of the building looked dark and little used.

'And if you're really intent on breaking in,' he'd added, 'all that ivy growing up there is a burglar's delight.'

Deb's response had been instant. 'I'm no burglar!'

'You're planning on getting inside,' Francis had said quietly. 'Though why you're so intent on taking such a risk when the owner's a Justice of the Peace and has already threatened us all with prison remains a mystery to me.'

If Francis had known that Hugh Palfreyman was her uncle, he'd have been quite speechless. But by Deb's reckoning, desperate times called for desperate measures.

'I'm not turning back now, Francis.' Deb spoke with utter calmness, utter certainty. 'I'm always grateful for your advice, believe me. But I hope you've not forgotten that you promised my stepfather you'd trust me.'

'I also promised your stepfather that I'd keep you safe, Deborah,' said Francis, who was distinguishable always by his wide-brimmed hat and his ancient, rust-red coat. 'But I'll do as you say. Young Luke and I will be here, waiting for you—'

'No!'

'What?' This time Francis looked really outraged.

'*No.*' Deb shook her head decisively. 'I've changed my mind about you waiting for me here. It's just too risky.' No one at all was around, but it was very possible their luck wouldn't hold, especially if this rain eased off. And in that case—better for only her to be captured, rather than all three of them. 'I've decided,' she went on, 'that it would be a good idea for you and Luke to return to the horses and wait for me there.'

They'd ridden from Oxford by cutting through the Ashendale Forest and taking a track which brought them almost to the edge of Palfreyman's estate. There they'd left their three horses, carefully tethered, although the sturdy old creatures were most unlikely to gallop off.

Francis clearly didn't think much of Deb's instructions. 'You want us to just leave you here? But what if you get caught? By the servants, or by Palfreyman himself?'

As if she hadn't thought of that. 'And how on earth could the two of you do anything if I did?' she pointed out. 'You can help me get started—but then you must go, do you understand?'

'But…'

'What would my stepfather, Gerald, have said, Francis? What *did* he say to you, when he called the Lambeth Players together and spoke to us all for the very last time?' It was two years since Gerald O'Hara had died, but there was still a catch in her voice whenever she spoke his name.

Francis too looked affected. 'Mr O'Hara said he was leaving the Lambeth Players in your charge.'

'He also told you, I believe, that you were to all work

with me and heed me in every way.' Deb surveyed them both with her cool gaze. 'So are you going to wait for me in the woods?'

Luke glanced anxiously at Francis, who still hesitated. 'Very well,' Francis said at last. 'But—'

'Thank you—*both* of you,' Deb cut in quickly. 'And if I don't turn up in the woods by five, you're to ride back to Oxford and the others. Do you understand me?'

Francis's brow was growing dark again and he looked as if he were about to utter some fresh warning. Deb couldn't blame him for having doubts, because *she* certainly did. 'Remember, Francis! I only let you come with me on the condition that you obeyed me in *everything*. And what's the motto of the Lambeth Players?'

'Triumph over adversity!' declared Luke.

'Exactly. Now, the sooner I get up there—' she pointed at the rambling ivy '—the sooner I'll be back with you, safe and sound.'

To Deb's relief, not another objection was uttered. She could sense Luke's and Francis's tension as she grasped the ivy and began to climb, but she turned round from her perch and gave them a cheerful nod. 'Go, both of you. I'll be fine.'

She saw them cross the lawns in the rain, then weave through the sodden shrubbery. Any minute, she feared she might hear the barking of Hugh Palfreyman's guard dogs, or the shouts of his groundsmen, but, no; Luke and Francis made it to the wall and inwardly she cheered them on. *Up and over. That's the way.*

Taking a deep breath, Deb pulled down her cap over her thick chestnut curls and pressed on with the scariest and most necessary climb of her life.

* * *

Triumph over adversity. That was an apt motto for the troupe of travelling actors who moved between fairs and country markets each year from March to December, with their old carts full of costumes and scenery. The Lambeth Players were Deb's family and her life.

She'd initially resolved to complete her task today without telling a soul. But as ill luck would have it, sharp-eyed Francis, the senior actor, had spotted Deb saddling one of their horses outside the Angel Inn on the outskirts of Oxford where the Players were staying, and of course he wanted to know exactly where she was off to.

In the face of his determination—*we swore to Gerald O'Hara that we'd take care of you and we will!*—she'd been forced at last to tell him that she was riding to Hardgate Hall. That she was, to be precise, planning to enter Hardgate Hall in secret—though she refused to tell him precisely why. Glibly she'd dismissed the dangers—it would be an easy matter, Deb assured Francis, for her to get in and out of the house in no time at all.

But Francis's face was a picture. In fact, he was horrified, and he made so much fuss that she at last consented to let Francis and Luke accompany her on the ride through the Ashendale Forest. And here she was; though she was beginning to have the sinking feeling that this whole idea of hers was a bad mistake.

And the rain didn't help. What if she slipped, or the ivy gave way? It was a long way to fall. Or what if someone came round this side of the house? A gardener, or even a gamekeeper with a gun... Stop it. *Stop it.* Carefully finding footholds with the toes of her lace-up boots—*don't look down, whatever you do*—she could only be grateful she was as wiry and nimble as a boy.

'Why, there's nothin' to you, lass. You're all skin and bone,' the innkeeper's wife had declared last night, slamming down a bowl of rather greasy stew before her in the shabby public room of the inn. 'You need to put on a bit of flesh if you're to catch yourself a man!'

Just at that moment, her own spouse—a surly creature who was over-fond of his homebrewed ale—had come in, and Deb thought, *Catch myself a man like yours? No, thank you.*

Deb didn't want a husband. Her dream was to establish a theatre for the Players—a *proper* theatre, in London—instead of them having to tramp round the country every season. And after today, she would be able to concentrate on her dream once more. *Hugh Palfreyman, you might be a Justice of the Peace. But you are nothing to me*, she breathed as she clambered on up the ivy. *And I will teach you that you interfere with the Lambeth Players at your peril*!

At last, the small window was within her reach. Heaving it open, she hauled herself in, knowing that at last she was in the forbidden domain of her uncle—and not a sound pierced the silence, except for the thudding of her own heart.

Her mother had wept after that visit to Hardgate Hall sixteen years ago and Deb had crept into her arms 'Mama? *Mama?*'

'My darling girl.' Her mother had hugged her tightly. 'I shouldn't have taken you there. But I'd thought—I'd hoped…'

Deb couldn't understand how anyone could want to make her sweet mother cry. 'Is he a bad man, that man in the big house?'

'That man is my brother,' her mother said quietly. 'He is many years older than me and became master of Hardgate Hall when I was still a child. I thought he might have changed. I was wrong.'

'But why was he so cruel to you, Mama?'

'I think he is very unhappy. I think he always was. He was a solitary creature and used to go out for long rides alone, or lock himself away in a room upstairs for hours on end. I think he had secrets.' She'd added, half to herself, 'And what those secrets were, I never wished to find out.'

Deb heard her mother recounting the same tale to Gerald O'Hara months later. *I used to wonder why he allowed no one but himself in that room up in the north wing. None of the servants ever entered it. The room was on the second floor; the door was locked and only he had the key…*

Deb progressed steadily along the passageway, trying door after door; only to find that not one was locked, and each room she peered into contained nothing but old furniture shrouded with dust sheets.

And then—just as she was beginning to fear that she'd got everything wrong—she came to a door that wouldn't open. Swiftly she pulled out her small, sharp-pointed knife, used it to slip the lock and stepped inside, alert and aware. In the centre of the room stood a big old mahogany desk, behind it a leather armchair. Heavy red-velvet curtains half-shrouded the windows and every wall was lined from floor to ceiling with books.

This was a private library, a secret library. But it wasn't

because her uncle Hugh Palfreyman was a scholar of the classics or some other clever subject. Far from it.

A little over a week ago Deb had visited the stall of a travelling bookseller at the Oxford market, for she was constantly on the lookout for any half-forgotten plays for her company to use. Comedies, tragedies, it didn't matter which, as long as they kept the crowds entertained.

'Aren't you the young lady from the Lambeth Players?' the bookseller had enquired. 'I saw your lot doing that fight scene from *Tamburlaine* on the village green the other night. By heaven, it was a treat.'

'I'm so glad you enjoyed our performance,' said Deb politely. She glanced through a few more books laid out on his stall—no, nothing much of interest there—then went to investigate a box at the back. But the bookseller dived across to stop her.

'Oh, no, missy. Those books in there ain't for the likes of you. They're—' he coughed '—they're some serious works of literature. For my private customers only.'

Deb had already glimpsed two of the titles. Serious works of literature? That was a joke. *Artistic Treasures of Venus. Classical Collections for Gentlemen of Discernment*... She would stake her life that every single one of them was packed with erotic prints and libidinous tales.

'I'm sure you'll get a very good price for them,' she told the bookseller demurely and moved on.

But a little later, when she happened to be passing back that way, she saw the bookseller deep in conversation with someone else, and her heart began hammering against her chest. She'd been only six years old when she last saw him; but Hugh Palfreyman had changed very little, in Deb's opinion, except that perhaps his beaked nose was more protuberant and his little pursed-up mouth even tighter. As Deb watched, she saw the glint of coins being passed. Saw the bookseller reach furtively into that box at the back for several slim volumes, which he proceeded to wrap in brown paper, then give to Hugh Palfreyman.

Palfreyman hurried away, while Deb stood absorbing the full impact of what she'd just witnessed.

Her mother's brother—a Justice of the Peace—was a connoisseur of the kind of literature that was described in polite circles as 'stimulating'. *Well, button my boots*, as her stepfather, Gerald O'Hara, would say.

Deb found herself thinking rather a lot of other things about her Uncle Palfreyman as she stood in the confines of his secret library while the rain pounded against the window. *Hypocrite* was the most polite of them. Still listening hard for the sound of anyone approaching, she tiptoed over to the bookshelves and eased out some volumes to lay on the desk.

Not all the books were English—some were in French and some in Italian, but—*oh, my*. It didn't really matter in the slightest what language they were in, because there wasn't much writing anyway, and the pictures were just—*well*. Deb's eyes widened, but at the same time triumph swelled within her heart. For she'd realised that—incredibly enough—each volume had a gilt-edged bookplate just inside the front cover on which was carefully inscribed the owner's name— Hugh Palfreyman.

What a fool, Deb marvelled. To keep all this so secret, then provide such glaring evidence of possession.
What a gift, for her.

She'd hoped never to have to come into contact with
her uncle again, since he'd banished her and her mother
from his house. But all that had changed; for one Satur-
day, almost two weeks ago, a sweet old lady had sought
Deb out at the inn and told her that Shakespeare was her
husband's passion, but he was too frail to visit any of
the Players' outdoor performances. Would one or two
of the actors be kind enough to visit him, she asked, and
perhaps read out some of his favourite lines?

Deb and three others had gone to him the very next
afternoon and had performed the last, lovely scene of
The Tempest. The old gentleman's faded eyes had lit
up with pleasure, and afterwards his grateful wife had
tried to press money on the actors, but they'd refused.
Apart from knowing anyway that it was illegal for them
to perform on a Sunday, they wouldn't have dreamt of
taking the coins, because that sort of performance and
the pleasure it brought was beyond price.

But somehow, Hugh Palfreyman had got to hear
about it. And he was chairman of the local magistrates.

'Acting, on the Sabbath Day,' he'd apparently
stormed—Deb had heard talk of his rage all around
Oxford. 'It's a direct contravention of the law!' And
he'd threatened the Lambeth Players with a crippling
fine, or even gaol.

*Thank goodness Palfreyman didn't know that the
leader of the Lambeth Players was his own niece.*
Swiftly Deb selected three small but explicit volumes,
then she sat at Palfreyman's desk and, after pulling a

clean sheet of notepaper and a pencil from her inner pocket, she carefully wrote a letter.

To Mr Hugh Palfreyman
This is to inform you that it is very much in your
interest to take back the accusations that you re-
cently made against the Lambeth Players. I en-
close something to explain why. Please confirm
in a letter that the threats you made will be com-
pletely withdrawn, and leave the same letter be-
neath the stone horse trough beside the wall of
St Mary's churchyard, by ten o'clock tomorrow
morning at the latest.

Then Deb drew out her pocket knife and leafed through the pages of the books she'd selected. Oh, my goodness—the Italian one was the worst, she decided. It was illustrated by someone called Aretino, and her eyes widened again as she looked at picture after picture. Was that really anatomically possible? Carefully she detached one page—*I'm not going to look at it, they're all just too dreadful*—then she folded the sheet inside her letter, sealed it with a wafer she'd brought, and wrote Palfreyman's name on the outside. The books and the letter fitted—just—into her inside pocket.

After that, climbing back out through the window and down the ivy-clad wall was easy. Running stealthily to the front door—keeping to the wall and ducking below windows—wasn't so easy, and she heaved a sigh of relief as she pushed her sealed message into the letter box there. Then she ran as fast as she could for the shrubbery, weaving through the tangle of lilacs and rose bushes as the rain poured down, and giving a flash of a smile as she climbed nimbly over the boundary wall.

Job done, she silently congratulated herself.

As Damian Beaumaris rode steadily along the track through the woods, the rain streamed off his multi-caped greatcoat and down the flanks of his big bay gelding as if someone was hurling buckets of water over both of them.

A lesser man might have been put off—but not Beaumaris, who was known as Beau to his friends. When he'd first written to Palfreyman two weeks ago, to demand an immediate meeting in London, Palfreyman had tried to wriggle out of it by pleading that ill health prevented him from leaving his Oxfordshire mansion. So Beau had promptly ordered his business secretary, the ever-efficient Nathaniel Armitage, to write back and explain that since Palfreyman found himself indisposed, Beau would travel to Oxfordshire.

My employer trusts, wrote Armitage in his careful script, *that it will be convenient if he arrives at Hardgate Hall on the thirteenth of June, at four o'clock precisely.*

Armitage had pointed out to Beau that the thirteenth of June just happened to be a Friday. Beau had swiftly responded that as his long-standing secretary, Armitage ought to know that superstition played no part whatsoever in his meticulously ordered life. Though after Armitage had gone, Beau reflected that the day and date certainly boded ill for Hugh Palfreyman, who Beau had concluded was as cowardly and conniving a wretch as he had ever come across.

On the morning of the twelfth of June, Beau had set

off on the journey to Oxfordshire in his brand-new and speedy travelling carriage, driven with great pride by his faithful coachman, William Barry. After spending the first night at the Greyhound Hotel in Reading, Beau and William departed early with fresh horses, Beau's plan being to lunch at noon in Oxford, then proceed to Hardgate Hall. But as the spires of Oxford came within sight, the rear axle of the coach began to make ominous grinding noises.

William Barry took any such event as an insult to his own skill and, after pulling the horses to a halt, jumped down to investigate. Beau quickly followed.

'It's not good,' William pronounced, shaking his head. 'Not good at all.'

He proceeded to nurse the vehicle as far as a blacksmith's on the outskirts of Oxford, where the proprietor, Joe Hucksby, also examined the curricle with a deepening frown.

'I'd say this axle needs a new cross-pinion, sir,' he said to Beau, after scrambling up from beneath the vehicle. 'And three hours is about the fastest time that my lads can do it. You see, with a top-notch vehicle such as this, everything has to be right and tight as can be, so maybe, sir, you'd like to go on into town and take a nice meal at one of the inns there? Especially since it's starting to rain.'

'I'm afraid I can't wait. I have an appointment at Hardgate Hall this afternoon.'

'You're visiting Mr Palfreyman?' Joe Hucksby looked surprised. 'Well, if that isn't the oddest thing! We just happen to have a fine riding horse of his stabled here. Mr Palfreyman left it yesterday to have it shoed, and—'

'You've got Palfreyman's horse here? Is it fit to ride?'

'Why, yes, sir! In fact, Mr Palfreyman asked me to send one of my lads over to the Hall with it this very afternoon, as it happens.'

'Then there's no need to send one of your lads. I'll ride his horse to Hardgate Hall myself.'

Joe Hucksby looked startled. 'It's a spirited beast, sir. Took two of my lads to hold it while I did the shoeing—'

'I'll take it,' Beau repeated decisively. He was clad anyway in buckskins and riding boots and was impatient to get on with his journey. But he could see that William was fretting.

'Should I see if there's another horse, so I can come with you—sir?' his coachman suggested quietly.

Beau shook his head. 'Better if you stay around here, William, and check that the job's being done properly. Oh, and you could take the opportunity to find a decent inn nearby. Book us two rooms for the night and get yourself a meal while you're at it.'

'But you, sir? You haven't eaten since breakfast!'

'Hugh Palfreyman's bound to offer me refreshment of one kind or another. And, William—don't tell them any more than you have to about me or my business at Hardgate Hall, you understand?' He'd already instructed William to address him by nothing but *sir* for the whole of this journey.

As William nodded, Beau turned back to the blacksmith. 'I'll return for my coach later this evening, Hucksby. Here's some payment in advance.' He'd thrust his hand in his coat pocket and drew out some coins to put in the man's big fist.

'Well, that's mighty obliging of you, Mr...'

'My name's Beaumaris.'

The blacksmith nodded, clearly disappointed that he wasn't a lord at the very least. 'Thank you kindly, Mr Beaumaris, sir. And I've no doubt that Mr Palfreyman would himself suggest that you take his horse if he were here, yes, indeed.'

Beau privately doubted it very much. But within ten minutes, the horse in question—a handsome bay gelding with a white blaze down its forehead—was saddled up and ready, though just as Beau was about to mount, the blacksmith darted away and returned with a sturdy whip.

'You might be needing this, sir,' Joe Hucksby pronounced. 'Mr Palfreyman warned us this bay can be a stubborn brute and don't like being told what to do.'

Already realising that the horse was trying to back away in pure terror at the sight of the whip—and that the blacksmith's lads had gathered to watch the entertainment—Beau pushed the implement back into Joe Hucksby's hands. 'A man who needs to use a whip like that,' he said flatly, 'doesn't deserve to be entrusted with any animal.'

William nodded his approval and Beau mounted, aware that the horse, on feeling his weight in the saddle, was already sidling and snorting with fear. Beau soothed the beast and thought, *Damn. What has Palfreyman done to this animal?*

He had a pretty good idea, for if he looked back at the horse's flanks, he could see the marks where the whip had been used to lash the beast only recently. *Palfreyman,* he thought grimly, *if my opinion of you wasn't already at rock bottom, it certainly would be by now.* He tensed his muscular thighs to let the gelding know that he was in control, while at the same time he stroked its neck. 'There. There,' he murmured. 'Easy does it, now.'

The horse at last moved forward, showing obedience, even willingness. Beau was rather pleased to see the blacksmith and his boys gazing after him, openmouthed. 'Which is the best way to reach Hardgate Hall?' Beau called to them over his shoulder.

'The track through the Ashendale Forest is quickest, sir,' one of the lads piped up. 'You'd best take the road for Reading—you'll see it just past the church. At the first crossroads you turn left, and then you want to head over the bridge and follow the path into the woods—'

At that point the blacksmith interrupted him. 'Oh, I wouldn't advise that way *at all*, Mr Beaumaris, I really wouldn't. It's easy to get lost and there are sometimes footpads.'

'Is this track through the forest quicker than the turnpike road?'

'Much quicker, sir.' The lad was still eager. 'It takes—oh, at least a mile off your journey!'

Then that's the path I'll take. And Beau was on his way.

The lad's instructions were easy to follow and Beau was pleased to discover that the big bay, once he had its trust, was an energetic and speedy mount. He was even more pleased when he looped the reins over one hand and with the other delved for his pocket watch, to find that it was not yet half past three—there was still time to arrive punctually at Hardgate Hall. The one factor he hadn't bargained on was the rain, which drove straight into his face and was becoming heavier by the minute, slowing his pace; but he never once thought of turning round, because this meeting with Palfreyman was long overdue. Palfreyman had questions to answer and consequences to face.

Beau's frown deepened as he remembered the day of Simon's funeral just two months ago, when the rain had fallen as relentlessly as it did today on the cortège of black funeral carriages and his brother's oak coffin.

Enough of that wretch Palfreyman's feeble excuses. It's time to meet the coward face to face. Beau urged the bay gelding on through ancient oaks, aware that the trees were growing thicker all around him; but the path was clear enough and so he was taking little heed of the dank undergrowth on either side, which was foolish of him.

Because in his haste he had completely failed to see the two shadowy figures who had watched him earlier from behind a thicket of birch when he'd stopped to check the time. Failed now to see the twine tautly stretched between two saplings on either side of the path ahead of him—until it was too late.

One moment he was making good speed along the forest track. The next—disaster. The big bay stumbled badly and, though Beau wrestled to keep the beast upright, within moments he'd gone crashing to the ground.

Chapter Two

Loping steadily through the woods, Deb paused to brush down her kersey jacket and corduroy breeches, which had picked up a fine coating of pine needles when she'd landed on the other side of Palfreyman's boundary wall just now.

On the *safe* side of Palfreyman's boundary wall. She crammed her cap more securely over her curls and set off again towards the clearing where their horses were, weaving her way between the oak trees and the birch saplings, and even allowing herself a quick smile as she imagined Hugh Palfreyman's face when he read that letter. When he saw the page she'd cut out.

She grinned, but she felt revulsion too. Ever since she'd got clear of that place, she'd been vigorously inhaling the fresh air to rid her lungs of the musty odours that lurked in Palfreyman's secret room. And she found herself wondering again—why would her mother have even *wanted* to be reconciled with a brother whose cruelty had driven her from her home in the first place?

It wasn't as if her mother had been unhappy with her new life. In fact, Deb remembered her as being full of

love both for her daughter and for her husband, Gerald
O'Hara, actor and manager of the Lambeth Players.
Deb too had loved her caring and intelligent stepfather
dearly; but two years ago had come a fresh blow, for
Gerald had fallen prey to a debilitating lung sickness
and had left the responsibility of the Players to her.

'No. You can't leave me in charge, Gerald. I'm too
young!' she'd pleaded as she'd crouched by his sickbed,
feeling frightened and alone. *Don't die*, she'd murmured
under her breath to the man who'd truly been a father
to her. *Please. Don't you leave me as well.*

'You can do it, my brave lass.' Even though Gerald
was desperately weak by then, he'd reached to clasp her
hand tightly. 'You've been holding the company together
ever since my damned sickness started—don't think I
haven't noticed how everybody comes to ask for your
opinion. *Ask Miss Deb,* they say. *She'll know.*'

'But Francis Calladine—shouldn't he be in charge?
He's the senior actor, and he used to perform at Drury
Lane...'

'And he never tires of telling everyone so.' A wry
smile lifted Gerald's wan face. 'No—Francis is a fine
man for tragedy, but what the people want is *entertainment*, and you have an instinct for providing it. In addi-
tion, you can act every bit as well as any of those fancy
ladies at Drury Lane.'

'But to be in charge, Gerald. I couldn't—'

'One day,' Gerald interrupted, 'you'll take London by
storm, my lass. One day...' He'd begun coughing again
and Deb, distraught, had held a glass of water to his lips.

The Lambeth Players were no more than a humble
travelling company. But Deb and Gerald dreamed of
establishing themselves in London and a rich backer

was the answer, Gerald had often told her; a rich and generous backer who would buy them a lease for one of the numerous small theatres on the edge of the city. 'It needn't be a fancy affair,' Gerald said. 'But think, Deb, of the plays we could put on, in our very own place!'

The rest of the actors were content with touring the usual theatrical circuits every year, setting up their stage at fairs and race meetings to entertain the crowds with their varied miscellany of comedies, songs and drama. Shakespeare was always a favourite of Gerald's, but an ancient statute forbade minor theatrical companies like theirs to perform any Shakespeare play in full, so Gerald O'Hara had taught his players to pick out prime scenes only: Macbeth and the three witches, Henry V's speech before the battle of Agincourt, and the balcony scene from *Romeo and Juliet*. By starting their shows with brief acts of comedy and acrobatics, Gerald was able to describe their performances as 'entertainments' and the crowds came in droves.

'It's like offering an all-too-brief taste of a banquet,' Gerald had once said to Deb. 'But some day, when we get that theatre of our own, we'll perform the whole play—and we'll have all of London society at our feet!'

But then Gerald died. Losing her mother at such a young age had been heartbreaking, but now Deb had to face life without her beloved stepfather, who had been her guide and her inspiration for as long as she could remember. Kneeling by his graveside the day after the funeral, she'd whispered aloud, 'I can't take charge of the Players, Gerald. I know it was your wish—but I'm only twenty and I'm too young. I can't follow you. I simply cannot do it.'

She'd tried to explain as much to the others later that

evening, when the Players had gathered in a tavern to solemnly discuss their plans now that Gerald was gone. It was Francis, loyal Francis, who'd raised a cheer for her and called out, 'Who else but an O'Hara should be in charge of us all?'

And they wouldn't take no for an answer. The Lambeth Players had given her their trust and in return she was prepared to risk everything for them—it was as simple as that. She'd been truly touched by the loyalty of Francis and Luke in coming with her today to Hardgate Hall, obeying her orders even though Francis clearly had grave doubts.

I've succeeded, she looked forward to telling him. *I've succeeded*.

She quickened her pace as she realised that the trees were beginning to thin out a little. There they were, Luke and Francis, standing in the clearing with their backs to her, engrossed in conversation, while a little distance away the old mare and the two ponies gently grazed…

Deb froze.

Beside them was a horse she'd never seen before. A fine big bay, with a white blaze down his forehead. A horse of quality. She felt her heart-rate falter; then she caught sight of something that really made her blood freeze in her veins. In the centre of the clearing lay the prone figure of a man. His wrists and booted legs were bound with cord, and a white silk neckerchief— *his own*?—had been used to blindfold him. He wasn't moving.

Dear God, was he even breathing?

Deb turned slowly to her two companions, who had seen her now and were hurrying towards her. 'Luke, Francis. What on earth…?'

'We got him, Miss Deb!' cried Luke jubilantly. And Francis was nodding towards their captive. 'We had to act quickly. You see, he was galloping along the track, making straight for Hardgate Hall. And we knew we had to do something, Deborah, or you would have run into him.'

Deb looked at the bound, blindfolded man with a growing sense of—no other word for it—panic. 'Who exactly do you think that man is?' she breathed.

'Why, he's Hugh Palfreyman, of course!' Luke delivered this news with an air of triumph.

Deb gazed down at their captive and found herself speechless again. The man was around thirty, she guessed: lean, fit and long-limbed. Even though he lay sprawled and unconscious in the mud she could see for herself that he was dressed like a gentleman, a *rich* gentleman, in a heavy cambric greatcoat, handcrafted leather boots and a lawn shirt with lace ruffles at his wrists. His hat had fallen off and he had black hair, gleaming and thick. As for his face...

She couldn't see his eyes because of course he was blindfolded. But the rest of his features—his uncompromising jaw, his long nose, his firm mouth—were so downright *arrogant* that she felt her stomach lurch with renewed fear.

'That man,' she pronounced to Luke and Francis, 'is not Hugh Palfreyman.' Her every word was etched with a sincere and furious despair.

Luke's jaw dropped in youthful dismay. 'But he must be, Miss Deb.'

'Why?' she asked with deceptive calm.

'Because he was on Palfreyman's horse!' explained Luke. 'Do you see it?' He pointed. 'Francis and I were admiring it only this morning in Oxford. A blacksmith was shoeing it and it took two lads to hold the beast steady. One of them told us afterwards whose it was…'

His voice trailed away when he saw Deb's expression. 'And do you really, truly think, Luke, that there's only one bay horse with a white blaze in all of Oxfordshire?' Both of them stood silent; Deb pointed at the man wearily. 'He is *not* Hugh Palfreyman. He's nothing like Hugh Palfreyman. And anyway, what if he was? Since when have we been highway robbers? Why did you have to knock him out cold?'

Francis looked affronted. 'We only wanted to stop his horse and perhaps delay him a little in case he met you. But he was going at such a pace, and so—and so…'

'He fell off with an almighty crash, Miss Deb,' supplied Luke.

Deb shuddered. 'And then?'

Francis took over the tale. 'And then we thought we'd better blindfold him and tie him up, of course. Because we couldn't let him see us when he came round, could we?'

'*If* he comes round,' said Deb. How could they? How could they have done something so foolhardy?

Luke looked nervous now. 'He's still breathing and everything. We checked!'

Deb sank to her knees beside the prone man and ran her hands swiftly over his arms and shoulders.

As far as she could tell, he didn't appear to be badly hurt. None of his limbs looked twisted or broken. There was no blood anywhere, and when she put her fingers to his wrist, his pulse was strong and even. But—oh, God, what would happen when he regained his senses and found himself trussed up tight as a turkey? And—who on earth was he?

Feeling even more flustered after touching him—*goodness, he was big, he was powerful*—she reached gingerly into his coat pocket, where she found a gold fob watch on a chain. She turned it carefully in her fingers. It looked old and very valuable, and on the back was a faded inscription. She held it up to catch the murky daylight and read the name aloud: *Damian Beaumaris*.

Whoever Damian Beaumaris might be, Deb knew with absolute certainty that they'd just made themselves a new and extremely dangerous enemy.

Beau was aware of aches and pains in every limb. His head hurt as if someone had swung a hammer at it. The last thing he remembered was riding through Ashendale Forest on Palfreyman's horse, making good speed, until he'd spotted, too late, a length of cord stretched right across his path. And now he found that he was blindfolded, he was well and truly tied up, and he was lying on the cold, muddy ground.

Muttered voices drifted across the clearing, and the owners of those voices sounded mighty worried. *So they should be.* Beau's jaw was tightly set. Then he frowned again, because some other faint memory lingered in his mind: a memory of the lightest of hands fluttering over his clothing, a finger touching his wrist. He thought he'd inhaled the delicate scent of lemons, and remembered a woman's soft hair brush his cheek...

And he needed to pull his thoroughly scattered wits together this minute—because the voices were moving closer. He lay very still, assessing his predicament—bound, blindfolded and half-stunned—*not good*. His

borrowed horse had been deliberately tripped up, and
Beau had been thrown; but seconds before he fell, he'd
glimpsed two men peering at him from the undergrowth—a middle-aged man in a scruffy red coat and
black hat, and a callow fair-haired youth. It must be one
of that pair of scoundrels—he guessed the older one—
whom he heard now, muttering anxiously, 'But that bay
horse. We really thought it was Palfreyman's, you see.'

That was interesting enough; but the next voice Beau
heard set his senses into full alert. Because it belonged
to a girl, and she sounded very, very anxious—with
good reason, Beau reflected grimly. 'Francis Calladine,'
she declared, 'if I hear your excuses repeated once more,
I swear I'll tie you up with your own ropes. This man
is *not* Palfreyman. His name is Damian Beaumaris.
And what, in heaven's name, are we to do with him?'

A case of mistaken identity, then—they'd thought
he was Palfreyman, who it appeared was no friend of
theirs. One thing was for certain—he was, at the moment, completely in their power. But Beau did not intend
that particular circumstance to last for much longer.

He heard the voice of the older man again—he
sounded just as worried as the girl. 'Perhaps we should
untie him and leave quickly, Deborah. When he comes
round, he'll just imagine he was thrown by accident.
He won't even know he was our prisoner.'

'But what if he doesn't come round?' The girl
again—*Deborah*. Beau envisaged his trio of captors
scratching their heads. 'What if he's truly hurt, Francis?' she went on. 'What if we leave him here and—he
doesn't recover?'

In the silence that ensued, Beau found himself oc-

cupied by a thought that had been forming in his mind
since the moment he heard the girl's voice.

Most of the females who travelled with bands of
highway robbers were as rough as their menfolk. But
something wasn't quite right about this one. She spoke
well. She had an educated voice… He stirred as far as
his bonds would allow, and let out a slight groan. Almost immediately, as he'd hoped, he heard the girl gasping, 'Oh, no. Did you hear that? He is in pain!' There
was a rustle of clothes close to his ear, and once more
he inhaled the faint lemon scent of soap and freshly
washed hair as the girl bent down and placed her hand
on his forehead; a cool, tender hand…

She'll be ugly as sin, he warned himself. She was
bound to be a painted, snaggle-toothed whore who had
been bedded by the lot of them. Yet she spoke in a way
that would be more at home in the drawing rooms of
London than amongst a nest of vagabonds. He chided
himself mentally. Whatever she was up to, no female
was going to get the better of him. He lay very still,
feigning unconsciousness once more.

'We really should be off.' The older man's voice was
taut with anxiety. 'We could perhaps ride back to the
nearest inn and mention that we glimpsed a stray horse
in the forest. Then they would send someone out to investigate…'

'We cannot leave him while he's unconscious!' The
girl's voice was authoritative. 'This is my plan, Francis.
I'm going to loosen our prisoner's ropes and wait for
him to regain his senses. As soon as he starts to do so,
and we can be sure that he's going to be all right, we'll
ride off as quickly as we can.'

'But what if he gets on his horse and gallops after

us?' This was the younger lad speaking. 'That bay of his could catch ours in no time!'

The girl had an answer for that as well. 'We'll lead his horse with us—just for a half a mile or so. Francis, can you go and see to the horses *now*? And, Luke, it's really important that you remove every trace of our stay here—for example, the remains of that campfire you and Francis lit over there.'

Luke said suddenly, 'I left some of my markers in case you had trouble finding us, Miss Deb.'

Deb frowned. 'Markers?'

'The sign for the Lambeth Players,' explained Luke. 'You know—the initials L and P, made with twigs. I made a trail, from the track to this clearing. I was only trying to help!'

'You idiot, Luke,' said Francis.

'You'd better go and remove them,' said Deb in exasperation. *Luke and his games.* 'Every single one. And as soon as you've checked round everywhere, we'll leave—but *only* when I'm sure this man is going to be all right, do you understand?'

They left, and Deb walked slowly towards their prisoner. Only now that Luke and Francis were out of sight did she feel that she could allow herself to give way to true, sick anxiety.

She dropped to her knees at the man's side, noting that he lay as still as ever in his bonds apart from the rhythmic rise and fall of his broad chest—*thank God he was still breathing steadily.* She rapidly tried to summarise what she knew about him, which wasn't a great deal, except that his name was Damian Beaumaris, and he was rich—she could tell that just at a glance, not only because of his fine attire and gold pocket watch, but because of that indefinable air of arrogance the rich had, yes, even when they were tied up on the ground and unconscious.

Luke and Francis had only been trying to help her, she reminded herself rather desperately. And they'd been right, in that if he *had* been Palfreyman, and had met her climbing back over his boundary wall, he would have seized her on the spot, found the books on her, and her plan would have been ruined. She could have been in dire trouble indeed...

And wasn't she now?

Deb tried her best to control her panicking thoughts. At least Mr Beaumaris was alive, and had no idea who they were. And thank goodness there was no sign of blood. But she could see quite a lot else about him—a bit too much, unfortunately, for his expensive riding coat had fallen right back, and beneath his white shirt and buckskin breeches she couldn't help but note that he displayed a formidably muscled body. Her eyes were reluctantly dragged again and again to that strong, square jaw already dark with stubble, and she found herself thinking that Peggy Daniels, the pretty actress who played most of the heroines for the Lambeth Players, would have been in raptures over him. 'Now, *there's* a fine figure of a man,' she would have exclaimed.

Deb sighed, and prepared to put his gold watch back in his pocket; but just at that moment Mr Beaumaris groaned, and she almost shot into the air.

'My God,' he rasped. 'My God, whoever you are, I'll see the lot of you in Newgate for this.'

Quickly Deb shoved his watch in her own pocket and moistened her dry lips. *Thank goodness he was still blindfolded.* 'My friends made a mistake, Mr Beaumaris.' She found herself defiantly tilting her chin, as if he could see her. 'You see, they thought you were someone else. Someone who's done us a great deal of harm. That was why they tied you up, but it was all an accident, I do assure you, sir—'

'Accident! Now, there's a Banbury tale,' he exploded. 'Your friends tied a cord across the path.'

He heard her catch her breath. 'I'm sorry,' she said quietly. 'Truly sorry you were hurt. And please stay still, Mr Beaumaris, there's really no point in trying to fight your bonds. I'll set you free in good time, you have my word on it.'

'Your word? You expect me to believe your promises?'

'It would be as well for you,' she said in her sweet clear voice, 'if you did.'

Who the deuce was she? Beau wondered anew. She sounded well educated—and yet she was clearly in charge of the men who'd landed him in this mess. He'd heard them calling themselves the Lambeth Players, but what kind of vagabonds could they be? Two rogues and a girl... Cursing his blindfold, he wished he could cure himself of the delusion that this little witch actually sounded rather exquisite.

'You claim I was captured by mistake,' he said flatly. 'Perhaps you don't mind telling me how you know my name?'

She said in a very small voice, 'I found your watch.'

'You rifled my pockets.'

'Only to find out who you were!' She'd rallied now.

'And now you know,' Beau said. 'But I'll give you a warning. If you're planning on demanding a ransom, don't waste your time. Because if anything happens to me, you'll not be able to find a safe hiding place in the entire realm.'

There was a brief silence, then he heard her say quietly, 'I suppose that's what happens, when you're rich and important. You *matter*. You go through life issuing threats and never listening to what other people are wanting to tell you. Not even *trying* to understand.'

Beau found himself frowning at the intensity of her words. Then he froze again—because he felt small cool fingers fluttering around his shirt and his greatcoat, and he swore under his breath because his body was disconcertingly aware that this young, sweet-scented female was far too close for comfort. Deborah, they'd called her. Or Miss Deb. *She'll be a pock-marked Jezebel*, he reminded himself. She couldn't be anything else, living the life she must lead.

'There,' she announced crisply. 'Your watch is back in your coat pocket, Mr Beaumaris. Let me repeat that we are *not* thieves. And no one regrets this incident more than I do, believe me.'

He could almost have been amused. 'So that's it, is it? You offer your sincerest apologies on behalf of your two henchmen, and you expect me to forget this whole business?'

'That's more or less it. But I have to ask you a question first, Mr Beaumaris. Are you a man who can be trusted to keep his word?'

What sheer, incredible insolence! He clenched his teeth. 'Most would say so, yes. But let me give you a warning. I assume you're going to ask me to promise some kind of clemency—but I don't take kindly to highway robbery. And I'm not going to enter into any kind of negotiation until you unfasten these damned ropes.'

'Then I'm afraid we're at stalemate, Mr Beaumaris,' she answered calmly. 'You may as well know that I have a knife—a very sharp knife—in my hand, and I can free you in moments. But before I do so, I want you to swear not to set the law on my friends.'

Beau really didn't know if she was pretending to be innocent, or stupid, or both. Aloud he drawled, 'You're joking, I hope.'

'I'm hoping you are willing to accept that my men made a genuine mistake. Otherwise…'

Again she paused, and he tried to picture her face.

'I really am going to have to leave you tied up here in the woods,' she went on, 'until someone finds you. And I cannot imagine that a gentleman accustomed to life's comforts as you must be would relish the prospect of being out here as darkness falls. The woods can get *extremely* cold and damp at night, even in June. Well? Do you want me to loosen your bonds or not?'

She sounded almost cheerful.

Beau was usually calm in the face of danger, but this was an altogether different kind of peril; indeed, he was hard put not to flinch as she leaned close and ran her hands over the ropes at his wrists. Damn it, could he feel a few soft strands of her hair brushing against his forehead? What colour was it—black, brown, or a brassy blonde? What colour were her eyes? Was she tall and slender, or short and plump—and why in God's name was he even bothering to *think* of such absurd trivialities?

'I've probably caught a cold already,' said Beau. 'And

if I die of pneumonia, I hope you realise it will be the gallows for you and your partners in crime.'

She'd moved back a little, he sensed, but not because she was afraid, oh, no; in fact, he even heard her emit a husky chuckle. 'Pneumonia? An exaggeration, surely, Mr Beaumaris. As a matter of fact…'

He could just imagine her gazing down at him thoughtfully.

'I don't think,' she concluded, 'that I've ever seen anyone who looked as healthy a specimen as you. Now, if you want me to cut these ropes, you really must swear not to set the law on my friends.'

The silence that followed was deafening. 'Mr Beaumaris? It really could be *very* uncomfortable for you out here in the forest. And I have a dreadful feeling that it's going to start raining again, any minute—'

'I swear!'

'You swear what, Mr Beaumaris?'

'I swear,' Beau pronounced through gritted teeth, 'that I'll not set the law on your friends.'

He thought he heard her emit a satisfied little sigh. 'And you'll promise not to pursue them?'

'I'll not—' he clenched his bound fists '—pursue them. Where are they, by the way? I haven't heard their dulcet tones for a while.'

'And you won't hear them again,' she said airily, 'for they've gone, but where to is no concern of yours. Now that you've promised not to pursue us, you'll soon see that everything will be *quite* all right.'

Moments later she was sawing at the ropes at his wrists—carefully, he hoped—with a small, ebony-handled knife. He knew, because the blindfold that they'd used on him—his own silk neckerchief, for God's sake!—had worked loose, so that if he turned his head at a certain angle, he could see her. And as it happened, Beau's first view of her gave rise to a rather unsettling kick of interest.

She was young, as he'd expected. But she wasn't dressed as most miscreant wenches would be, in a flouncy cheap gown with colourful petticoats and a bodice designed to display her feminine charms. Instead she wore close-cut breeches and a loose linen shirt, on top of which was a raggedy short jacket with leather patches over the elbows. A red-spotted neckerchief was tied around her neck, and all in all, any outfit less likely to emphasise her femininity, he couldn't imagine. Yet somehow—*somehow…*

It was her face that really astonished him. It was heart-shaped, dominated by huge eyes that were almost golden, and was given added piquancy by a pert nose, a determined little chin and a cloud of curly chestnut hair. *She was surprisingly, unusually attractive.* She spoke well. She'd sounded almost apologetic about his ordeal. Then his thoughts stopped, because all of a sudden, the rope round his wrists parted and the girl sat back on her heels, pushing her vibrant curls from her face. *Now what?* Beau flexed his hands and adjusted his position in order to keep her within his narrow field of vision. She was a little scoundrel, with her rebellious rain-damp curls and smears of dirt on her cheeks. She and her companions were highway thieves, no doubt about it.

So how could Beau possibly imagine that he'd seen the same girl in the not so distant past, adorned with jewels and wearing the finest of ballgowns? How could he think for one minute that he had actually met her, in the salons of London's elite?

That fall from his horse must have shaken his brains more than he'd realised. *Keep your wits about you, you fool.* He realised that she'd positioned herself to kneel by his feet now, and was starting to hack through the ropes that bound his booted legs. Slowly he reached for his blindfold.

She turned to him calmly. 'Very well,' she said. 'Remove it if you must.'

She went back to her sawing, while Beau eased the silk neckcloth from his eyes. He was astonished that she was going to let him see her in full. Surely the wench was afraid that he would be able to describe her to the constables? But then he realised that she'd already anticipated his inspection by pulling up her own spotted neckerchief to cover the lower part of her face, though she couldn't hide her eyes—and what eyes, he marvelled again. Lambent gold and dark-lashed, they almost matched the colour of her gleaming gold and copper curls.

'That's it,' she announced. She rose to her feet, at the same time slipping the knife into a sheath on her belt. 'You're free now, Mr Beaumaris, but I most sincerely hope you're fully aware that my men have your horse, and that your situation is still precarious in the extreme...'

Her voice trailed away, as Beau drew himself to his full height while at the same time delving into an inner pocket of his coat—in order to pull out a small but lethal pistol, which he cocked and pointed straight at her heart.

'I rather think,' said Beau softly, 'that *you're* the one who needs to understand that your situation is precarious—Miss Deb. Give me that knife of yours. *Now.*'

Chapter Three

Oh, no. He was formidable, Deb realised, and not just because of his pistol. Everything about him—his pride, his height and his muscle power—shouted danger, as he stood looking down at her with the clearest, most captivating male blue eyes she had ever seen. And those eyes were full of pure scorn, as he pointed that lethal-looking pistol at her heart.

Deb's pulse bumped sickeningly. Why, oh, why hadn't Luke and Francis searched him? But they weren't the only ones to blame. She should have noticed the pistol's bulk when she pulled out his watch; she should have gone through everything he carried, except that it felt like a gross insult to his privacy…

More of an insult to him than taking him prisoner, you mean? 'Well,' Deb said, tilting her chin so she could meet his hard gaze. 'So much for your oath to let us go.'

A slow smile curved his arrogant mouth. 'Your memory is failing you somewhat. I did indeed swear not to set the law on your friends, but you forgot something rather important. You see, you didn't include yourself in the bargain.'

Deb stood very, very still. She concentrated on meeting his gaze without flinching. *Don't let him see you're afraid. You must never let an enemy see you're afraid…*

'Trickery with words,' she scoffed. 'Usually the last resort of a man who knows he's in the wrong.'

'I don't think there's any doubt about who's in the wrong here. Empty your pockets.'

'I don't see why I need to—'

'I said, empty your pockets—Deborah.'

Deb breathed hard and deep. 'Why? Unlike you, I don't carry a gun. If I did, I assure you you'd have seen it by now.'

'No doubt,' he retorted calmly. 'Nevertheless, I want you to empty your pockets. You see, I wouldn't be at all surprised if you'd been off on a thieving jaunt of your own while your friends were busy setting their trap for me.' Mr Beaumaris nodded curtly at her little jacket. 'What have you got in your pockets? I can see *something*. Stolen trinkets? Silver?'

Deb fought sheer panic. 'I've just got some old books, that's all. And I can't imagine you'll be in the least bit interested in them…'

'Let me see them.'

'What? No, they're nothing of value, *really*…'

Her voice trailed away as he took two steps towards her—*my, he was tall, he was big*—and jerked that wretched pistol towards her head.

With his free hand, Mr Beaumaris began to explore her pockets. His cool blue eyes never once left her face, and she couldn't help but marvel at the man. He'd been subjected to a dangerous fall from a speedy mount. He'd lain stunned and trussed up on the cold ground—and yet he could still have walked into a Whitehall club and not looked an inch out of place.

He could also, she thought rather wildly, have walked into a crowded ballroom and had every woman there falling at his feet. *Handsome* wasn't an adequate word for him. She'd spent a large part of her life in the theatrical world of fantasy, and Mr Damian Beaumaris, if he weren't so unpleasant, surely resembled every woman's dream of a hero. But at that exact moment, her rambling thoughts stilled into an awful realisation of doom as he pulled out the first of Hugh Palfreyman's books.

'Take it.' He shoved the book towards her.

She took the little volume without a word. He drew out the next one, and the next, handing them to her until she was holding all three.

'Old books,' he said softly, echoing her very words. 'Now, you've already assured me that you're not a thief. So what precisely *is* your occupation—Deborah?'

She stared up at him defiantly. 'My friends and I put on—entertainments.'

'Entertainments.' He repeated the word almost with relish. 'Well, I can only assume that these books are part of them, since you carry them with you all the time. Show them to me, will you?'

'Oh, I assure you, you'll find them very dull—'

'Will I? Let's see,' he interrupted. 'Open the top one—yes, that's right—and let me judge for myself.'

He'd lifted his pistol so close to her face that she could almost smell the cold, deadly metal. Slowly she opened the first book. *Please, let it be all writing. Please don't let it be one of those dreadful pictures…*

She heard the hiss of his indrawn breath. She'd

opened it, as luck would have it, at the most lurid illustration she had yet seen.

'Turn the pages,' he ordered.

She did, one by one, feeling his contemptuous blue eyes burning into her.

'Part of the equipment of your trade, I assume?' he said at last. 'Intended, no doubt, to arouse the interest of any prospective client who might find your feminine charms rather less than—overwhelming, should I put it?'

'No! I—'

He gestured with his pistol. 'Show me the next book. *Now.*'

Deb felt her cheeks burn. *Bastard. Bastard, to do this to me.* She turned the pages of the second slim volume, hoping it might be marginally less shocking than the first—but it wasn't. *Oh, heavens.* What on earth were those two in the picture doing? Yes. She saw *exactly* what they were doing. And so did Mr Beaumaris.

He regarded her with cool appraisal. 'You don't look like a whore,' he said.

Oh, what would she give to insult him in equal measure? Her skin tingled with fury. But right at this minute, it was her absolute priority to keep this abominable man unaware of the fact that she had just robbed Hugh Palfreyman's abode, so she gazed up at her captor and smiled sweetly. 'Such things are a matter of taste, sir, as I'm sure you're aware. And some men prefer to— *vary* their choice from time to time.'

His eyes glittered—blue, dangerous eyes—and they were so transfixing that she couldn't tell whether he was amused or madly angry at her gibe. 'Men might vary their choice of women, yes. But you look more like a boy,' he said, quite calmly.

She shrugged. 'I've heard that's what some gentlemen prefer.'

'You think so? Not me.' He briefly took his eyes from her as he checked his pistol and eased it back into his pocket. 'I can, of course, have the gun out again no time at all if you try to run. But now—tell me your favourite.'

'What?' Deb's heart hammered.

'Tell me which illustration is your favourite.' His brows tilted wickedly. 'Since you must know the contents of these books rather well.'

Oh, heavens. 'Well, of course,' she said, 'it all depends on what mood I'm in.'

'And what kind of mood *are* you in?' he asked in an interested way.

I just wish I had that damned pistol of yours in my hand, she muttered under her breath. 'Of course, I always endeavour to match my clients' inclinations rather than my own,' she responded sweetly. 'But my time costs money, Mr Beaumaris.'

'And I'm not usually in the habit of paying,' he replied smoothly, 'least of all for a travelling slut—'

He broke off when she flung out her hand to slap his cheek. Which was more than foolish of her, because before she'd time to reach her target, Beau had knocked aside her raised hand, cupped her chin and tipped her face up to his, while his hard blue eyes scoured her. He felt her go very still as he let his fingertips slowly caress the warm silken skin of her cheek. *She was so like—so very like—the other one…*

He was aware of the books dropping from her hand, one by one. And the idea—the idea that had been lurking at the back of his mind since he first set eyes on her—took firmer shape.

He said softly, 'Well, Deborah. How do you fancy a trip to Hardgate Hall—with me?'

He thought he saw a flicker almost of horror cross her face. But then she smiled up at him. She reached to touch his cheek with her fingertip. And gently, almost mischievously, she murmured, 'So you've a notion to take our acquaintance further, have you, sir? But first— why not try me here, for yourself?'

Beau gripped her tight and let his mouth come down on hers. Hard, relentless and demanding.

He wanted to teach her a lesson. He wanted to show her that her charms left him cold. He planned to kiss her briefly, than thrust her away with some icy insult.

But instead it was he who was being taught a lesson—that her kiss was sweet, sweeter than he could have believed possible. He found himself holding her closer, prising her lips apart, forcing his tongue inside her mouth to take sure possession, and he was mystified, because there was something totally unexpected about her. In spite of those outrageous books, she somehow carried the allure of innocence, and at the first touch of her lips desire had hit him like a punch in the stomach, momentarily winding him.

And now her arms were tightly around his waist; her lovely face was lifted expectantly to his and he was unable to resist caressing her lips with his again, feeling arousal thud through his loins as he drew her closer, thinking in wonder, *Her kiss is soft and sweet. She's not like the other one, even though she's the exact image. Not like her at all…*

In almost the very same instant, he heard two sets of footsteps pounding up behind him.

Before he could do a thing, the girl was already plunging her hand into his pocket to snatch out his pistol, and both his arms had been seized from behind.

Her two colleagues had returned.

You fool, he told himself bitterly. *You stupid fool*. To fall for her tricks…

The girl had retreated a few yards, but was pointing the gun at him steadily. 'Best not to struggle, Mr Beaumaris,' she called out. 'I'm not altogether sure that I won't fire this fine pistol of yours by mistake, you see.'

Beau stood there raging as Deb's friends searched every single one of his pockets. 'There's no other weapon,' they called out to her. Then they started swiftly binding his hands behind his back.

Damn it. 'You'll pay for this,' Beau breathed.

Those were his last words, before he found himself blindfolded—*again*—and wrestled to the ground. One of them—he guessed it was the younger one, Luke—practically sat on his legs in order to lash some twine around his ankles, and Beau began on a catalogue of prime insults, until the girl said thoughtfully to her colleagues, 'Oh, dear. You'd better gag him as well.'

So his insults were at an end, more was the pity. But most of all Beau regretted being blindfolded; because if she'd been able to see his eyes, she would have realised that the expression in them was one of pure and utter contempt.

First round to the Lambeth Players, Deb's stepfather, Gerald O'Hara, would have said. But Deb didn't feel the slightest sense of triumph. *That kiss. Oh, that kiss*. It was with only the greatest difficulty that she managed to keep her voice calm as she guided Luke and Francis away from their captive. 'Well done, both of you,' she said, 'for timing your rescue to perfection.'

Francis looked stunned. 'He had a gun. And he was molesting you. *Kissing* you. As far as I'm concerned that decides it. We'll leave him here.' Francis picked up his hat, which had fallen off during the struggle. 'Luke and I spotted some woodcutters at work further along the track. They're bound to come this way once they've finished for the day, and find our fancy gentleman—so let him fume in his bonds for a while. He deserves no pity from us.'

'And he won't get it,' said Deb swiftly. 'But I'm afraid we have to keep him under guard for a little while longer.'

'Why?'

'Because he's a friend of Palfreyman's.'

Francis stared; Luke let out a small yelp of horror.

'That's right.' *And that's not the least of it. Our prisoner has seen those awful, awful books, and once he's set free, he might recount the whole incident to Palfreyman. My plan to save the Players could be wrecked...*

'Mr Beaumaris was actually on his way to Hardgate Hall,' she went on. 'And you were right—that *is* Palfreyman's bay that he was riding. So you have to keep him a prisoner, I'm afraid, until I receive Palfreyman's written promise to drop all charges against the Players.'

'But that's not till...'

'I know. Not until tomorrow.'

'But he'll need feeding.' This was Luke speaking. 'He'll need somewhere to sleep, Miss Deb. He'll need—'

'We can do it if we have to,' interrupted Francis. 'But what about you, Deborah?'

'I've got to go back to Oxford, to the Angel, Francis.' Somehow she managed to sound calm. 'I'm booked to entertain the inn's customers for an hour, tomorrow at noon. Don't you remember?'

Francis looked gloomy. 'But the rest of the Players have gone on to Gloucester. Can't we just leave, now, and join them?'

'No! We've put posters up all around town for my show, and you know as well as I do that if we let our customers down, they won't turn up the next time we're here! Also, I *have* to stay in Oxford to get Palfreyman's reply tomorrow morning!'

'Do you really believe he'll write to say he's going to lift those charges against us?'

'I'm sure of it,' Deb replied confidently. Francis would be confident, too, if he knew what she'd stolen from Palfreyman's house. 'I've told him that I'll expect his reply by ten tomorrow.' From the corner of her eye, she glimpsed their prisoner stirring slightly; her spirits plummeted again. 'I don't think Palfreyman will dare to be late. But it does mean that you and Luke are going to have to keep our prisoner here until I get back to you, early in the afternoon.'

Both men looked appalled. Clearly she wasn't the only one to realise that they had a truly formidable opponent in Mr Beaumaris. 'If there was an alternative I'd use it, believe me,' she continued earnestly. 'But I'm afraid we've really no choice.'

Francis still looked deeply unhappy. 'Very well,' he sighed. 'I noticed there's a charcoal-burner's hut off the track back there, and it doesn't look like it's been used for years. If we get him inside it, he wouldn't have to lie out in the cold and wet all night.'

Deb remembered the insults that Mr Beaumaris had paid her and replied thoughtfully, 'Francis, do you know, I don't think I care very much if our prisoner *does* have to lie out in the cold and wet all night. But you're right, I suppose. Luke, you must ride over to Hardgate village and pick up a few provisions—it will all work out, you'll see. As an extra precaution, Francis, I'll give you Mr Beaumaris's gun.' She spoke with forced cheerfulness as she handed him the pistol. 'As soon as Luke rejoins you, you can take our prisoner to the charcoal-burner's hut for the night. By the time I've done my performance at the Angel, I'll have received Palfreyman's written promise not to prosecute us—then I can ride back here and we'll let Mr Beaumaris go free.'

'But then Mr Beaumaris will ride on to Palfreyman's, and he'll tell Palfreyman all about us!'

'By which time we'll be well out of the way, believe me.'

Francis glanced at their furious prisoner. 'I'd say that the more miles we put between ourselves and Mr Beaumaris, the better.'

Deb couldn't have agreed more. As she mounted her old pony, Ned, she tried to keep up her optimism, but she felt more and more afraid of the consequences of this ill-fated encounter. And yet it was hard to describe the almost crushing disappointment she'd felt when she realised that Mr Beaumaris was a friend of Palfreyman's.

Something about Mr Beaumaris disturbed her in a quite alarming manner. There was no denying that he was absolutely, compellingly male, with his brilliant blue eyes and his unruly dark hair and hard, lean jaw.

Gorgeous, Peggy Daniels would say. *Mouthwateringly gorgeous*. But shouldn't Deb have been immune to that?

Instead, what his kiss had done to her just terrified her. Yes, she'd lured him into the kiss because she knew that Luke and Francis would arrive any minute, and it had been the obvious way to distract him. She'd been prepared to feel revulsion and fresh fear. Instead, she'd been completely stunned by her own reaction to the touch of his lips on hers.

Damian Beaumaris was the kind of man she absolutely detested. He was arrogant. He was hatefully insulting. But as soon as his mouth came down on hers she'd felt shock flooding every nerve and her world had slowed. She'd wanted—no, she *needed* to be closer to him; she even heard her own little moan of longing. She still felt as though her world had turned upside down.

Deb drew a deep breath, and urged her ambling steed onwards.

Chapter Four

In less than an hour Deb had returned to the inn to find that the rest of the Lambeth Players had travelled on earlier as arranged, taking their carts of belongings and their other two horses. She was glad everything here at least had gone according to plan, but she missed their lively banter. After stabling Ned, she went to buy herself a hot meal to take back to the stables where she would spend the night, but she wasn't able to escape the sharp tongue of the innkeeper's wife.

'I'm hoping, young lady,' the woman said as she ladled out some dubious-looking stew, 'that a few people turn up for this speechifying of yours tomorrow. It's going to put us to a deal of trouble, you know, clearing our yard and setting up a stage for you.'

Deb took her plate and looked at her steadily. 'Your courtyard is always packed every year when I appear. You know that. And they pay.'

'Sixpence apiece, but *you* take half of that!'

'Ah, but the people who come to see me also drink your ale and buy your hot pies by the dozen.' *Which I'd guess you fill with the local butcher's sweepings,*

Deb added to herself. She'd tried one of them once—it was horrible. She turned to go, but the innkeeper's wife hadn't finished with her.

'The rest of your friends,' she said suddenly, making Deb almost drop her plate. 'They paid their bill and cleared out this morning. Now, where were they bound?'

'They've gone on to the fair at Stow on the Wold,' Deb lied glibly. 'A little muddying of their trail might be a good thing, all in all.' *Mr Beaumaris. Palfreyman. Oh, heavens.*

Still the woman hadn't finished, but came closer, her eyes gleaming with malicious curiosity. 'It must be a strange life,' she said, 'for a young woman, traipsing around with a bunch of travelling players. And I heard tell that you're all in trouble with the local magistrates—'

'You must excuse me,' Deb broke in, 'I really wanted to eat this delicious stew while it's hot—'

'In trouble with the local magistrates,' repeated the woman with emphasis, 'for putting on a play on a Sunday. They say the lot of you have been threatened with prison. There, now. What do you say to *that*?'

'It was all a mistake. And I assure you that the matter will very soon be sorted.' Deb gave the woman a dazzling smile, then marched out towards the stables. Once inside she kicked the door shut with her foot, sat on a hay bale and put her plate down.

She wasn't hungry any more.

Did everyone in the whole of Oxford know the predicament that they were in? Damn Palfreyman! She would come through this. They would *all* come through this. But now there was an added complication—their prisoner.

She had a feeling that Mr Beaumaris wasn't a man to either forgive or forget. *But he's no idea who I am*, she told herself. He has no idea of my connection with the Players or with Palfreyman. He thinks my friends are highway robbers, and that I'm a whore. *Hardly surprising, since he'd found those books on her…*

Oh, to blazes with Mr Beaumaris, Deb thought irritably. It was *his* fault that he was in such a pickle. But with both him and Palfreyman as enemies now, the sooner she, Francis and Luke were on their way to Gloucester to join the others, the better. And then she could push today's rather alarming events from her mind.

But she wouldn't be able to forget Mr Beaumaris's kiss quite so quickly. Or his wicked blue eyes and devilish good looks. She thought that she would quite possibly *never* forget the way her heart had jolted and almost stopped as his lips crushed hers and his hands had drawn her closer…

Enough. *Enough.* She picked up her plate and tried to convince herself that the greasy mess looked appetising. She hoped that Mr Beaumaris was vastly cold and miserable in the charcoal-burner's hut, and that Luke and Francis were making his captivity as uncomfortable as possible.

She forced herself to eat the stew, aware that she really needed to keep her strength up—because just at the moment, it rather looked as if her company would be lucky to survive the next few days without the lot of them being hurled straight into Oxford County Gaol, by either Hugh Palfreyman, or the even more formidable Mr Beaumaris.

* * *

As the sun began to sink in a haze of mist over the Ashendale Forest, Beau turned restlessly in his bonds and decided that he could not remember having been more furious in all his life.

Oh, he'd been *angry* before now. But there had always been something he could do—some counter-attack he could plan, some legal strategy he could devise. He'd been known in the past to use his fists if the circumstances were appropriate.

But now his impotence made him wild. He'd heard the girl riding off on her pony, leaving her two companions to guard him—and there hadn't been a thing Beau could do, since he was once more roped up and blindfolded.

His hearing, though, was acute, and shortly afterwards he realised that the younger fellow was riding off also. But Beau heard him return within half an hour, and then they both came over to offer him some food that the lad must have purchased. After some muttering between themselves, they removed his gag, so he was able to point out, in no uncertain terms, that they'd have to untie his hands as well if he was to eat.

They muttered to each other again, then unfastened the cord round his wrists to allow him to feed himself with the bread and cheese they offered. But when he reached for his blindfold the older one tutted and said, 'I hope you're not going to try and get your blindfold off, are you, Mr Beaumaris? That wouldn't be a good idea at all. It really wouldn't.' And—though Beau doubted if the fellow could use it—he heard the ominous click of his own pistol and decided it was, for the moment, more prudent to obey.

Of course, they didn't want him to see their rascally faces—but he guessed they were watching him all the time as he ate. Then they tied his hands again but loosened the rope at his ankles and led him about a hundred yards or so to what he guessed was some kind of rough shelter. And that was where, he gathered, they expected him to spend the whole of the long, miserable night.

It was apparent that their leader—Miss Deb, or Deborah—had had no intention of returning that evening, quite possibly because she had her own trade to ply in the streets of Oxford. And that troubled Beau.

She was a slut and a highway robber, by her own admission. But most dangerously of all, she was attractive in the kind of way that he just could not erase from his mind. Yes, she was a little on the skinny side, to be sure—but he'd quickly forgotten that when he'd held her close and realised that some very feminine curves were hidden by her boy's attire. Yes, she was scruffy, and her long hair could have done with a good brush, but what did that matter, when she possessed such ravishing chestnut curls and such enchanting, dark-lashed golden eyes?

And as for the kiss... Beau shifted uncomfortably on the beaten-earth floor of the charcoal-burner's hut, remembering her against his will.

He might be blindfolded again, but her image was etched on his memory. He couldn't help but remember how she'd let out a little gasp of surprise as he kissed her, how she'd clasped her hands tightly around his waist as if to steady herself.

He couldn't forget the feel of her pert and slender figure pressed so close to his, or the scent of her skin; nor could he fail to remember how her hair was a tumbled cloud of radiant hues that perfectly framed her flushed face. She'd looked *exquisite*—and innocent.

But it was all a sham. She'd deliberately pretended to be stunned by his caresses while secretly enabling her two henchmen to spring their trap.

He gritted his teeth as he remembered how she'd earlier flicked through the quite scandalous illustrations in those little books of hers and told him sweetly, *Of course, I always endeavour to match my clients' inclinations rather than my own.*

She was so like Paulette—who never dressed in anything other than silks and satins, but even so the similarity between the two of them had hit him like a body-blow. When darkness fell he lay there thinking, *Who is she?* And when he slept at last, he dreamed of her.

He dreamed that he had her in his arms, and her smile was enticing as he bent his head to kiss her. Then she squirmed with wanton relish in his arms, and fluttered her lashes with the skill of a practised coquette, breathing, *'Well, Damian Beaumaris. It seems that I have you at last.'*

Beau woke at dawn to a chorus of birdsong, and found that his muscles were cramped and stiff. The younger of his guards came to check that his blindfold and bonds were still in place. There was no sign of any imminent improvement in his situation.

He dozed again briefly, but woke to hear his two guards having a muttered argument. They tried at first to keep their voices to whispers, but as their tempers rose, so did their voices. He let out an almighty bellow. Moments later he heard hurried footsteps and the door creaked open. The older one said, 'Was there something you wanted, Mr Beaumaris?'

'I'm hungry,' Beau pronounced in a dangerous voice. 'I'm cold and cramped in here. Above all I want you to know that I'll have you all clapped in bloody Newgate for this.'

'We're sorry, Mr Beaumaris.' It was the younger one who spoke this time—he must have come to join his friend. 'But you have to stay our prisoner, see? For just a little longer, that's all.'

Beau could almost hear the lad shaking in fright. The girl was made of sterner stuff than the rest of them put together. He gritted his teeth. 'I don't recall your…*Miss Deb* telling you to let me starve. And there's something else. I've been shut up in here all night, and I need to relieve myself.'

'Now, let's see,' the older one was muttering. 'We have to keep his blindfold on, but we'll need to untie the ropes at his feet. Though it's best perhaps if we keep the long rope tied to *one* of his ankles, so he can't run… This way, Mr Beaumaris, sir!'

And Beau found himself being led a few yards away, still blindfolded and with his wrists tied behind his back, while the rope that connected him to the doorpost uncoiled behind him. He told himself, calmly, *Someone is going to pay dearly for this*.

'We'll leave you in privacy, sir.'

'My hands will need freeing,' Beau pointed out.

His guardian was clearly unhappy. 'I suppose so.' He untied the knot with nervous fingers. 'I'll be back in a few moments—sir.'

Beau almost had to laugh, it was all so ridiculous. What would his friends—Prinny and the Duke of Devonshire and the rest of high society—have to say if they could see him like this? Swiftly he eased off his blind-fold and stared around. His captors were busy over their fire again, but they were still near enough to spot instantly if he were to try to undo the knotted rope around his right leg. And the older one no doubt still had Beau's pistol in his belt.

He assessed the two men swiftly. The older one, a lanky fellow, wore a long coat in a peculiar shade of red, and a black hat with a feather in it. The younger was—well, the younger was just a fair-haired lad, pleasant-looking enough, wearing breeches and a leather tunic.

He spotted their horses—a pony and an old grey mare—over on the far side of the clearing, and tethered beside them was Palfreyman's bay horse. After a few moments Beau called out to his captors and allowed them to lead him back to the charcoal-burner's hut.

They were clearly upset that he'd removed his blind-fold, but after conferring together decided there was little point now in replacing it. They tied his wrists again, but his legs were left free. Preferring to remain standing, Beau leaned against the doorway and watched the two men bend over their small fire—he could smell bacon cooking. He wondered how Palfreyman had felt yesterday when Beau failed to turn up for his four o'clock appointment. Most likely he'd opened a bottle of his best wine to celebrate.

'You take the food over to him, Luke,' he heard the older one say. As the younger one approached, Beau stared down at him fiercely.

The lad cleared his throat. 'Here's some bread and bacon for you, sir. Is there anything else you need?'

'Yes,' said Beau curtly as he took the hunk of hot

bacon wrapped in two slabs of bread. 'I need to be set free. I want my pistol back and that bay horse, so I can ride to Oxford and report the pair of you for kidnap and violence.'

'It's not kidnap!' The lad sounded terrified. 'And we're only to keep you here until Miss Deb gets back, she said so. Then we can let you go, I swear...'

'You take orders from a *girl*?' said Beau with contempt.

The lad flushed to the roots of his fair hair and hurried off. Beau ate the bacon and bread, then settled himself on the floor and pretended to be asleep again. They came over to check him, then stood outside, talking. They talked for quite a while; then the older one said, 'Best get going with our jobs, lad. The horses need feeding and watering for a start—I'll see to that, and lead them down to the river. You go and explore the track—in both directions, mind. Make sure there aren't any search parties out looking for our prisoner, do you understand?'

'But shouldn't one of us stay to keep an eye on—*him*?'

'With his wrists tied, and that rope round his leg? Our Mr Beaumaris is going nowhere in a hurry. Besides, he looks to be sleeping again...'

Their voices faded. Lying by the open door of the hut, Beau opened one eye and watched the younger one set off anxiously towards the track, while the other made for the horses.

They'd left the fire burning low.

As soon as they were out of sight, Beau began to get to his feet, smiling grimly to himself.

Chapter Five

Deb O'Hara was sitting on a bale of hay in the Angel's stable, dressed in a white shirt and black velvet breeches, with her long chestnut hair pinned up tightly. She was doing her breathing exercises, which consisted of swinging her arms from side to side, taking a deep breath, then expelling the air from her lungs in a steady hum—Gerald had taught her to do this, to warm her vocal cords. At the same time she was trying hard to concentrate on the words she would be reciting out there in about—oh, no—in about twenty minutes.

Miss Deb O'Hara's '*entertainments*' always gathered a crowd. It had been her idea years ago to present selections of their repertoire by herself, keeping the content short and lively. After considerable practice she'd mastered the art of playing two parts at once—in this case, the clown from *Twelfth Night* and the lovelorn heroine, Viola. By the time she'd skipped from one side of the stage to the other, changed her hat and her voice as necessary and sung a few comical songs as well, she usually had her audience captivated.

But at this precise moment, she couldn't even remember her lines.

'I will build me a willow cabin...'

She stopped. She wasn't getting a headache, was she? She'd slept badly last night in the stable loft, but there was a good reason for that—Mr Beaumaris. And his kiss. *He's safe in the woods,* she kept assuring herself. *Francis and Luke have him tied up...* After taking a deep swallow from the flask of water she'd put on a nearby hay bale, she began again.

'Build me a willow cabin—'

She broke off once more as her old pony, watching from its stall, stretched to nip playfully at her shirt sleeve. 'I've no apples for you, Ned! Now leave me be—*you're* having a nice long rest, but I've got all these words to remember!'

And an awful lot on my mind, if truth be told, she muttered to herself before starting her breathing exercises again. 'Hmmm...'

A crowd was already gathering out in the yard. They sounded to be a noisy, ale-swilling lot, but that was only to be expected, and besides, she'd been used to stepping out in front of lively audiences since she was little. Her very first role had been as one of the young, doomed princes in *Richard III*, and some raucous onlookers had started jeering the moment she appeared. But they'd gone absolutely silent when she'd made her poignant little speech—*God keep me from false friends!*—and the sense of sheer power over people's emotions had enthralled her.

'You're born to it, Deb,' Gerald O'Hara had said proudly afterwards. 'Some day they'll be calling out your name in Drury Lane or Covent Garden.'

Perhaps. But meanwhile here she was, struggling to remember her lines for a performance in an inn yard,

and the surly innkeeper was banging on the stable door.
'You nearly ready? All this lot out here are making an
almighty nuisance of themselves.'

Deb thought of all the sixpences he would have been
busy collecting from them and bit back a sharp retort.
'I said I'd appear at midday.' She kept her voice pleasant. 'And that's what I'll do.'

'Well, see that you keep to it, missy.'

He left before she had chance to reply.

*Don't waste your time and effort arguing with the
wretch. Don't.* A feeling of deep dread lurked in Deb's
heart—but it wasn't the crowd she was afraid of.

Her business with Palfreyman was more or less resolved. At ten this morning she'd hurried to St Mary's
churchyard, watching out for any trap that might have
been laid—after all, she wouldn't put anything past
Palfreyman. But everything was quiet there, and relief
swept through her when she spotted the letter under the
horse trough by the church wall.

Deb sat in the sun on the village green, and carefully opened the letter, which promised that Palfreyman would lift the charges he'd laid against the Lambeth
Players. The wording was brief and gave away little,
though she thought she could detect Palfreyman's fury
in the jagged penstrokes of his signature.

After buying herself a fresh currant bun from the
nearby baker's by way of celebration, she enjoyed it in
the sunshine before wandering thoughtfully back to the
inn. What could go wrong now?

Nothing—as long as they could set Mr Beaumaris
free and get away before he could catch up with them.

To have been forced to keep him a prisoner overnight
was an appalling turn of events—especially as he was

a friend of Palfreyman's. His kiss—and her reaction to it—had disturbed her badly. And there was something else. She could not forget how when he'd first seen her, his incredible blue eyes had opened wide with something that almost shouted aloud: *I know you. I know you from somewhere.*

Deb continued to pace the stables carefully, swinging her arms and trying to calm her racing thoughts. Palfreyman had a daughter, an only daughter called Paulette, who was the same age as her. And Deb knew for a fact that between the grown-up Paulette and herself there was an uncanny resemblance, because she'd seen her, last year.

Deb and Francis had gone to the Vauxhall Pleasure Gardens on a hot July afternoon. There was a display of Moorish acrobats and the London crowds had thronged to see them, but Deb and Francis had been there for a different reason—they'd come to ask the manager of Vauxhall if they could put on one of their plays for a week in the autumn.

Deb's mind had been wholly on the negotiations. But when she saw the young woman wandering by with a group of female friends, she'd quite forgotten what she was about to say, because it had been like gazing into a looking glass—a magical looking glass, that turned your clothes from cheap cotton to silks and satins, and your leather boots to dainty kid shoes. The lady Deb was staring at was clad in a lovely pale green pelisse and a neat bonnet that set off her chestnut curls exquisitely. She carried a matching parasol, and everything about her declared that she was rich and proud and privileged.

The manager had gone off to fetch his appointments book. The young woman in green had disappeared among the summer crowds. But despite the blazing sunshine, Deb had felt as cold as if a ghost had walked over her grave, especially when Francis said with wonder, 'That young lady who went by just then, with all her friends. She bore a remarkable resemblance to you, Deborah!'

'No,' Deb had said, shivering. 'No, you're mistaken, Francis.'

But afterwards, when the business with the manager was successfully completed and Francis had strolled off to admire the acrobats, Deb spotted the woman and her friends in the crowds again, and found herself unwillingly drawn closer to them.

'Paulette,' one of them was calling out. 'Paulette, do come over here, they're selling ices, and we *must* have one!'

The years had rolled back. Once more she was a six-year-old child clinging to her mother's hand as they were driven by an angry Hugh Palfreyman from his house—but before the great front door was finally slammed on them, she'd caught sight of a small girl about her age, who happened to be crossing the vast, marble-tiled hall with her nurse.

The girl had tugged at her nurse's hand when she saw Deb and her mother. 'Nurse,' she'd said in a clear, piercing voice, 'Nurse, who *is* that dirty girl who's staring at me so?'

Then the door was closed, with Deb on one side, and the little girl on the other. Even at such a young age, Paulette had been dressed in expensive and elaborate finery—a complete contrast to Deb, in her cotton frock. But Paulette was the same age as Deb, her curls were the same shade of chestnut—and such was the similarity that Deb had heard her mother utter a low cry on seeing her.

What different paths the two girls had taken, thought Deb. It was inevitable, really, since one of them was the privileged daughter of a rich country gentleman and the other was a travelling player. Yet even so, to see her cousin at Vauxhall looking so very like her in feature and figure had shaken Deb badly.

She had wandered away into the crowds that day reminding herself that Paulette Palfreyman had no relevance whatsoever to her own life. Palfreyman had disowned his sister and her child completely, all those years ago; he hadn't even come to his sister's funeral. Deb had heard occasional news of Paulette; she'd married well last autumn, and was presumably content. No one was ever likely to link the two girls, were they? And did it matter if they did?

It might matter now. As she prepared to go out on the crude little stage, Deb was thinking—*Mr Beaumaris may very well have met Paulette Palfreyman, since he is a friend of her father.* What if he had spotted the likeness in the woods yesterday?

Mr Beaumaris would, she knew, be more than angry with his captors. In fact, he would be furious. But she'd comforted herself up till this moment with the knowledge that he would be unable to identify them.

Now, she had to think again.

The bells of the nearby church were beginning to strike midday. Picking up her two hats—the clown's black-and-white pointed one and Viola's jaunty green cap—she drew a deep breath, then stepped outside to a chorus of cheers and the occasional jeer. The inn yard was packed, she realised. Giving them a jaunty bow, she climbed lightly up to the makeshift wooden platform set in the inn's courtyard, and several of the men whistled appreciatively at the way her breeches and hose displayed her legs. She grinned, gave them another extravagant bow, put on the clown's hat and skipped lightly across the stage to begin one of the lively songs.

When that I was and a little tiny boy,
With hey, ho, the wind and the rain…

They fell silent. They *listened*. After that they roared with applause, but silence descended anew as she went to put on the green cap, sat on a bale of hay placed at the corner of the stage and began Viola's speech, recounting her sadness in finding herself stranded in a foreign country. The magic of the words took over, and her troubles were—for the moment—forgotten.

Deb was as amazed as ever to see how these country folk—rough and uneducated, most of them—completely melted on hearing Viola's lovelorn words. After dextrously entwining the two parts and feasting her audience with some of Shakespeare's loveliest verse, she rounded her performance with the clown's last song.

A great while ago, the world began,
With a hey, ho, the wind and the rain;
But that's all one, our play is done,
And we'll strive to please you every day.

They roared their approval. 'Ladies and gentlemen,' she called above the din. 'Thank you, so much!' She bowed again and again as they applauded, blowing them kisses. *One day*, she vowed, *I'll have a theatre of my own in London. I will.* It didn't have to be big, or in an expensive part of the city. She wouldn't be able to charge a fortune and seat hundreds, as the three big London theatres did—Drury Lane and Covent Garden and the Haymarket. But she would find the Lambeth Players a permanent home; one that her stepfather, Gerald O'Hara, would have been truly proud of.

Almost skipping back to the stable, she found Ned the pony poking his head over the stall and she fed him a handful of hay. 'It went well, Ned,' she whispered. 'Really well.' Taking off her jester's hat, she smiled with reflective pleasure—*oh, it was the best of lives, to be an actor*! Then she froze.

Because she'd just realised that she and Ned weren't the only ones in here.

'Bravo, Miss O'Hara,' someone said softly behind her. That very male voice was followed by the sound of ironic applause. Deb whirled around. No. No, *please…*

It was Mr Beaumaris. Free, here and larger than life.

Deb felt the colour drain from her face. 'You got away,' she whispered. Her mouth was very dry. 'But how…?'

He shut the stable door and bolted it, just as she made a dart for freedom. Faced with his formidable figure, Deb backed up against Ned's stall. An ominous fluttering started low down in her abdomen. Goodness, he was tall. He was strong. He was…almost sinfully handsome. *Irrelevant, Deb. Irrelevant.* She jerked her head up to meet his hooded blue gaze, while he folded his arms across his chest.

'In answer to your question,' he said, 'your two accomplices were foolish enough to leave me unattended.'

'But surely, you were tied up…' She moistened her dry lips.

'They'd left their fire alight. While they weren't looking, I burned through my ropes.'

She glanced at his wrists, and saw that the fine Brussels lace beneath his coat cuffs was charred and soot-stained. Her heart drummed. *This man was truly ruthless.* 'But how did you know that I'd be here?'

'Your friends told me, Miss O'Hara. In fact, they really had no alternative. You see, I reclaimed my pistol—which they'd carelessly left lying by the fire—so they had no choice but to do whatever I said. I found out from them that you were here, then I made them saddle up Palfreyman's horse for me. Oh, and before I left, I sent their two nags trotting off into the forest.'

Deb felt herself go very pale. 'Have you hurt my friends?'

'Much as I'd have liked to—much as they *deserved* it—no. I told them to make no attempt to pursue me, but to join their colleagues in—Gloucester, I believe it was. I hope they realise how lucky they've been to get away so easily.'

Deb looked around rather wildly for a means of escape for herself, while he proceeded to issue a lethally eloquent diatribe against highway thieves and robbers. And all the time her despair grew. 'They are *not* robbers.' She clenched her fists at her side. 'They only captured you because they thought—they thought that you were an enemy of ours!'

'Because they thought I was Hugh Palfreyman,' he said flatly. 'Who I believe has every intention of prosecuting you and your players for performing on a Sunday. And before you ask how I know that, the story is all over town.'

'But that story is wrong. You see, it was all done in private—'

'Really?' Beau drawled. 'I wonder what other— *private performances* you have in your repertoire?'

As he spoke Beau watched the girl with detached interest. When he'd spotted the playbills put up around the place, promising an entertainment by Miss Deb O'Hara of the Lambeth Players, he'd expected—*what* had he expected? The Angel was a rough place at the best of times. He'd thought perhaps to find her offering some sort of song-and-dance act, followed by a bit of banter with the raucous, mostly male crowd. He guessed she'd likely be drumming up some lucrative private business for herself later on.

Instead, he'd arrived to find her holding the admittedly rough crowd in the palm of her hand with—Shakespeare. Beautifully, eloquently spoken Shakespeare. Up on that stage, she'd looked slim and calm. She was possessed of a lovely speaking voice and a kind of magical charm that held the crowd spellbound. He'd listened to her with near-wonder.

Shakespeare, for heaven's sake. Two parts at once, woven together with ingenuity and skill.

And—as he'd noticed before—she was damned attractive. Her boy's breeches and hose showed just how shapely her slender legs were, while that white shirt didn't do a thing to conceal the curve of her breasts. He'd stood at the back of the crowd with his arms folded and his jaw set. He saw and heard for himself how the noisy whistles and occasional mocking jeers had died away at almost her first words.

No doubt every red-blooded male in that crowd would be wondering what it would be like to hold her and to kiss her rosy lips. But he *knew*. He knew, because he'd done it, and despite everything, despite his sheer anger with her, he felt desire rear anew. He remembered those books she carried, and wondered how she could, at times, look so very innocent.

It was because she was an actress, he told himself curtly. That was why. But he didn't think she was acting now, not in the slightest little bit. He'd seen how the colour fled from her rather exquisite face, as she realised that he knew about Palfreyman and the charges he had laid.

'I thought you would have gone straight to Palfreyman,' she said tonelessly. He noticed that she'd backed up as far as she could against some bales of hay at the other end of the stable.

'There's time enough for that,' he answered. 'I wanted to make sure of tracking you down first. Though I imagine Palfreyman will be very interested to know that I was kidnapped by a trio of vagabonds on my way to visit him. He'll be especially interested to learn that one of my kidnappers was—his niece.'

If they'd been in a boxing ring, she would have been on the ropes by now, thought Beau. On the floor, even— but this one recovered quickly. Feeling reluctant but increasing admiration for her, he saw how she tossed back her hair and flashed her golden, dark-lashed eyes until he almost wanted to applaud again, then she declared, 'You think that I'm Palfreyman's niece? Why, that's simply *laughable*...'

'Well, you'd better start laughing, then.' His voice was silkily lethal. 'And you may as well start telling the truth too. It's futile to lie, Miss O'Hara. You see, you bear a quite astonishing resemblance to your cousin—the beauteous Paulette.'

Although he'd just landed her a body-blow, she again recovered her poise almost miraculously.

'Hugh Palfreyman,' she said, 'drove my mother—his sister—from Hardgate Hall when she was only seventeen.' She was meeting his gaze steadfastly. 'As for me, I met Palfreyman once only, sixteen years ago. I haven't met him since. My uncle is a cruel and hypocritical man, and I have no wish to ever encounter him again.'

For a moment, Beau hesitated—until he remembered she was a scheming little actress, who'd kept him trussed and bound in the forest. So she and her uncle didn't see eye to eye? Hardly surprising, since each was as bad as the other. And how much of her story did she actually expect him to believe?

He folded his arms across his chest. '*Bravo* for another fine performance, Miss O'Hara. Nevertheless, you're coming with me, *now*, to Hardgate Hall and—'

He broke off because she'd spun round to make with surprising agility for the door. But he reached out to grasp her tight around her slim little waist. 'My God, listen, will you? You haven't a hope in hell of getting out of this unscathed. I can ensure that you and your friends are put in gaol, however far they try to run. You and your men assaulted and kidnapped me. There's nowhere on earth you'll be able to hide if you escape me now.'

She struggled and he gripped her shoulders, hard. Her skin was soft and clear, and her lips looked every bit as luscious as he remembered. And even though she was panting with fright, there was no doubt that the proximity of her slender body was having a totally inappropriate effect on his pulse rate, amongst other things...

Abruptly he let her go. She dragged herself unsteadily away and smoothed down her boy's shirt. 'You promised,' she breathed. 'You promised not to prosecute my friends.'

'But that was before they roped me up a second time. And if you remember, I said nothing about letting *you* go free. You're going to come witn me, to Palfreyman's house. But first of all I want you to tell me exactly what you know about Paulette, your cousin, and I want you to tell me the truth.'

The girl was looking around rather wildly. 'But... the stable boys, the innkeeper. They'll all wonder what on earth we're doing in here...'

'They'll guess exactly what we're doing in here,' he replied. 'I told the innkeeper that I'd admired your performance greatly, and I wanted a little time alone with you, in order to arrange a meeting later.' He gave a cold smile. 'For our mutual pleasure, you understand.'

Deb felt as though all the air had been squeezed from her lungs. *Keep him talking; that's all you can do. Keep him talking, and watch for any chance of escape...* She only wished she could banish the rather sick panic churning in her stomach.

'Well, Mr Beaumaris,' she said, 'arranging an appointment with me will do wonders for your reputation, I'm sure.'

He shrugged. 'Is it so unlikely that a gentleman's fancy should be caught by a young lady who carries books of erotic prints in her pocket?'

She leaped again for the door, but he was there first. He secured her by pinning her wrists at her sides before saying softly, 'Do you know, Miss O'Hara, I thought that you rather enjoyed our kiss in the forest.'

The way he looked at her made her insides churn anew. *Oh, that kiss. The way he'd made her feel, with that face, that body, that mouth…*

She shivered. 'You are despicable.'

'So you've already informed me. Now—as I said before—I want you to tell me what you know about your cousin. Your uncle Hugh Palfreyman's only daughter.'

Deb steadied her breathing. *Stay calm. Watch and wait for your chance.* 'I know very little about Paulette. I did hear that she married well last autumn, but I've no idea who her husband is. We do not, as you'll have gathered, move in the same circles. What my uncle did to my mother…'

'So you've said. I take it you didn't realise that Paulette's husband died this spring?'

She looked astonished. Slowly she shook her head. 'No. No, I didn't. How could I?'

He stared at her a moment longer, then glanced at his pocket watch. 'We've been in here long enough,' he announced with an air of finality. 'My coach should be ready by now.'

To take her to Palfreyman's. 'You—you have a coach?'

'I do. I had to leave it to be repaired at a local black-smith's, yesterday. That's why I was riding Palfreyman's horse.'

Beau went to open the door. He expected her to vociferously object again—to struggle, and make one enormous fuss. Instead, she closed her eyes briefly, but then she squared her shoulders and said calmly, 'Are you going to tell Palfreyman that my men and I kidnapped you?'

'I see no need.'

'Are you going to tell my uncle that I'm one of the Lambeth Players?'

'I'm not.'

This time, he thought he saw something jolt through her—shock? Relief? Certainly her voice was steady enough as she said at last, 'Are you—going to tell him about the books?'

'No,' he said again.

Her eyes widened. 'Then why take me there? I don't understand...'

His hand was already resting on the stable door. 'You will.'

She nodded slowly, biting her lip. 'I—I have a few possessions here, some clothes.'

'Bring them with you.'

He went outside, closing the stable door again to shut her in.

Think. Breathe, Deborah. Her belongings were in the loft; swiftly she climbed up there and started packing them into a shabby brown valise that had been Gerald's. She stopped, hearing the clatter of hooves and the jingle of harness outside, and voices—those of the grooms and that of Mr Beaumaris. Who was giving orders, of course.

She turned back to her task. She had Palfreyman's books and couldn't leave them, so she pushed them in the bottom of her bag beneath some petticoats, then she scrambled down the ladder just in time to see that he was back. He was carrying a long black cloak draped over his arm, and he held out a black gown, and a black bonnet with a veil.

'Here you are,' he said. 'Put these on.'

Her pulse started thudding ominously. Black? He wanted to shroud her in black?

It's to make you look respectable for the journey, she told herself quickly. Respectable and invisible—dear God, she might as well wear a shroud… She took the clothing from him. 'What about Ned, my pony?'

'I'll pay for his stabling here, until our plans are clarified. Is that your bag? I'll see to it.'

Deb stood very still. Our plans? *What plans*?

He was inspecting her again. 'Now, pinch your cheeks to bring some colour to them—you're deathly white. Try smiling.' He leaned closer. 'Look as if you're enjoying yourself with me, for God's sake. And—get those clothes on.'

Chapter Six

Deb got changed—*all black, she hated black*—then came out slowly into the stable yard, conscious of the grooms and stable boys turning from their work to steal covert glances at her. Just then, Mr Beaumaris—who was rapidly supplanting Palfreyman as her worst enemy—saw her and came to meet her.

What was he intending to do with her, at Palfreyman's?

'My bag…' she began.

'It's in the carriage.' He tugged at her veil sharply. 'Keep that down.'

The grooms, who were clearly disappointed to see that the subject of Mr Beaumaris's amorous attentions was swathed up in such a fashion, quickly lost interest in her—but no one ignored Mr Beaumaris. Already, he was striding purposefully towards the extremely fine travelling carriage that stood in the middle of the yard, with two horses harnessed up to it. A coachman in grey livery who'd been checking the horses turned towards him, touching his hat.

'Everything all right, William?'

'Indeed, Mr Beaumaris.'

'Time for us to be off, then.'

'Right you are, sir.' William swung himself up on to the driver's seat, while one of the hovering grooms hurried to open the passenger door. At the same time a packed public coach had just pulled up beside the inn, and three middle-aged women were alighting from it and staring at Mr Beaumaris in open-mouthed admiration.

Yes, he's handsome, Deb thought bitterly. He was also very, very dangerous. She realised that he was holding out his hand to help her inside, but she ignored it and stepped quickly up to seat herself at the far side. Seeing her bag on the floor there gave her a small sense of relief.

He followed her and leaned out of the window. 'Drive on to Hardgate Hall when you're ready, William,' he called.

The ostlers uttered a shrill warning to all the onlookers, the coachman William urged on the horses and the carriage began to clatter out of the Angel's courtyard.

Deb sank back into her seat. Mr Beaumaris was sitting less than three feet away. *Too close. Far too close.* Deb allowed herself to panic quietly. The man was inhuman. Despite his night of captivity in the forest, his coat of fine broadcloth appeared to have survived his ordeal without a blemish, as had his pristine white shirt. He'd tucked those scorched ruffles out of sight, and…

He'd reached up to open the window and as he did so, his coat sleeve fell back, to reveal that his wrist was tightly bandaged. She looked swiftly at his other wrist and saw the same. Her pulse began to thud. 'Your wrists—those bandages…'

He turned those beautiful, ice-blue, ruthless eyes directly on her. 'When I burned the ropes off, the flames caught my wrists. The skin's a little blistered, but it's nothing much.'

Deb gasped aloud. It must be *exquisitely* painful. She whispered, 'I'm sorry.'

He turned to her, his gaze scouring her. 'Are you? Am I mistaken to think it was your idea to keep me captive all night?'

She clasped her hands in her lap. 'I didn't mean you to be hurt.' She shot a quick look up at him. 'And you wouldn't have been, if only you'd been patient. We were going to set you free—eventually!'

'Perhaps you were,' he said calmly. 'But be warned. It's the sort of thing I neither forgive nor forget.'

She turned away to stare out of the window. *Hateful, hateful man.* She sat in silence as the countryside rolled by, thinking of her friends and wishing she was with them. Unfortunately, the horses were speeding along the turnpike road towards Hardgate Hall as if they were actually eager to get there.

She closed her eyes and pretended to be asleep, although she was aware of the moment they crossed the boundary into Palfreyman's land, because the coach came to a brief halt while the lodge-keeper hurried to open the gate. Then the coachman was urging the horses on down the long driveway, and Deb found herself gazing at the hall in the distance, remembering how as a child she'd vowed never to set foot in Palfreyman's domain again.

She'd broken that vow yesterday, in order to steal the

books. But how hollow the sense of triumph she'd felt seemed now. As Hardgate Hall drew steadily nearer, she reached down to make sure that her leather valise was still tightly fastened, and when she looked up again, Mr Beaumaris's eyes were on her.

He said, 'Best leave all the talking to me.'

'Very well. But I hope you realise that your friend Palfreyman won't be in the least pleased to see me—'

His next words knocked her sideways. 'You think that I'm Palfreyman's *friend*?'

She stammered a little. 'I assumed so, yes. Otherwise, why would you be on your way to—?'

'On my way to visit him? Because I have a few issues to settle with Mr Hugh Palfreyman.' He glanced out, as did she, to see that the house loomed close. 'Enough,' he finished curtly. 'You and I will talk later.'

The carriage pulled to a halt in the gravelled forecourt outside Hardgate Hall, and grooms were hurrying out to take the horses' heads; the gruff voice of Mr Beaumaris's coachman could be heard, giving them orders. Deb put her hand briefly to her temples.

So Mr Beaumaris and Palfreyman were not friends, but enemies. Did that mean Mr Beaumaris was on her side? Far from it, apparently. *Very* far from it. She glanced around quickly. The shrubbery was nearby. And so was the wall, over which she'd clambered to freedom yesterday...

'Don't even think of it,' said Mr Beaumaris, then he climbed out and came striding around to her side of the carriage to open the door. As she stepped down, Deb clutched her valise close and was aware of a cluster of curious faces—the grooms and several footmen—all gazing wide-eyed.

Mr Beaumaris was reaching to tug down her veil—
again—and then his arm was around her, wrapping her
black cloak tighter. 'Allow me to take your bag.'

She shook her head.

'Very well,' he said in a curt voice. 'But let's get inside. Quickly.'

A butler came hurrying up.

'I'm here to see Palfreyman,' Beau told the man. 'I
should have arrived yesterday, but I was delayed. And
I have someone with me, as you'll see.' He gestured to
the girl swathed all in black and Deb saw the butler's
eyes widen with astonishment.

'Mr Palfreyman is upstairs, sir,' he began. 'In his
study—'

'Then fetch him,' Beau cut in. 'We'll wait through
here.'

He guided Deb swiftly into an ante-room, away from
prying eyes, and she swung round to face him. 'Why
are you doing this?' she breathed. She'd seen the looks
on the faces of those grooms as she'd climbed down
from the carriage. They'd thought she was someone
else. They'd thought she was—

'Stay here,' he warned. 'I'm going to have a word
with Palfreyman—alone. Don't speak to anyone.'

And then he was gone. She sat rather weakly on a
chair, putting her bag down by her feet. *They'd thought
she was Paulette. Paulette, all in black, in mourning
for her dead husband.* Moments later she heard voices
outside—Mr Beaumaris and her uncle—and just a
few words were enough for her to realise that, as she'd
guessed, the two men detested one another.

'We expected you yesterday,' Palfreyman was saying. He sounded flustered. 'And I had no idea that you

were bringing *her* with you. Surely you can imagine the effect all this will have on my wife, and...'

The rest of Palfreyman's words were lost to her. Mr Beaumaris spoke next, but again she couldn't hear, then Palfreyman started stammering something that ended with, 'Paulette is ill. She was overcome with grief when her husband died, and now she's resting in the country. In Norfolk—everyone knows it...'

'Wrong, Palfreyman.' Mr Beaumaris's voice was clear enough now. 'What your daughter does to wreck the rest of her life is of no concern to me. But there are matters to be attended to. Business left unsorted.'

'So you bring *her* to my house?' Palfreyman's voice was etched with scarcely controlled fury—and fear, Deb thought. Yes—he sounded terrified of Mr Beaumaris.

She could hear Mr Beaumaris's voice again now, and she strove desperately to catch his words. 'Listen, Palfreyman,' he was declaring. 'You know what will happen if you don't do exactly as I say. I want you to bring me your daughter's letters, and anything else at all that sheds light on your daughter's time in London.'

'But...'

'I remember that your wife was obsessed with keeping news cuttings, theatre programmes, party invitations. I want to see everything, do you understand?'

She heard nothing more, because the door to the room she was in opened suddenly. As Deb whirled round, a woman with a thin, pinched face and eyes oddly bright with excitement came hurrying towards her. 'Paulette?' she whispered. '*Paulette*? Oh, my darling daughter...'

The dawning of hope in her eyes was painful to see. Deb backed away. 'No,' she said, as steadily as she

could. 'No, Aunt Vera, I'm not Paulette. I'm your niece.
I'm Deborah, Emily's daughter—'

She broke off as Vera Palfreyman lunged towards
her, tearing the veil from her face 'Get out of my house,'
she breathed. 'Get *out*. You filthy, deceiving creature.'
And she slapped her so hard across the cheek that Deb
stumbled and fell, striking her forehead on the corner
of a low table.

She opened her eyes slowly, realising as she looked
around that she was lying on a day-bed in a spacious
upstairs chamber. The door to the room was wide open
and Deb saw a young maidservant standing there, ner-
vously holding a tray.

'My lady?' The maid was staring at her. 'Here is
some barley water for you.'

'Thank you. Please leave the…'

The maid put the tray down and almost ran from the
room. '…the tray,' Deb finished. *Oh, my goodness.* She
pulled herself up against the cushions of the day-bed.
Her head still throbbed from where she'd fallen against
that table, but her mind was quite clear now—which
was as well, considering the predicament she was in.

My lady, the maid had called her.

Rising to her feet, she hurried to the window, only to
find out that she was at least two floors up. And there
was no ivy clambering up the wall outside. No escape
that way. As for her bag… Where was her bag?

She went to sit on the day-bed again. The servants
had thought that she was Paulette, from the moment she
arrived. Mr Beaumaris must have known they would.
Why was he doing this?

And then the door opened, and he was there.

* * *

When Palfreyman had told him that the girl had fallen, and had to be carried upstairs unconscious, Beau was incredulous. 'She *fell*?'

'My wife…struck her.' Palfreyman was angry and nervous. 'She fell against a table. It happened because the girl was insolent.'

Beau had actually felt quite cold with rage. She had apparently recovered, but as he walked towards her, he thought he saw a slight reddening on the left side of her brow, and she was backing away from him, folding her arms across her chest as if to protect herself. He didn't intend her to be hurt. Actually hurt. But then again, he couldn't weaken—he had to do what he was doing. Her temporary fragility was surely an illusion. *She's an actress, you fool*, he reminded himself. *And worse.*

He said, 'Are you all right, Miss O'Hara?'

Her gaze was steady. 'Do you know where my bag is, Mr Beaumaris?'

That bag… He suppressed an exclamation. 'One of the footmen left it out in the corridor.' He went to bring it in, putting it on the floor close to where she was sitting. 'I'll ask you again—are you all right?'

He saw her catch her breath. 'So far,' she answered, 'I could say that the last twenty-four hours have been almost the worst of my life.'

'At least you weren't forced to spend the night tied up in the forest.' He sat down, at a safe distance from her, and scrutinised her carefully.

She coloured slightly. 'That was because of a dreadful mistake. I told you, and I apologise. But all of this— you bringing me here. *That* wasn't a mistake. You decided it from the start. You wanted me to look like

Paulette and I don't understand why. Is it some cruel joke of yours? Because you sound as if you absolutely hate her.'

'I have good reason to,' Beau replied levelly. 'Paulette Palfreyman seduced my brother into marriage. And it's because of her that he's dead.'

Deborah O'Hara gazed up at him with wide, shocked eyes, as he spelled out to her in a clear, cold voice how his only brother, Simon—two years younger than he was—had married Paulette last autumn. 'They lived in London,' he told her without emotion, 'where Paulette began almost immediately to take other lovers. She retreated to Norfolk in January this year, supposedly on grounds of ill health. Early in March, she ran off to Venice—to live with her latest lover, an Italian count. I believe she's now married to him.'

He guessed the girl was about to say something. If so, she thought better of it as Beau pressed on relentlessly with his tale.

'Both my brother and Paulette's parents,' he went on, 'worked hard to maintain the story that she was still convalescing in the country, being looked after by an old nurse of hers. Rumours of a possible miscarriage were deliberately whispered around the *ton*. But I knew the truth. And then, two months ago, my brother died in a riding accident.'

She was gazing steadily up at him. 'I'm sorry. Truly sorry. I had no idea that Paulette…' She spread out her hands. 'But what has all this got to do with me?'

'Paulette *betrayed* my brother,' he said in a lethal voice. 'She lured him into marriage, then left him, and I cannot forget it. And there's something else.' He walked across the room to point to a portrait on the wall. 'Who do you think this is, Miss O'Hara?'

Deb came slowly over to join him. 'Paulette,' she breathed.

'Indeed. Do you see the jewels she's wearing?' He pointed in turn at the earrings and necklace she wore, of diamonds and rubies. 'They're known as the Brandon jewels, and Simon gave them to her. I want them back.'

'From—*Venice*?'

'No. I have men of discretion, who work for me quietly and well. They suspect that Paulette left those jewels in a place of safekeeping in London, before her flight. And I want *you* to retrieve them for me.'

Her eyes turned slowly from the portrait to him. She said, 'I'm sorry that your brother died, Mr Beaumaris. But I'm not sure that I quite understand. You're telling me that it's only two months since your brother's death—yet now you're spending your time in trying to obtain some jewels that were a gift from your brother to his wife?' She drew in a deep breath. 'Most men would still be in mourning. Most men would be more concerned about honouring their brother's memory, rather than going to what I can only describe as quite extraordinary lengths to recover some—possessions.'

'The jewels,' he said, 'have not only got a monetary value. They represent my family's honour.'

'Well, Mr Beaumaris, you said you have men working for you. So why not get *them* to retrieve these jewels?' She said the words almost with scorn. 'Get your minions to do your work. I am not one of them.'

There was a moment's silence before Beau said, 'I

need you, Miss O'Hara. You must know that you bear an extremely strong resemblance to Paulette—'

'But that is ridiculous!' She shook her head. 'When I saw Paulette in London last year, she was dressed to perfection. I was raised to wear patched-up cast-offs; I have no idea how to look like a lady…'

Her voice trailed away as Beau put his hands on her shoulders and adjusted her stance. 'Look,' he said. 'Look properly at that picture of Paulette.'

He felt her tremble a little in his grasp, but she said steadily, 'I'm looking. And I can see that everything about her speaks of money and privilege.'

'Listen to me.' Beau turned her to face him and shivers tingled down her spine. At the same time she felt a sharp jolt of awareness implode quietly yet disturbingly deep inside her. *Again. Again.* She wasn't supposed to feel like this. She'd sworn no man would make her feel like this…

'There's nothing,' he was saying, 'absolutely nothing about your appearance that can't be dealt with. You both have the same colour of hair. The fact that hers was carefully coiffured and yours has been allowed to run wild can soon be remedied. You both have unusual gold eyes with dark lashes. You're around the same height and build…'

Remedied. She wouldn't forget that in a hurry. Remedied. Steadily she replied, 'But our faces aren't the same. My nose is shorter, my chin is more pointed. I'm not as plump as Paulette…'

'Once your hair is cut, and you're dressed and veiled in black, no one will think to suspect that you aren't who we say you are. People see what they expect to see, Miss O'Hara. No one has seen Paulette for months—'

'That's just it! People must *know* that she's gone!'

'No. She cut herself off deliberately from her friends when she retreated to Norfolk in January. If there *have* been any whispers about her flight abroad, then your reappearance in London as a grieving widow will convince the *ton* that those stories were completely wrong.'

She made herself meet his gaze steadily. 'So you're going to force me into all this?'

'If necessary, yes.'

She was shaking her head dazedly. 'But my uncle and aunt hate me—they will never agree to this plan! And I'm not one of your minions!'

'Your uncle and aunt will do whatever I say. Because unless Palfreyman does exactly as I command, I'll make sure all of England knows the story of his daughter's scandalous behaviour during her marriage to my brother. As for you not being one of my minions—' and his voice was suddenly, lethally soft '—I've got news for you. You are now.'

All the colour suddenly seemed to leave her face. She walked slowly over to the window and gazed out at the late afternoon sun shining on Palfreyman's gardens.

She would agree to his proposition, Beau was completely sure of that. He certainly wasn't going to have his plan thwarted by yet another member of this tainted and treacherous family. But as she turned back to him, Beau felt a sudden tightness in his lungs. She looked young. She looked vulnerable. She said, 'Your plan is absurd.'

'It's no more absurd than the fact that Palfreyman has managed to keep the whole of society from guessing the truth of Paulette's disappearance,' he answered. 'I believe we can convince London that you are her. But we have to proceed with this matter—*now*.'

She was shaking her head in disbelief. 'And you're prepared to go to all this trouble—this *risk*—merely to get some jewels back?'

'I've told you, the jewels are only a part of it. My brother has been grievously wronged by Paulette's behaviour—and I want all of London to see, if only for a short while, Paulette as she should have been—a grieving widow.'

She tilted her chin. 'So you want revenge.'

'You could call it revenge, Miss O'Hara. I prefer to call it paying my dead brother the honour that should be his due. And I need your answer. Your consent.' He looked meaningfully over at the door. 'We haven't long before Palfreyman comes back.'

She closed her eyes briefly. Then: 'Tell me this, Mr Beaumaris. What was your original plan? Before I turned up? Why, exactly, were you on your way here?'

'To make sure Palfreyman knows that Paulette can never lay claim to anything of my brother's. In other words, I was coming here to warn Palfreyman that I won't tolerate his connivance with his absent daughter, in any way whatsoever.'

'But then—*I* appeared.' Her voice was bitter. 'And presented you with an entirely new strategy.'

'Oh,' he said, 'you presented me, Miss O'Hara, with a whole new range of possibilities.' He walked over to that bag of hers and picked it up. 'I take it you have those books of yours in here?'

She said nothing. Clearly he didn't need to spell out that he could have her prosecuted for kidnap and assault, as well as possibly selling herself. He put the bag down again. 'Your answer?' he prompted with lethal softness.

For one wild moment, Deb thought of telling him the truth about the books. But then—then she would have to confess she was a burglar, and the punishment for breaking into a house like Palfreyman's was hanging. Besides, would he even believe her story? And wasn't it safer anyway to let him go on despising her as a whore, since this lethal man only had to *touch* her and all her self-control fled to the four winds?

'I will do what you say,' she whispered.

'Good,' replied Beau. 'Then let's get on with it. Shall we?'

Chapter Seven

At that very moment the door swung open and Palfreyman stood there, his arms laden with sheaves of paper which he deposited on a nearby table. After taking one scornful look at his niece, he began talking in a low voice to Mr Beaumaris, and Deb backed slowly away from them, her mind reeling. A few hours ago, she'd been full of quiet triumph at her apparent victory over Palfreyman. She'd outmanoeuvred her devious uncle by getting hold of those books, and she'd negotiated freedom from prosecution for her fellow actors.

Now, a whole new nightmare faced her. Sitting down carefully in a chair by the window, she heard Palfreyman talking to Mr Beaumaris in a voice that was a mixture of resentment, petulance and downright fear.

Unless Palfreyman does exactly as I command, she remembered Mr Beaumaris saying, *I'll make sure all of England knows the story of his daughter's scandalous behaviour during her marriage to my brother.*

Now she heard Palfreyman muttering as he leafed through the various items he'd put on the table. 'My wife —*hoards* things. Everything and anything to do with

Paulette. Here are some party invitations and dance programmes. And there are newspaper cuttings too, all relating to Paulette's Season last spring.'

'Do you have the details of the place where she's supposed to be staying now?'

Palfreyman's expression was still grim as he searched. 'Yes.' He pulled out a printed card. 'Here is the address of the Norfolk house where she is still, supposedly, in residence.'

Deb saw Mr Beaumaris inspect it. 'Well,' he said, 'now you'll be able to start spreading the word, Palfreyman, that your daughter has decided to leave her rural retreat and return to London—with me. Won't you?'

Palfreyman glanced furiously at Deb. 'But people will wonder why—?'

'People have never stopped wondering why your daughter didn't even attend my brother's *funeral*,' Mr Beaumaris cut in. 'You informed everyone that Paulette was prostrate with grief. Now you can say that at last your daughter feels sufficiently strong to visit her husband's grave and to pay her last respects. I've played along with all your subterfuge, Palfreyman, but now I've had enough. I want due honour given to my dead brother's memory.'

'But I still don't see how this girl can…'

Mr Beaumaris—tall, powerful and impossibly autocratic—had already turned his attention to Deb. 'Stand up,' he ordered.

She hesitated, and instantly he eased back his cuff, so slightly that it might have been unintentional. But she glimpsed the scorched lace at his wrist and knew that it was a reminder of the bandage there. *Look what you did to me.* She rose very slowly, putting as much defiance as she could into her stance.

'Turn around, Miss O'Hara,' said Mr Beaumaris. She did so, cheeks aflame.

Mr Beaumaris transferred his gaze to Palfreyman. 'I take it, Palfreyman, that your family and all your acquaintances here and in London will have long forgotten that your niece exists?'

'Well, yes,' began Palfreyman, glancing at Deb with mingled anger and contempt. 'Since this girl's foolish mother chose to disgrace herself by running off and getting herself pregnant by some ne'er-do-well. But you'll never get away with this—'

'Won't I? Even you must be aware,' Mr Beaumaris cut in softly, 'that the servants are already saying that the girl who arrived here today is your daughter. Your *wife* thought she was your daughter.'

'Yes. But…'

'The girl will be Paulette,' said Mr Beaumaris, 'but not the Paulette that you and the fashionable world know. She will instead appear as a devastated young widow who is only reluctantly beginning to appear in society again, under the protection of her brother-in-law. Me. And if you breathe one word of the pretence, Palfreyman, you'll regret it deeply.'

'What about *her*?' Again Palfreyman pointed at Deb. 'The little tramp could blackmail you for the rest of her life over this, and no doubt she's already planning it—'

'Stop it,' Deb breathed. 'Stop it, both of you.'

She was making for the door, and Beau was charging after her. 'You cannot run,' he said. 'Are you forgetting we have an agreement?'

She gave him a look of pure scorn. 'I'll keep to our

agreement, don't worry. But I warn you now—there is a limit to what I will tolerate.' She pointed to a narrow room leading off the corridor. 'I'll wait for you in here, Mr Beaumaris—but I won't be subject to my uncle's insults a moment longer.'

She walked, head high, into the neighbouring room, leaving Beau standing there.

Most men would still be in mourning, she'd said. *Most men would be more concerned about honouring their brother's memory.*

His brother's memory was in fact what all this was about—but since her opinion of him was clearly at rock bottom, perhaps it was better to keep it that way. Safer to keep it that way, especially as he kept remembering only too vividly the way her slender body had felt when he'd kissed her in the forest.

And thoughts like that had no place whatsoever in his plans.

Deb found herself in a narrow room that was sparsely furnished with a sofa, a low table and some chairs pushed into various dark corners. She put her hands to her cheeks, feeling agitated and cold. How could she possibly be Paulette?

Then she remembered how the servants had backed away in shock as she'd emerged from the coach, veiled and swathed in black. Even her aunt had thought that she was Paulette, and her rage when she'd discovered she wasn't had been vicious—Deb's temple still throbbed from where she'd hit the corner of the table after Vera Palfreyman struck her.

Mr Beaumaris had planned it all so carefully. She hadn't realised how safe she felt with the Lambeth Play-

ers. Now, she suspected that she would never feel safe
again.

This room was dark and airless—unlike the other
room, the window was too high up for her to be able to
look out. The walls were lined with paintings that were
of little value, she guessed, since they were hung carelessly and without any order or neatness.

She walked to and fro for ten minutes or more, thinking, *I am trapped, like an animal in a cage.* At last—to
distract herself from her agonising thoughts, if nothing
else—she began to look at the various pictures. And suddenly, amongst some small portraits that were almost
lost in the shadows of a deep alcove, she saw one that
made her hold her breath as she stooped to look at it.

It was an old and faded portrait of a young girl with
chestnut hair, perhaps ten or eleven years old, looking
sad and unbearably alone. Deb felt her chest tighten
as she lifted it carefully from its hook and carried it
over to the meagre light. *That hair. The sadness in
those eyes…*

She spun round with a gasp as the door opened, and
Mr Beaumaris entered.

When Beau saw her there, with the light from the
small window slanting across her slender figure, he
thought that he glimpsed in her unguarded expression
some terrible unspoken grief, and it pierced him with
unexpected force. But he needn't have worried. As soon
as she realised he was there she faced him squarely, with
defiance etched in every line of her stance. In every
lock of her unruly hair.

She'd been holding a small picture, he'd noticed.
He also noticed that she swiftly put it face down on a

nearby table the minute he came in. Beau made a mental note to take a closer look at that picture just as soon as he could. He said, 'I'm sorry that you were subjected to—certain of Palfreyman's phrases.'

'Are you?' she answered softly. 'I warned you that Palfreyman long ago banished my mother from this house. How, exactly, did you expect him to react to my arrival here?'

Beau exhaled sharply. 'Palfreyman accepts,' he said, 'that he had no right to speak to you like that. I extracted an apology from him, which I told him I would convey to you. Palfreyman won't make any trouble, you may rest assured—'

'Stop,' she breathed, interrupting him. '*Stop.*' She was gazing up at him almost desperately. 'Tell me the truth. From the moment you first saw me, in the forest, you planned all of this, didn't you? You came to me at the Angel with the black cloak and gown and bonnet. You *knew* that I would accept.'

'I knew that, like Palfreyman, you had little choice,' he answered. 'As we've already discussed. And I don't see how you can even think of making judgements on the morality of my tactics.'

He was thinking of the kidnap. And those books—*again.* She drew a deep, shuddering breath, then suddenly looked up at him with her clear, bright gaze. 'What about my friends, Mr Beaumaris? They are a company of actors, as you've surely realised, and I look after all their bookings and the money. I keep the records of which plays we've put on and where. I'm also the one who decides on our programme for the coming season—'

'You sound invaluable,' he cut in drily. 'But I'm afraid they'll have to manage without you for a short while.'

'You're not—making me stay *here*? At Hardgate Hall?'

'For tonight, yes. There's no alternative. Write to them in Gloucester—that's where they've travelled to, isn't it? You can make up some excuse and I'll see that your letter is delivered.'

'What about Ned?'

Ned? He almost laughed when he remembered. 'Your pony.'

'Yes—my pony! What will happen to him?'

'Naturally,' he said, 'I shall arrange for him to be… reunited with your friends.'

'But that will cost a… You would really go to so much trouble?'

'To defeat your objections, Miss O'Hara, yes.'

At first, he thought she wasn't going to say anything at all. She walked to the end of the room and stood there a moment with her head bowed, and only then did she turn back to him.

'What can I say?' There was a hint of bitterness in her voice. 'You seem to have everything planned, Mr Beaumaris.'

'It's essential that I have everything planned,' he replied, 'since I'm going to be the one taking you back to London. I'm going to be the one who has to explain to society that you have finally summoned the strength to return to the public eye in order to pay my dead brother the respect he is due.'

'And to get back those jewels.' Her voice was harder now.

'Let's call it all a matter of my family's honour, Miss O'Hara. Now, I believe there's a housemaid waiting out in the main hall to show you your room upstairs—it's been prepared for you. Will you dine later?'

'With my uncle and aunt?' She shook her head. 'I think I'd rather starve.'

'Then I'll have your supper sent to your room. And we'll have no more talk about starving, if you please. Let me make it clear from now on that you can save your melodramatics for the stage.'

She smiled sweetly up at him. 'Oh, you've seen very little of my melodramatics yet—Mr Beaumaris.'

And Beau realised something else he'd forgotten. Damn it all. *She still didn't know who he really was*.

Beau dined with Palfreyman and his wife that evening, in an over-furnished dining room that shouted of new wealth. The fellow had gone mad for *chinoiserie*—there were dragons and nodding mandarins painted on the walls, with blue-and-white porcelain pots on every possible surface. The footmen were icily efficient, the food was elaborate and the wine rich—but Beau would rather have had supper in his room, like the girl, or a meal in the nearest alehouse with William Barry, come to that.

To have to spend even one night under the roof of the man whose daughter had trapped Simon into marriage churned like acid in Beau's gut.

The liveried footmen brought in course after course, and during the progress of the meal Palfreyman veered in his attitude to Beau between downright sycophancy and barely concealed hatred. His thin-faced wife—*she struck the girl*, thought Beau, *she struck the girl*—ate very little and hardly spoke a word.

Shortly before the meal, Beau had gone to visit Deborah O'Hara in the bedroom that had been allotted to her. He'd asked for pen and paper to be provided in there, and he wasn't surprised to find that she'd already made use of it. 'I've addressed my letter to Francis Calladine,' she said tonelessly as she handed him the sealed envelope. 'He is the longest-serving member of the Lambeth Players, and I've told him that he's in charge now. I had to lie, of course. I told him that I heard in Oxford today that a relative of my mother's had been taken very sick, and that I needed to visit her. I told Francis that I hoped to rejoin them all soon.'

'I'll make sure your letter reaches him,' he promised. 'And, Miss O'Hara—I'll certainly ensure that all this is worth your while.'

She stared at him. 'Are you talking about money? I thought I was doing all this to save myself and my friends from a prison sentence or worse.'

He shrugged. 'I'll reward you as well. I assume some money would be useful?'

'And I used to think,' she said softly, 'that there were limits as to what I'd do to earn it.'

Damn it, she ought to be grateful. This girl wrong-footed him at every turn, and he couldn't afford to let her. Beau was still brooding an hour later as he tinkered with the dishes of food that Palfreyman's servants set before him. Yes, she should be grateful; apart from anything else, there was the fact that he wasn't prosecuting her companions. And she would see London in style, wouldn't she?—all right, so she would be in mourning, but for a few weeks she would be able to lead the kind of life she wouldn't normally even dream of!

Clearly a similar thought had gone through Palfreyman's mind, since after Vera had left them to their port, Palfreyman dismissed the servants and said to Beau, 'You'll have to watch that girl, if you ask me. Letting her loose in London. Her mother had little sense of morality, and you know what they say. Like mother, like daughter.'

'Her mother,' Beau said, 'was your sister. And be careful what you say about your niece. Do I really have to remind you about your daughter's truly scandalous behaviour?'

After that he left Palfreyman almost immediately and headed up the stairs towards his allotted rooms. By his own estimation, family loyalty and family devotion did not tend to be universal qualities. His father and mother had detested one another, and been completely indifferent to their two sons.

But the girl bothered him. He couldn't forget her voice as she'd whispered to him, 'You're not making me stay *here*?'

She'd appeared vulnerable—even innocent. That had to be an illusion. But she had been so sweet to hold, and her lips were shy, almost...

She's an actress, he told himself bleakly. A fine actress. That's all. But the way back to his own room led past her door, and some wayward impulse made him stop—and listen.

What the devil did he expect to hear? The sound of her sobs? He knocked, then again, harder. 'Miss O'Hara?' His voice was almost harsh. 'Miss O'Hara?'

There was no reply. With a darkening brow, Beau put his shoulder to the door and found himself inside an empty room, lit only by the glow of a low fire in the hearth. The bed itself was pristine. The black cloak, the dress and the bonnet lay neatly upon it. But—*she wasn't there.*

Chapter Eight

Beau felt filled with a furious frustration that his plan
might yet go wrong. He'd thought—surprising himself
with his verdict—that he could trust her. Then suddenly
he remembered the room lined with portraits, one floor
down, where she'd sought refuge from Palfreyman—
and from him—earlier today. She'd been looking at a
picture there when he came in…

Guessing that Palfreyman would be surlily intent
on finishing that bottle of port by himself in the dining room, Beau descended the stairs and strode along
the corridor, working out where the room was. When
he reached it, the door wasn't shut. And she was inside.

He could see her sitting cross-legged on that old
chintz sofa, gazing in the soft light of a single candle
at the small framed picture she'd been looking at before. She was wearing the white shirt and black velvet
breeches that she'd worn to play Viola. Loose tendrils
of chestnut curls curtained her forehead and billowed
around her shoulders.

He felt the blood start to beat heavily through his
veins. She looked lovely. Quite lovely.

He must have moved slightly, because she suddenly looked up to see his figure blocking the doorway and she sprang to her feet. 'Mr Beaumaris…'

She still didn't know who he was. He came slowly into the room. 'I thought you might have run away,' he said.

She was certainly standing as if poised for flight, glancing at the door behind him. But her words were stalwart enough. 'I told you,' she said. 'I keep my word.'

He nodded and cleared his throat. 'Have you had a meal?'

'A maid came with some supper. And then I had a bath, and got dressed again. But I didn't want to wear that black gown. I'm much more comfortable in my old clothes.'

He said, more tersely than he meant to, 'You *must* wear mourning. You must wear a veil. From now on, you must be Paulette, *always.*'

'I know.' She met his eyes unflinchingly. 'I know, and I didn't intend to break the promise I made. No one has seen me like this tonight except you, but you're right. I'd better go back to my room.' But she was still clutching the picture close to her chest, just as she had when he came in.

He said, 'Hadn't you better put that picture back first?'

She gave a start, then nodded and made for the alcove, where the picture had hung; Beau followed her. 'Here,' he said. 'Let me.'

She didn't want him to see it, he could tell. She didn't want him to even touch it. He hung it carefully back on the wall, giving himself time to take it in. It was a portrait of a young girl whose chestnut hair was pulled back tightly beneath a plain straw bonnet. She had a strained, unhappy look on her face. And both her bonnet and her gown were of the type that was fashionable thirty or more years ago...

The girl had to be Palfreyman's sister. This girl's mother. He turned to her and said, 'Are you very tired, Miss O'Hara? Can we talk for a while?'

'If you like.' Her expression told him, *I'd much rather not.*

Beau said, 'I *do* like, as it happens.' He gestured towards the small sofa. 'Please sit down. Please make yourself comfortable.'

She cast him a glance that expressed pure incredulity at the idea of being comfortable in his presence, then she crossed the room to sit on the sofa again. Beau dragged up a chair and sat opposite her, then pointed across to the portrait he'd just replaced and said without expression, 'Was that your mother?'

'My mother, yes.' She was gazing at the picture. 'My uncle—Hugh Palfreyman—was twelve when she was born, and my mother told me that he never forgave her for the fact that their mother died while giving birth to her. Eight years later, a winter fever carried their father also to his grave, and Hugh became the master of Hardgate Hall. My mother ran away when she was seventeen.'

'Do you know why?'

'I thought I'd told you, back at the inn. I gathered—though she spoke of it only rarely—that Palfreyman *drove* her away, with his coldness and his emotional cruelty.' She looked up at him with her wide, anguished eyes. 'And then—he banished her a second time when she visited him with me, years later.'

'So she brought you *here*?'

'When I was six.'

'Had she come for money?'

This time her look was full of contempt for him. 'Far from it, Mr Beaumaris. She had come to propose a reconciliation, because she knew she was dying.'

Now, *that* shook his composure at last. 'She was *what*?'

'She knew she was dying,' she repeated. 'Of a lung sickness. My mother thought—' and a small, bitter laugh escaped her '—that Hugh Palfreyman might feel a little actual *regret*, if he heard some day that his only sister had died, while he and she were still estranged. I was six years old, and I shall never, ever forget that visit.'

Silence fell, except for the distant steps of a servant carrying coals and hot water to some bedroom upstairs. 'Please,' said Beau. 'Tell me more.'

'Do you really want me to?'

'I do.'

He saw her shiver, then she continued, 'My mother had put me in my very best dress for that visit. She had brushed my hair till it shone. She knew that she had only a few months to live, but I didn't realise it at the time, though I used to be upset because she couldn't stop coughing.' Her gaze went to that picture, then she looked back at him. 'I didn't want to enter this big, strange house, even though my mother told me that her brother and his wife were bound to be kind to me.'

'And were they?' Beau prompted gravely.

Her voice was steady again. 'We were allowed in as far as the entrance hall. But my uncle stopped us there. My mother—her name was Emily—said something like, "This is my daughter, Hugh. My only daughter, Deborah. I thought you might have been thinking of her." Hugh Palfreyman almost pushed her away. He said to her, "*Thinking* of you? Are you mad? You made your own choices, Emily. And now you're no sister of mine. Get out of my house, and take your brat with you.""

Beau was silent for a moment. 'So you and your mother had to leave? That was it?'

'Almost,' Deb said quietly.

'Almost?'

'Palfreyman told a footman to see us off the premises. We'd nearly reached the door, when suddenly Paulette appeared, with a woman who was her nurse. This nurse clearly realised that we weren't to be spoken to, and tried to drag Paulette away.

'I remember thinking, when I saw Paulette there in the entrance hall, how very pretty she was, and how lovely her clothes were. My mother had told me about my cousin the night before. "You are almost the same age," my mother said to me. "And you might become friends."

'Paulette wore a turquoise dress trimmed with satin ruffles and lace—I can still picture it—and I smiled at her. But she scowled at me and said to her nurse, "Who is that dirty girl who's staring at me so?"'

Mr Beaumaris appeared to be absorbed in some unspoken thought or memory. 'That sounds like Paulette,' he said at last. 'Did you leave after that?'

'We left, yes. Although we were just setting off to walk away down the drive when the old housekeeper—she must have retired from here long ago—came hurrying after us with some little cakes. I remember her whispering to my mother, "The master, Miss Emily—he's not changed one little bit. God bless you and your daughter!" My mother died six months later.'

'But you still had your father?'

'I had my stepfather, Gerald O'Hara. I don't actually know who my real father was, and I have no desire to know. As far as I was concerned, Gerald was the best father I could hope to have, and the Lambeth Players were—*are*—my family.'

She looked up at Beau with clear, open eyes. 'I hate this house. I hate Hugh Palfreyman and his wife. And although I've promised that I'll do exactly as you say, I'm…I'm *afraid* of going to London, as Paulette.'

Beau thought to himself, *This should have been easy, damn it.* This girl—this travelling actress—was completely in his power thanks to her men's assault on him. Anyone else would have been grateful for his leniency, and been eager to explore the opportunity her new situation would offer along the way. Any other woman might even have slyly tried to raise her price—one way or another.

Instead she was sitting there in her boy's clothes looking as if the proposal he'd made was every bit as bad as being thrown in gaol.

He acknowledged now that he'd misjudged her, in many ways. He could see why she hated her uncle, and who could blame her? Hugh Palfreyman had treated both mother and daughter quite shamefully…

And he himself, Damian Beaumaris, was treating her no better.

His mouth hardened. He needed to do this. His whole life centred around doing this.

'You will be in mourning,' he reminded her sharply. 'You will be a grieving widow, and in my care. You will be very much protected, in my London house—'

'I'll have to live with *you*?'

'Where else? You're my sister-in-law, after all. Though I'm afraid that in the circles in which I move it's inevitable that you'll face a certain amount of curiosity. Shall I remind you again of the story you must tell if questioned?'

She sat down again and leaned back on the sofa. 'If you wish.'

'You were taken ill in January, three months after your wedding. There were, I believe, rumours of a miscarriage. You retreated to the countryside to convalesce. When the news was brought to you of your husband's accidental death in April, the shock made you so overcome with grief that you weren't even able to attend the funeral in London. Since then you've remained in rural retreat, too stricken to face society. Will you be able to remember all that?'

She said wearily, 'I regularly have to remember whole *plays*, Mr Beaumaris.'

He nodded. 'I shall let it be known that at last you feel strong enough to come to town, to make your appearance as my brother's grieving widow and to accept society's condolences.'

'And to reclaim those jewels,' Deb added quietly.

'And to reclaim the jewels.' His voice was iron-hard again. 'I told you, I think, that I've reason to believe Paulette left the jewels secretly in London before she went to Venice early in March. She perhaps did it as a kind of insurance for herself—in case her plans didn't work out. It appears likely that Paulette gave them to a London jewel-dealer for safekeeping.'

'But how do you know that? Oh, I was forgetting. Your minions.' She was still looking at him in that way that unsettled him. 'But I thought you said Paulette would *never* return to England.'

'And nor will she—openly. But it's just possible she might come to London secretly, to collect the jewels and return swiftly to her new husband, her new life. I want to make sure she doesn't get them.'

Deb felt a rush of sudden dread compressing her lungs. *This man was pitiless.* Heaven help anyone who was his enemy. 'May I ask you a question, Mr Beaumaris? How many hours of sleep has Paulette Palfreyman cost you?'

'I want justice for my brother,' he replied.

'No, you don't,' she answered him coolly. 'It's your pride making you do this. It's my belief that you just cannot bear anyone getting the better of you.'

Beau's eyes were narrow slits. 'My motives, Miss O'Hara, aren't yours to question.'

'But your strategy is, since I'm to play a major part in it! How can I seriously pretend to be Paulette?' Her composure appeared to be cracking at last. She got to her feet and walked to and fro.

He too rose and came slowly towards her, and she was utterly shaken by the lithe movement of his lean body, by the sense of his power and strength. She'd never met anyone like him, and she knew she was in deep, deep trouble.

'You *will* be Paulette,' he said. 'We shall make you Paulette, in every way.'

She tossed her head almost scornfully. 'You sound as though you remember her well.'

'I shall never forget her,' he said. Then he glanced at his pocket watch as if the conversation was beginning to bore him. 'Of course, Miss O'Hara, I'll make it all worth your while.'

Her head jerked up at that. 'You told me that before.'

'And I'm saying it again. There'll be a reward for you, if you're successful. It's up to you, what that reward is.'

She was walking slowly across the room again, her hands thrust in the pockets of her breeches, her head bowed in thought. As Beau watched her, he felt an unwelcome stirring of interest again. In those slim-fitting breeches, her *derrière* looked exquisite. Her chestnut curls were in glorious disarray, her waist was slim enough for him to grasp in his hands…

She swung round suddenly, and he hoped to God she hadn't seen the darkening of arousal in his eyes. Lifting her head, she said, 'You're rich, aren't you, Mr Beaumaris?'

He shrugged. 'Rich enough.'

'Then I want you to provide my actor friends with a London theatre.'

'A theatre?' He was astonished.

'Yes! You could buy a lease, giving us a small theatre south of the river, perhaps, where my friends will have the freedom to put on whatever plays they wish.' She was gathering speed now. 'I want it in writing, Mr Beaumaris, and—and oh, my *goodness*…'

Her voice faded away.

'What?' Beau asked sharply. 'What is it?'

Only then did he realise that her gaze had dropped to his hands.

'You've unwrapped the bandages from your wrists,' she breathed. 'Those burns—they look so painful!'

'They're nothing,' he lied. Impatiently he pulled down the ruffled cuffs of his shirt to cover them.

But she'd already stepped quickly up to him, and she pushed back the lace again. 'The skin is blistering. You must protect it. You need some sort of salve—we used to use witch-hazel…'

Her fingers were gentle on his hands. Her slim body was warm next to his. He could so easily have pushed her away, but he didn't.

He'd wanted to stay rational throughout this encounter. Wanted to stay cold-bloodedly in control—he was *used* to being in control, always. It was the sweet scent of her hair that did it, he told himself harshly, and now he was struggling to command his senses.

'You sound as though you care,' he said with a cynical curl of his lip. 'Is that because my injuries were your fault?'

Her eyes shot up to meet his. 'You did this to *yourself*, remember! Yes, I told my men to keep you prisoner. But that was because—because…'

It was because she'd had to wait till the morning for Palfreyman's letter. It was because she'd thought this man was Palfreyman's friend. It was because… Oh, heavens, what an utter, abominable mess.

She jerked away from him. 'I'm going back to my room.'

'I don't think we've finished our conversation yet,' he reminded her. 'Yes, Miss O'Hara—you'll have your theatre.'

She looked rather dazed. 'I—I will?'

'We'll sort the details later, when our bargain is concluded—you have my promise. But you've not answered all my questions yet.' His hand reached out to catch her arm. 'You've still got those books, haven't you? In that shabby bag of yours?'

Her insides churned with shock and dismay. 'Yes. What of it?'

He was surveying her tight-fitting breeches and shirt. 'Why do you guard them so carefully? Is it so you can study them by candlelight? So you can—perfect your professional skills?'

She caught her breath. Would he never forget those books? And then—*what*?—he was using his lean fingers to raise her chin, forcing her to look up at him. He was drawing his thumb slowly over her lower lip, and…

No.

She couldn't breathe. She couldn't think. She felt as if his dark eyes were burning into her soul. Then he cupped her face in his hands and brought his mouth down on hers. As her heart jolted and stopped, he parted her lips with sweet strokes of his tongue; he plundered her mouth with skilled caresses, stirring up feelings that she hadn't realised she possessed. His hand had slipped round her hips to draw her close to his hard, unyielding body and flames of shock tore through her.

She hadn't known. She hadn't even guessed it could be—like this. The taste of his mouth and tongue was so dangerously good that she gave a low moan. Her breasts, pressed against the hard contours of his chest, were melting, yearning for more. Then his fingers slipped beneath the soft lawn of her boy's shirt and roved upwards, finding bare flesh, and she felt her whole body tremble. Especially when his hand brushed the lower curve of one small, sweetly swelling breast…

The clock on the mantelpiece chiming twelve brought her back to her senses. Somehow, though her heart was pounding and her blood was drumming through her

veins—somehow she pushed him away. *My God, Deb.*
You might have decided to suffer his taunts and let him
think you a whore. But you're playing your part a lit-
tle too well.

Beau was breathing hard. He could have done more
than kiss her, he knew. Her lips were rosy and swollen. Her hair was a tumbled cloud, half covering her
flushed face. She looked quite irresistible. He knew he
could have drawn her into his arms and kissed her again
until she melted, then carried her upstairs to the suite
of rooms Palfreyman had reluctantly provided for him.
He could have made love to her all night long. It was
perhaps what she wanted. What she expected.

And his palm still tingled from the feel of the silken
skin of her breast...

He saw her start to smooth down her shirt and her
breeches—but her hands were trembling.

'I'm sorry,' Beau said.

Her eyes shot up to his—wary eyes, full of defiance,
yet unexpectedly fragile. 'You're apologising? For the
kiss, or for the insult?'

'For both,' he said. He exhaled sharply. 'That
shouldn't have happened. I didn't *mean* it to happen.
And there won't be a repeat of it. We'll leave for London in the morning. And we'll both of us remember that
ours is purely a business arrangement.'

'But *of course.*' There was more than a hint of scorn
in her voice now—as if she knew how his blood was still
drumming through his veins, how harsh desire was still
thumping at his loins. 'But I think *you're* the one who
needs to recollect the exact nature of our arrangement
—Mr Beaumaris.'

She'd already started towards the door, but at the last moment she swung round on him. 'I keep my word,' she said. 'I hope you do, too.' And with that she left.

Beau paced the room, cursing himself. She was just what he needed. She looked so much like Paulette that, dressed in mourning, anyone who spotted the differences between her and her cousin would swiftly forget them. She was an actress. She was shrewd and tough—she had to be, thanks to the life she'd led. And he was going to *make* it work—damn it to hell, he wasn't going to let this chance get away.

But he was going to have to be careful. This one was as beautiful as Paulette, but far more of a threat, because she puzzled him more and more. Those books of hers would shame some of the street walkers of Covent Garden. She blithely admitted they were tools of her trade. And yet she'd seemed so innocent—*shocked*, even, when he kissed her just now.

Another trick? A pretence of shy reluctance, to entice him into lust? She was a wicked little temptress. A clever actress, that was the sum of it. And that made her, he concluded bitterly, all the more fitting to play her cousin Paulette.

Because—before his brother died, and before she ran away—the beautiful Paulette had done her very best to seduce Beau himself.

Instead of going to bed, Deb sat shivering on a chair by the window, wearing the expensive silk nightgown the maid had laid out for her. She couldn't help wondering whose it was. Was it an old one of Paulette's? She pressed her hand to her throbbing forehead, thinking that at least she should be grateful Mr Beaumaris hadn't spotted the bruise that was hidden by her unruly hair, for it was beginning to turn an ugly shade of purple. After glancing at it again in the mirror—*oh, no, it looked even worse*—she went to pull back the curtains and gaze at the night sky.

Anything, to take her mind away from the horrifying fact that she was completely in the power of Mr Beaumaris.

She'd saved the Lambeth Players and she'd made her bargain. But it wasn't supposed to be like this. Beaumaris was her enemy, every bit as much as Palfreyman was, yet she just couldn't stop remembering how she'd felt when he'd held her just now. How she'd felt when he kissed her.

He'd done it to humiliate her—he'd made that clear. Her aim had been to keep him at arm's length—to let him persist in thinking her a woman of the world, well able to take care of herself—but instead she'd made an utter fool of herself by submitting to his wiles.

Deb curled up on the chair by the window, feeling cold and wretched. Mr Beaumaris was surely the most cynical man she'd ever met. He'd talked on and on about his family's honour, but when it came to *her* honour, he clearly thought her beneath contempt. Which was hardly surprising, since when he'd lured her into that wickedly delicious embrace, she'd melted. Just melted.

She shivered. *You aren't going to get any sleep at all if you keep thinking about him, you fool.*

Well, since she didn't feel she would get to sleep in this hateful house anyway, she might as well do something useful. Deb rose to her feet and went back towards her bed, because laid out on the counterpane was

the heap of documents Palfreyman had reluctantly provided; Mr Beaumaris had brought them to her earlier.

'You might find it useful to look through these if you
can,' he'd said in his usual brusque manner. 'The more
you know about Paulette, the better.'

Now she settled on the bed, propped herself up
against the pillows, and flicked through the items list-
lessly. Who had collected them together? Her aunt Vera,
probably. Mostly they were ephemera such as party invitations and dance cards; although some theatre programmes from Covent Garden and Drury Lane held
her interest for a little while longer.

Some day, if Mr Beaumaris kept his promise, she
would have a small theatre of her own. Some day, when
all this was over…

The bruise on her forehead seemed to be making her
whole head ache. She sat cross-legged on the bed, pressing a cold damp cloth to her temple, trying to will the
pain away. Then she realised that a pile of papers had
tumbled to the floor. Sighing, she bent to pick them up
and was about to put them to one side, weary of reading, when she realised that these items were different,
because they were about Paulette's wedding in London
last October.

Today saw the marriage of Miss Paulette Palfrey-
man, only daughter of Hugh Palfreyman of Hardgate
Hall in Oxfordshire, to Lord Simon Beaumaris, of Hert-
ford Street, London. The bride, who was given away by
her father, was attended by six bridesmaids; while his
Grace, the Duke of Cirencester, Lord Simon's brother,
gave an eloquent speech at the wedding feast…

For the next few moments Deb felt very strange, as
though everything around her had somehow altered

irretrievably. To all outward appearances, everything remained the same as before. She was still in Palfreyman's house. She still felt afraid and alone. But really, nothing—*nothing* was the same. Everything was much worse.

What had Mr Beaumaris said to her earlier? *I'm afraid that in the circles in which I move, it's inevitable that you'll face curiosity…*

She'd heard of the Duke of Cirencester. *Everybody* had heard of the Duke of Cirencester. She remembered, all too clearly, the name by which he was known up and down the country—*the Dangerous Duke*. He'd earned his reputation because of his sharp tongue, and because of his renowned skill with both duelling sword and pistol. Also because of the beauteous mistresses he was rumoured to keep in sumptuous style, only to cast them aside, leaving broken hearts scattered in his wake.

Nobody—but *nobody* got the better of the Dangerous Duke.

Slowly Deb began to gather up all the programmes and cuttings and went to put them carefully on the dressing table. Then she blew out her candle and climbed beneath the counterpane of the bed, her bruised head throbbing so fiercely that she feared she might be sick. It was sixteen years since she'd last been inside this hated house, and here she was again. But this time, she was old enough to truly fear what lay in store for her.

Chapter Nine

By eight o'clock the next morning Beau was out in the stableyard, where his coachman was putting the last touches to the preparation of his carriage for the journey ahead.

'With respect, your Grace,' opined William, 'I wouldn't trust Palfreyman's stable boys with a pony and trap, let alone your new travelling carriage.' He paused to look around. 'I take it that it will be just you and me heading back to London today?'

'Not quite. You see, the young lady we brought here yesterday is coming to London with us also.'

William struggled. Then he said, with an effort, 'Very well, your Grace. Miss O'Hara seems a quiet enough young creature—'

'Here's the point, William,' interrupted Beau. 'From now on, you will address the lady in question as Lady Simon.'

William's honest face was a picture. 'But Lady Simon was your brother's—?'

'My dead brother's wife,' nodded Beau. 'Just so. The lady we "collected" from the Angel yesterday is Lady Simon's cousin, hence the likeness. But for purposes of my own, she's now Lord Simon's grieving widow.' He patted his stunned coachman's shoulder. 'I trust you to be discreet, William.'

Just then Hugh Palfreyman came out into the yard, looking flustered. 'Your Grace. May I have a word—in private?'

Beau had breakfasted in his room, since he was of the opinion that the less time he had to spend with his host the better. But now he listened intently as Palfreyman explained that his niece was indisposed.

'One of the housemaids took her some tea this morning,' he muttered, 'and the girl tried to keep her eyes covered with her hand. She had a slight megrim, she explained. But then the maid caught sight of her, and the sight was shocking, she said. So she ran down to tell the housekeeper—who told me—that one of the girl's eyes is half-shut, and the skin around it is as black and blue as can be. I warned you, your Grace. I warned you that she is nothing but trouble—'

Beau said sharply, 'I wonder if you recall that she bruised herself because your wife struck her, Palfreyman? And perhaps I need to remind you that you'll treat the girl with respect—unless you want me to reveal to the world how the *real* Paulette has disgraced herself.'

Palfreyman's pursed mouth opened and closed. Beau almost pushed the man aside and swept back into the house. *Damn.* It was a slight bruise to her forehead, she'd told him yesterday, and he'd not thought to question her about it. But he should have done.

He headed for her room.

Deb had woken early, taken one glance in the mirror and gasped. The bruise on her temple had darkened and spread, and now the eye beneath it was almost shut, with the skin around it an interesting mixture of black and blue, with a hint of purple.

At first she tried to brush her hair forward to hide it, as she'd done yesterday, but there was no concealing *this*. When a young maid came in with her morning tea, Deb tried to keep her hand over it; but the maid, as she went to draw back the curtains, caught sight of her and fled the room.

Deb sat there, her heart sinking. Oh, no. The maid would tell everyone, including Mr Beaumaris. Only he *wasn't* Mr Beaumaris, he was the Duke of Cirencester…

There was an ominous rap at her door. Then it opened, and Mr Beaumaris, no, the Duke was there. She clutched at her nightrobe and saw him taking in her startling appearance.

Dear God, thought Beau, *she would hardly be able to see anything from that eye.* 'You should have told me yesterday,' he rapped out. '*Why* didn't you tell me yesterday?'

'I saw no need to,' she answered coolly. 'I assure you, it's not nearly as bad as it looks.'

Dear God, she *had* to be in pain. That swollen eye looked atrocious. He made up his mind swiftly. 'You're going nowhere near my house in London while you look as if you've been floored in a prize fight,' he pronounced. 'Instead we'll go to Brandon Abbey, my country home in Hertfordshire.'

She looked quite distressed. 'But that will delay your plans. I would rather get all this over with—'

'I'm sure you would,' he said curtly. 'But my mind's made up. We'll stay in Hertfordshire for a few days, until I judge that you're fit to be presented to society.'

Except for the darkness of her bruised skin, her complexion looked paler than ever. 'Fit to be presented to society?' she echoed softly, almost mockingly. 'I'm afraid it might take me more than a few days to make me a suitable companion for a duke—*your Grace.*'

He looked up sharply. 'So you've learned who I am?'

She nodded. 'Was it your idea of amusement not to tell me?'

He pressed his lips together. 'Often I prefer to travel incognito, as Mr Beaumaris. It makes life easier.'

She nodded, but found that her hands were shaking slightly. 'Would it have been so very difficult to announce your rank to me at some point in the proceedings?'

'Would it have made any difference?'

Deb shrugged. 'I might have bowed and curtsied to you a little more, I suppose.'

She heard the rush of his indrawn breath, then his gaze swept over her, cold and expressionless. 'We'll depart for Brandon Abbey in an hour,' he said, and with that he left.

Deb sank back on to her bed with her eyes closed. *Oh, no.* This was going to be even worse than she expected.

She dressed with the help of the maid, though she would have preferred to manage by herself, because the maid kept glancing at her bruised face in horror. When the maid held out her black bonnet and veil, Deb almost snatched at it, glad to pull the veil down; then finally she swathed herself in the black cloak and hurried down the stairs, clutching her brown valise.

Only to realise that in the entrance hall, most of the

staff appeared to have been summoned there, to pay their due respects on her departure.

'Lady Simon, ma'am,' they murmured to her, the footmen bowing and the maids curtsying as she walked slowly past them.

The travesty had begun, thought Deb with a faltering heart.

It was going to be a hot day. As a footman took her bag and escorted her out to the waiting carriage, she saw that the sky was a clear blue, the breeze gentle; it was just the kind of summer day, in fact, when she and her friends would travel through towns and villages with light hearts, eagerly discussing future plans.

Today, her destiny was spelled out for her by the clothes she was wearing. She was shrouded—buried alive—in widow's weeds.

His Grace the Duke of Cirencester assisted her personally inside his travelling coach. She wondered how ever she could have missed his pre-eminence yesterday, for now the servants seemed to be bowing and scraping, and addressing him as *your Grace* every time they came within a few yards of him.

She settled herself in the far corner of the carriage, leaning back against the velvet upholstery with her bag at her feet. Thankfully there was no sign of her aunt, and though Palfreyman had come outside to see them off, Deb noticed that the Duke made no effort to shake his hand. As for her, Palfreyman had come up to her just before she stepped up into the coach, and said with a hideous attempt at affection, 'Goodbye, my dearest Paulette. We'll meet again soon, I've no doubt.'

Deb had turned to the Duke in horror once he'd gone.

'He's not coming to London, is he? I won't have to see him there?'

'He has a London residence,' the Duke told her icily. 'But I think he's aware that he'd be well advised to stay away from it for a while.'

At first Deb had been afraid that the Duke would sit inside with her, but she was spared that at least, because he chose to sit up at the front next to his coachman. She watched the scenery rolling by and tried to think calmly. *The Duke is a man of action. His plans will be concise and effective. All I have to do is be Paulette for a matter of a few weeks only. Then I will be free…*

The whole side of her face ached, but her mind was clear. Clear enough for her to be able to foresee, with a sense of considerable doom, that she would probably never be free of the consequences of all this, for the rest of her life.

They stopped twice to change horses, and at one of the better inns Deb was guided to a private parlour to partake of a light lunch. The Duke did not join her, so she ate in solitary splendour.

Onwards they went. The Duke remained outside, up on the driver's seat; Deb could hear the two men talking intently about horses and axles and harness, and the Duke sounded just as knowledgeable as his coachman. By the early evening they'd passed through St Albans, and Deb must have nodded off, because when she opened her eyes the carriage had left the turnpike road and was rolling along a sweeping drive that was set between sheep-dotted pastures and lush woodlands. In the distance, but growing nearer every minute, was perhaps the most beautiful house that Deb had ever seen.

House? It was more like a palace built of golden-grey stone, with a great, sweeping façade flanked by stables, and a crenellated roof which glittered in the sun. Fountains played in ornamental ponds on either side of the vast forecourt, while ancient statues watched from their plinths as the carriage slowed and drew to a halt before the pillared entrance.

The horses were instantly surrounded by a flurry of grooms, while a footman hurried to open the carriage door. Deb realised that ranks of servants were already lined up by the steps leading to the entrance; it was probably someone's full-time job to watch for the Duke's arrival, she thought rather faintly. Then the Duke himself was holding out one firm hand to help her descend, and she realised that all eyes were on her.

'They're expecting me?' she whispered to him.

'Naturally,' he said. 'I sent a rider on ahead. Welcome to Brandon Abbey—Lady Simon. And please keep that veil over your bruised face. Or there really *will* be talk.'

She tugged the veil into place and reached for her bag. 'Leave it,' he said sharply. 'A footman will carry it up to your rooms. Take my arm.'

Deb would much rather have got down by herself. She would much rather not have been aware of the tremor that jolted her body at his firm, warm touch. No doubt he'd already forgotten last night's kiss—but she hadn't. She reached, panicking slightly, to touch the bruised skin around her eye.

'Keep your veil *down*, I said.' The Duke's instructions were curt. 'Say absolutely nothing to anyone as I introduce you. The staff won't expect it. I've explained to them all that you are still in fragile health.'

He was already leading her towards the servants.

'Lady Simon, as you all know,' she heard him explain to them, 'has suffered a most grievous loss with my brother's sudden death. I trust that you will all make her stay here a comfortable one.'

The footmen bowed and the housemaids curtsied. Finally the housekeeper, Mrs Martin, after murmuring respectful words of concern, took Deb up a vast staircase and along a carpeted corridor to her own suite of rooms.

Yes—a *suite* of rooms. Deb smothered a gasp. She found herself being shown around a bedroom, a bathroom, a dressing room and a small but beautiful sitting room with tall sash windows that overlooked a pastoral scene of carefully tended gardens, with rolling green hills dotted by stands of ancient oak woodland in the distance.

She looked around again slowly. All this just for her? The true irony was that she'd rather be in a barn with the Lambeth Players any time, or sleeping under the stars, for that matter. Her heart clenched in sudden anguish. *She was going to miss her friends so badly.*

Mrs Martin hovered. 'We are all so very sorry for your tragic loss, my lady. If there's anything at all you require, please let us know.' She pointed to the bell-pull, curtsied and left.

As soon as the housekeeper had gone Deb pulled off her black bonnet with its veil and put it on the bed. Her bag was here already—a footman must have *run* up the back stairs with it. She pushed it into a corner, out of sight, then gazed out of the window again.

The distant road curling over and beyond the hill taunted her with the prospect of a freedom she no longer had.

* * *

She was the Duke's prisoner, Deb acknowledged to herself over the next few days, but she was a very *comfortable* prisoner. Mrs Martin was the only person allowed to tend her—the elderly housekeeper had gasped when she first saw her bruised face, but in the discreet tradition of household staff, Mrs Martin asked no questions, but instead provided a bowl of warm arnica solution together with some soft lint. 'Bathing it with this should help ease the discomfort a little, my lady,' she had said kindly.

All in all, Deb could not have been better treated. Her meals—deliciously light soups and salads and jellies—were brought up to her regularly by Mrs Martin herself, whose demeanour softened even further with Deb's shy praise of the care she was receiving. Of the Duke himself, there was no sign; but Deb couldn't complain that she was confined to her rooms, for on her third day there Mrs Martin asked if she would like to be shown around the main part of the house, and Deb followed the housekeeper through the great hall and the banqueting chamber, her eyes growing wider beneath her ever-present veil.

A home fit for a duke, indeed. From the banqueting chamber they went on to the sculpture room, which was filled with statues of Italian marble, and at a higher level Deb noticed there was a mezzanine gallery lined with imposing portraits of the Duke's ancestors. Mrs Martin pointed up to them, and told her that the gallery led to the private quarters of the Duke himself.

The life of an aristocratic lady did, Deb acknowledged reluctantly, have its advantages. The baths alone were luxury—never before had she had enough hot water to submerse herself deliciously; never before had she been provided with so many clean, soft towels piled high. When her bruises had faded so as to be almost invisible, she had a visitor, a small, dapper Frenchwoman called Madame Celine, who came to measure Deb for new clothes. Only two days later, the modiste brought the first of them.

Deb gazed at them as they were unwrapped from their tissue paper. They were all in black, of course—there were two day gowns, an evening gown and two pelisses—and they were exquisitely made. Deb looked up at the modiste in amazement. 'You have made them so very quickly.'

'I have several *assistants*, my lady,' said the cheerful Frenchwoman, 'and for this task I put all of them to work, night and day. If the Duke of Cirencester makes a request of me, nothing is too much trouble. He is one of the finest gentlemen in the land, *n'est-ce-pas*? So handsome, also!'

And the modiste cheerfully left her to survey the wealth of black garments that bedecked her room.

'Ma'am. My lady?'

Deb swung round to see that a young maid had come in.

'Mrs Martin sent me,' the maid stammered. 'My name's Bethany, ma'am—my lady—and she thought you might perhaps want someone to help you with your new clothes.'

So Bethany—she was a sweet, timid girl—brushed out Deb's long hair, then helped her into one of the new black gowns. And as Bethany buttoned it up and adjusted its silk collar and cuffs, Deb caught sight of herself in the looking glass, and her stomach pitched.

Unlike the gown the Duke had thrust upon her at the Angel in Oxford, this one was made to fit; this one was made to flatter in an entirely feminine way. Every seam, every pleat, every ruffle spoke of craftsmanship and artistry. And—her blood chilled—there had to be a mistake, because the neckline of the gown was appallingly low.

'I cannot wear this,' she said quickly to Bethany. 'I'll put on another gown.' But every garment was the same, she saw with rising panic as she inspected one after another. *Madame Celine had made an error.*

'I'd better keep this one on,' she said wearily to Bethany. But she would speak to the Duke as soon as she could. Already the little maid was finding her a soft black shawl to wear, from another box of garments that Madame Celine had brought.

'How very tragic for you, my lady, to lose your husband so young,' Bethany whispered as she helped her to adjust the shawl around her shoulders. 'And you have been very ill, the Duke says. He told us all that only now can you face society again, and we are all to treat you with the very greatest care.'

Your master, thought Deb, is the biggest hypocrite going. 'Did you ever meet my husband, Bethany?'

'Oh, no, my lady, Lord Simon hasn't been here for years, as you'll well know. We all guessed that his lordship much preferred London to the countryside.'

Bethany began to tidy up Deb's dressing table, while Deb reeled again a little. *Simon hadn't been here for years? Hadn't been to visit his older brother with his bride?* But this must have been Simon's family home. He must have grown up here, surely…

like that. With that fire in your eyes, you look just like Paulette. My God, you *are* Paulette.' He reached out to touch her arm and she froze; then he seemed to shake himself. 'The way you walk isn't quite right,' he said flatly. 'You move too confidently, too assertively. Paulette's every move was calculated to attract men, not to challenge them. Paulette made the most of her *décolletage* always, and would have done so even at her husband's deathbed—had she troubled to be there. And that,' he concluded calmly, 'is why I ordered Madame Celine to—emphasise your assets.'

'But—even now?' she whispered. 'Paulette would dress like this even in mourning?'

'Oh, yes. What better chance to extract sympathy and catch herself a new husband? As for you, I thought you of all people would be used to dressing up in almost anything, whether for the stage or for your clients. Though I don't suppose, now I come to think of it, that you've been paid to dress in mourning very often. But Paulette's would have been an *unusual* kind of mourning.'

He went casually across to the drinks cupboard and poured out a small glass of sherry. 'You've made a good impression on my housekeeper, by the way. Mrs Martin for ever murmuring her pity for you. *A poor, heartbroken soul*, she calls you.' He handed her the sherry, and she was aware of him examining her face beneath her half-veil before he spoke again. 'I trust that you're fully recovered from the injury that Vera Palfreyman caused? That, incidentally, was why I wanted to see you. To check that you were all right.'

Deb hated sherry. She put the glass down. 'My thanks,' she said coolly. 'But I'm perfectly recovered. So

And she told herself, *You are supposed to know all these things about your husband already. Be careful.*

'Shall I put your hair up, my lady?'

'No. No, thank you, I prefer it loose.'

Swiftly Bethany pinned on the widow's cap and half-veil that Deb knew she had to wear indoors, and Deb drew the shawl more tightly across her bosom. 'Do you like it here, Bethany?'

'Oh, yes, ma'am—my lady. Brandon Abbey is such a beautiful house. And all the others tell me that his Grace the Duke is the best employer they could wish for.'

Deb listened incredulously—*so his abrasive rudeness was stored up for her, then*. Little Bethany chattered on while Deb tried to listen, tried to concentrate.

Already she was Paulette, in the eyes of so many. Perhaps playing the part of the stricken young widow was not going to be as hazardous as she'd feared.

Or so she thought—until the Duke demanded that she be presented to him.

Chapter Ten

$$\mathcal{C}\mathcal{D}\mathcal{C}\mathcal{D}$$

Bethany had only just left Deb's room when Mrs Martin came in. 'My lady, his Grace wishes to see you in his library. In half an hour's time, if you please.'

'Is he there now?'

'He is. But...'

'Then I see no point in delay, Mrs Martin. I wish to see him also. I'll go to him straight away.'

The housekeeper looked anxious. 'As you wish, my lady. I'll take you there, shall I?'

That was one advantage, thought Deb, in being, as she now was, a person of importance. No one dared to argue with you. Although there was one notorious exception, and that exception was standing in the library with his rather forbidding back to her, gazing at some items in a tall, glass-fronted cabinet, apparently lost in thought; though as soon as he heard the door open, he swung round on her with astonishment in his blue eyes. 'Lady Simon. What are you doing here?'

She faltered, then tilted her chin defiantly. 'I was told you wanted to see me.'

'In half an hour,' he corrected her sharply. 'Di[...] my housekeeper tell you so?'

'Yes, but—'

'I would prefer you to follow my instructions in [...] ture.'

Breathe. Breathe steadily and calmly. Bethany mi[...] think him kind, but as far as Deb was concerned, [...] was as hateful and as autocratic as ever, with his c[...] elled jaw and his utterly cold blue eyes beneath jet-b[...] brows. She felt rebellion surge in her chest.

So she'd responded to his summons a little ea[...] but did it really matter? Inwardly she cursed th[...] that physically he towered over her, but she forc[...] self to look up and meet his raking gaze. 'I came [...] your Grace, because I have an issue with the [...] you instructed Madame Celine to make for [...] are unsuitable.'

'Really?' He was examining her figure c[...] she felt the warmth rise in her cheeks. 'Ma[...] line is, I'm told, a modiste of some experi[...] precisely, are the gowns unsuitable?'

She found his drawling tone utterly prov[...] at this one.' She parted the shawl in an ext[...] ture and his blue eyes glittered—with amu[...] relish, at the sight of her half-naked bos[...]

Oh, no. She shouldn't have done t[...] shouldn't.

'It—it's too low,' she stammered. 'A[...] with all of the gowns you provided f[...] posed to be dressed decorously! I a[...] in mourning—'

She broke off because he was v[...] wards her. 'Stay there.' He pointe[...]

are you saying that the design of these gowns was your idea? And that I have to dress like this—in London?'

He drew even closer, so she could almost feel the warmth of his muscle-packed body. 'I was only reminding you that Paulette was open to the highest bidder—always.' His eyes raked her again. 'You will, I assume, be familiar with the feeling.'

She raised her hand to slap him, but he caught her wrist easily, and smiled. It wasn't a pleasant smile. 'Something else you've got to practise,' he said. He let her go and went to pour himself brandy. 'Use some self-control, for God's sake. My little sister's for ever throwing tantrums, but she's only seventeen.'

'You—you have a sister?'

He sipped some of his brandy. 'I do. Her name is Laura, and I'm her guardian, since our mother died even longer ago than our father did. Shortly after Laura's birth, in fact.'

'I'm sorry.'

'Don't be. Our mother had little time for her children—neither did our father, come to think of it. Anyway, you're unlikely to meet Laura, since she's staying with some good family friends in Brighton for the next month. At least—' he regarded her steadily '—I hope you *don't* meet her.'

Deb found herself almost shaking with humiliation. *Of course he wouldn't want her to meet his sister.* He no doubt assumed that the presence of a low-born actress such as her would, after all, contaminate the girl. Her gaze flew to that display cabinet, and her breath caught once more as she saw—weapons. A sabre, with a glittering hilt. A pair of pistols. An officer's sash, and a row of medals. A watercolour portrait, of a man in uniform…

'They're my brother Simon's,' the Duke told her quietly. 'When he was a boy, he always dreamed of being a soldier, and he did indeed join the army for a while. But it didn't work out as he'd hoped.'

There was something in his voice—grief, regret—that made Deb's heart turn over. Silently she acknowledged that if this powerful man cared for someone, be they brother, friend or lover, he would doubtless go to the ends of the earth to protect them.

'We'll travel to London in a few days,' he went on. He finished his brandy, then put the glass down and glanced at his watch. 'You may return to your room. I have to go out now, to attend to some business in St Albans. I'll summon Mrs Martin to escort you back upstairs—'

'No!'

He turned to stare at her.

Deb was gazing at the tall window, through which she could see that the sun was shining and the garden was colourful with flowers. 'I need to get out,' she said. 'I need some fresh air. I'm so tired of being shut up in here.'

The Duke frowned, then nodded slowly. 'You may, I suppose, sit out on the terrace. You could read, or do some embroidery—'

'I hate sewing.'

'As you wish. But whatever you do, make sure that you stay in the shade. Since you're meant to look…' he paused, to give his words added irony '…delicate, and fragile.'

She opened her mouth to argue, but saw his freezing glance and closed it again. He gave a small nod and said, 'Good. You're learning. By the way, I've asked

Mrs Martin to arrange for a hair stylist to come and cut your hair at four o'clock.'

'But I don't want—'

'Your hair,' he said, jabbing his finger at the loose mass of chestnut curls already tumbling from beneath her widow's cap, 'needs taming. Be back in your room at four.' And with that he walked out, leaving her furious and trembling and terribly afraid of what lay ahead of her. Of what this man was *doing* to her.

An hour later Deb was sitting out on the terrace with a copy of *The Lady* magazine lying on a table at her side, together with a glass of iced lemonade and some chilled grapes from the Duke's hothouse. A light breeze fanned her cheeks, but she still found the black clothes of widowhood almost unbearably hot. Perhaps there was something to be said for her *décolletage* after all. At least that part of her anatomy was pleasantly cool, although she would die rather than admit that to the Duke. Hateful, hateful man.

Restlessly she picked up her magazine then put it down again, reflecting that she could write an article of her own for the next issue.

Here is a word of advice for all recently bereaved ladies. In the summer, black bombazine can be the most relentless of fabrics, for it clings to the skin, and absorbs all the sun's rays. Wear as little as possible beneath it. Avoid exertion, and above all never allow your emotions to become heated…

She sat there in the sunshine, while the Duke's beautifully kept gardens spread away in all directions, and found herself filled with perhaps the greatest apprehension she had ever known.

All she had to do was be Paulette. Easy, according to the Duke. All she had to do was reinvent herself completely—change her hair, her clothes, even the way she moved. She had to alter everything that gave her individuality and independence. She had to submit to his will.

The problem was that she'd never met anyone like him before. She'd never thought that anyone like him existed.

Physically, of course, he was perfect and he knew it. No wonder society called him the Dangerous Duke. Any woman would have to have iced water running through her veins not to feel at least a flicker of desire on seeing those dazzling blue eyes, set in such a perfectly aristocratic face. On finding herself as close to his lean, rangy body as she had been. On feeling his lips caressing her own…

He'd kissed her twice. Clearly he'd forgotten those kisses. She, unfortunately, hadn't, and didn't think she ever would. And she'd put herself completely in his power. How was she going to survive this? Was this really better than being in Newgate? Dear God, she was almost beginning to wonder.

You're twenty-two years old, she told herself sternly. *Your life has been far from sheltered, and you should be able to cope with your situation.*

She should be able to cope with Mr Beaumaris—the Duke—in other words. But if Lord Simon Beaumaris had been anything like his older brother, Deb was almost beginning to feel sorry for her cousin Paulette, who had clearly gone straight from the bosom of one hateful family—the Palfreymans—to another.

When she'd first started to act many years ago, she'd had girlish dreams of a handsome hero coming on stage and sweeping her off her feet. Well, she'd met a man who'd swept her off her feet now, all right, and Deb found his carefully laid plans to foil her cousin quite frightening. She remembered how her mother occasionally used to wish aloud that she could buy Deb pretty things—but if this was what wealth did to people, they were welcome to every penny of it.

Deb thoughtfully sipped the last of her lemonade, then stood up and wandered slowly across the terrace, thinking, *I do not envy this harsh man at all. I do not envy him his money, his estates or his power.*

The Duke had warned her to stay close to the house, but over there on the far side of the garden were acres of cool, leafy woods. And—was that the gleam of distant water?

It took her only a few minutes to cross the perfectly manicured lawns, and after following an enticing path between the trees, with lichened stone statues at every turn, she came at last to a wilder part of the garden, and gasped with delight on seeing, at the end of the path, a lake fringed by a cluster of weeping willow trees.

At the far side of the lake was a stone pavilion. Without hesitation, Deb hurried over to it, opened the door and peeped in. *But this was perfect. Absolutely perfect.* Everything in it was exquisite, from the marble tiles on the floor to the porcelain cameos of frolicking water nymphs that adorned the walls.

Instantly Deb closed the door and started pulling off her widow's garb, casting everything on to a rattan *chaise longue* that stood in one corner. Moments later, wearing nothing other than her thin white chemise, she tiptoed to the water's edge and experienced the utter bliss of sinking into the cool, cool water of the lake. She floated on her back with her eyes closed and a smile of utter contentment on her face.

At precisely that moment, Beau was riding back from St Albans, and his thoughts were focused on matters that made him oblivious to the beauties of the landscape around him. He'd been to meet his secretary, Nathaniel Armitage, who'd travelled up from London the night before; they'd had a private sitting room booked in the Bull, where his secretary was staying, and Armitage had, in his usual quiet but efficient way, got straight to the point by setting out a sheaf of papers.

'I've already mentioned to you, your Grace,' he said, 'that shortly before her flight abroad in March this year, your sister-in-law—when she was believed by everyone to be in Norfolk—secretly visited a London jeweller who is, in fact, more of a dealer and pawnbroker. This man, Thomas Newman, has premises in Gresham Street in the city.'

'How do you know that she visited him?'

'People will talk, if they're paid enough, and one of Gresham's clerks recognised Lady Simon. It would appear that she may very well have deposited an item of value with Newman.'

Beau was leafing through the documents Armitage had set before him. 'So the man is a dealer. I hope you've also been investigating if anything else has been heard about the jewels? If there are any rumours about them?'

'Rumours of them having been sold, you mean? There's nothing, your Grace.'

Beau put the papers down. 'Very well. I'm intending to return to London within the next week or so, and it looks as if Newman will be our first target. He doesn't realise that he's being watched, does he?'

'No. Oh, no, your Grace. My men are very careful.'

'Keep them that way. Keep them looking, and listening. Though of course the only person who can deal with Newman over this particular business is Lady Simon herself. Miss O'Hara, in other words.' Decisively Beau got to his feet.

Armitage was standing also, but more hesitantly. 'She's young, isn't she, your Grace? Are you quite sure that she'll be able to emulate a lady of quality?'

'As well as Paulette Palfreyman did,' Beau answered drily. 'The real test, of course, will be when I bring her to London. But wait till you see her, Armitage. Believe me, you'll be amazed.'

After riding at a spirited trot through the lodge gates, Beau let his big horse slow down as the crenellated roofs of Brandon Abbey came into view beyond the woods.

He saw, as he always did, how beautiful it all was. Remembered as he always did that he'd been entrusted with the estate by his father; just as he'd been entrusted with the care of his younger brother, and failed.

Beau had been fourteen when their mother died, after giving birth to Laura. Simon had been twelve, and the news of her death had been brought to them by their house master at Eton. Beau had accepted the news in silence. '*Emotion is weakness!*' their father the Duke used to preach to his two sons as he stalked the corridors of Brandon Abbey. *'Emotion is the sign of a feeble character!'*

Certainly their father had shown little sign of emotion on any occasion to either of his sons, or to his wife. Beau remembered her as a distant, vain, flippant creature, who, he guessed, had found her marriage to the Duke a source of great unhappiness.

So at Eton, when the news came of their mother's death, Beau was relatively untouched by her loss, but Simon, two years younger, was distraught. Simon had been deeply unhappy anyway at Eton; he was weaker than Beau, and were it not for his older brother's intervention, he would have been a constant victim of bullying. 'You must be strong, Simon,' Beau urged him as he tried to console him over their mother's death. 'You must be brave.'

Emotion is weakness, he might have added. Just as their father would have said. Beau had learned the lesson—Simon hadn't. But...*I let you down, Simon*, he acknowledged silently. *I was supposed to protect my family, and I let you down. But I will see justice done, whatever it costs, whatever it takes.*

Beau's grim expression lightened a little as he turned from the main drive to take a track that wound through the woods. He was trying to picture his clever secretary's face when he saw Miss O'Hara in her widow's weeds. How could Armitage be anything but impressed? She would fool everyone into believing she was Paulette—London society, the lawyers, the lot.

And he would keep his side of the bargain. He'd give her the little theatre she wanted. But if she even hinted at wanting any more, he would come down on her with

the full force of his wealth and his title, no doubt of that.
He would remind her none too gently that her men had
kidnapped and imprisoned him. Yet he found, suddenly,
that he'd be *disappointed* if she tried such tricks. Yes,
she was a rogue all right, but she had a certain honesty,
surely—together with a forthrightness and a courage
that he found curiously appealing.

He frowned. Unfortunately, she had quite a lot of
other qualities that appealed to him also. Those eyes.
Those breasts, that had been deliciously revealed by the
low neckline she'd professed to hate. Those lips, that
had returned his kiss so sweetly on two occasions that
he would be far better forgetting…

He pulled his horse to a juddering stop.

The track Beau had taken was actually a shortcut
through the woods, and it was one he often used. But
less than a quarter of a mile from the house the track
forked, and a much narrower path led down to the woodland lake. When they were young, he and his brother
used to swim there often, though to his knowledge no
one used the place now. And yet, from the corner of his
eye, he realised that *someone was in the water*.

'No,' he found himself breathing aloud. 'No.' For a
moment he imagined that the past had rolled hideously
into the present; he thought that he saw arms threshing
in the lake and heard desperate cries for help…

Then he realised it was the girl. She was swimming,
and swimming well, apparently oblivious to the fact
that she was being observed. Beau urged his horse on
down the path to the lake's shore; but she must have
either seen or heard him approaching, because by the
time he'd got to the water's edge the girl was clamber-

ing out on the far side, heading for the pavilion, wearing practically nothing.

His jaw grimly set, he set off around the lake to meet her there.

Chapter Eleven

All the way to the pavilion, Deb was only too aware of her wet chemise clinging to her skin and her long hair dripping water down her back. He'd seen her. He was coming after her. *Damn the man*, she thought as she slammed the door of the pavilion and leaned her back against it, gasping for breath. Wasn't she safe from him *anywhere*?

She froze, because she could hear steady footsteps drawing nearer. The nymphs and sea demons on the tiled walls were laughing down at her, and she only wished she could summon up their mythical powers and disappear.

Springing towards the *chaise longue*, she snatched up her clothes; but already the door was opening. She whirled round and he was there, blocking out the light; then he'd pushed the door shut. And he looked angry. So very angry.

'If any of the staff or groundsmen should have seen you,' he bit out. 'Seen you out there swimming. Dressed in next to nothing…'

'But no one was there to see me!' she retorted hotly.

'Everything would have been completely *all right*, if you hadn't come galloping through the woods like that! I thought you wouldn't be back till much later…'

'I'd finished my business in St Albans. There's a shortcut I use through the woods, and from there I could see the lake. I could see *you*, Miss O'Hara.'

She faltered, then faced him steadily again. 'How was I to know there was a shortcut? Any man in his right mind would use his…miles of private driveway! But then again, any man in his right mind would *not* be forcing me to pretend to be his sister-in-law!'

He said, 'I assumed you were used to being paid for services rendered.'

Deb tried to slap him. He gripped her raised wrist. She lifted her other hand to strike him, but he grasped that one also and marched her steadily backwards until she was pressed against the exotically painted wall.

Water from her loose wet hair rolled down her shoulders and back. Only her soaking wet chemise protected her nakedness. And he hadn't once taken his eyes off her. Deb was all too aware that even if he wasn't blocking her route of escape physically, then his gaze would have incapacitated her.

It appalled her to realise once more just how shockingly attractive he was. It appalled her to realise that she couldn't drag her gaze from him. She should *not* be in awe of his chilly yet beautiful blue eyes framed by black lashes. She shouldn't be even noticing the beginnings of dark stubble on his lean jaw. And she definitely should *not* be looking at his broad shoulders, his long, muscular legs encased in those tight buckskins and riding boots…

Her ribs ached with the need for air. Her stomach

pitched. *Being paid for services rendered.* She'd let him think she was a whore, because of those damned books of Palfreyman's—and with his damned arrogance, he wouldn't risk polluting an inch of his aristocratic skin by laying another finger on her. Would he? *Would he*?

'I suppose,' he was saying softly as his eyes raked her, 'that I should be compensating you—financially, that is—for lost clients.'

'No!' She struggled again to escape, but he still grasped her wrists.

'Do you miss the pleasure of your trade?' he went on quietly—*cruelly*. 'Is that why you were swimming so energetically? Were you perhaps trying to tire yourself out so you'd forget—what you were missing?'

She could feel the warmth of his body, and her senses were being seduced by the citrus scent of the soap he used. But his blue eyes were cold and menacing.

I am not afraid of him, Deb told herself desperately, pulling her hands from his grip and reaching behind her to find the wall and steady herself. *He's a brute and a bully, but I'm not afraid...*

She was deceiving herself and she knew it. There was a raw male quality to him that came close to terrifying her. She didn't for one minute think that he'd do her physical harm, but being near to him like this made her feel vulnerable in a way she'd never, ever known before—and that was *bad*, she thought, heaving air into her lungs. Very bad. She should have been cold, in her wet chemise that clung to her skin and her breasts; but the aura of raw sexuality emanating from this man's powerful body made her feel as if she was standing in a furnace.

She tossed her wet hair from her face. 'I came in

here to get my clothes back. My *widow's* clothes, in case you'd forgotten. I'd be grateful if you would leave me alone, so I can dress myself.'

He said nothing, but his eyes were on her breasts. She glanced down at them swiftly. They were shockingly outlined by the clinging wet cotton, and her nipples were hard and protruding. They might as well not be covered at all.

'I think,' the Duke said silkily, 'that you realised I would be able to glimpse you in the water as I rode homewards. Any of the servants could have told you that the lake is visible from the track I often use. And so you decided to swim at the very time you guessed I'd be returning—because you wanted me to find you.'

She was shivering badly. 'That's ridiculous. Why should I want you to find me?'

'Because you wanted me to…warm you up?' he offered gently.

He rested his strong hands on her shoulders. Already backed against the wall, Deb began to shake her head. But his hands were warm and persuasive, and another far more dangerous kind of heat was spiralling through her body, stealing through her breasts and loins, curling inside her like a fire ready to burn everything in its path.

She was fighting for her very survival here. Deb tried to push past him, but he caught her and hauled her hard against him. Their bodies collided, and in that terrifying moment she realised that this man knew exactly what he was doing, knew exactly what she was feeling. He knew about the fire of longing that burned deep inside her, and had done ever since she'd seen him lying bound in the forest. He'd probably known it, she realised, even before she'd known it herself.

When his mouth came down on hers, she melted. She found it quite impossible to breathe or think. He was right; she was warm in his arms, her body yearned for his strength, and already his mouth was heating her cold lips with light but intense caresses…

'No.' She struggled to drag herself away. 'No, this is *wrong*…'

He drew a ragged breath and his blue eyes still blazed with dark emotion. The front of his shirt had been soaked by its contact with her damp body, so the linen clung to and outlined the rippling sinews of his chest and abdomen. 'You're right.' His voice sounded thick with desire. 'Perhaps this is *not* a good idea.'

'Then let me—' Her lips burned from his kiss, her body trembled.

'Let you go?'

'Yes. *No.* I…'

She was in his arms again. Begging for his mouth again. She wanted him so much that she couldn't help herself. *Just this once*, she kept telling herself. *Just this once*…

He kissed her again, lethally. His mouth swept once, twice over hers; his tongue was prising her lips apart with quick, sensuous strokes. Then their mouths were enmeshed, and without breaking the kiss, Beau, still holding her tightly, was easing her back to the couch in the corner where all her clothes lay, while tangling his fingers in her soaking wet hair so that he could drag her face closer and intensify the kiss.

Her fingers were gripping the folds of his shirt, otherwise she would have fallen—oh, no, now she *was* falling, back against the couch, colliding softly with the heaps of cushions there. He was arched over her instantly, one knee planted between her thighs, and now his kiss was bone-melting and his tongue was plunging into her mouth, stoking the flames inside her that were already white-hot...

This is so wrong, she thought in despair, even as she dug her fingers deeper into the hard muscle of his shoulders. She shouldn't be feeling like this. She should absolutely hate what he was doing to her—but all she wanted was more. Her damp hair was all around them both, and now he was running his hands through its soft mass; she let out a low moan and he took her mouth again hungrily, while his hands slid around her hips, pressing her against him so that she could feel his lean, hard body, could feel how very aroused he was.

One of his hands had slipped round to cup her breast, and for all the protection the muslin petticoat gave her, she might as well have been naked. Her nipple leaped at his touch, and then a bolt of pure, white-hot desire was shooting down to that tender place between her thighs...

'Let me go. *Please* let me go.' She pushed at him hard, and struggled to get away from under his weight, knocking her hip against the carved mahogany armrest of the *chaise longue* and wincing at the pain. *Another bruise. Another damned bruise.*

But that didn't hurt as much as when he drew himself up from her, his eyes still ragged with desire, and said, 'As you wish. But I do hope, Miss O'Hara, that you're not going to make some ridiculous claim that I've insulted your—*virtue*.'

She gasped and heaved herself upright, aware of his eyes raking her slender form, taking in her breasts, the curve of her waist, the place between her thighs where the damp muslin clung.

The Dangerous Duke. Too dangerous for her to handle, that was for sure. Fighting for control of her voice, her breathing, her existence, she drew herself up to meet his hard blue gaze. 'Whatever my past, your Grace, it doesn't stop me from exerting some choice over my immediate future. Now, I'm cold, and wet, and I need to get dressed. So would you please just—*leave me alone*?'

She'd already started floundering at random through her clothes that had somehow slipped in a heap to the floor, pulling out the black gown and preparing to heave it over her head. Her chemise was still soaking wet. But how could she remove it, with the Duke still standing there? No, all she could do was cover herself up, as quickly as possible, or he'd get all excited…

And he wasn't the only one to be excited, she reminded herself in dismay. Her insides still churned, her pulse still raced from his kiss, from the feel of his hard, powerful male body pressing against hers. She'd thought she would be safe from him, if she let him think she was—*used goods*. She'd thought wrong. She pulled on the gown and began to search with clumsy fingers for the buttons. *Go. Please just go.*

He was watching her calmly from a couple of yards away, his arms folded across his broad chest. He said, 'You shouldn't be putting those clothes over your wet chemise. You'll catch a chill.'

She stopped what she was doing and tilted her chin to meet his gaze. 'Really? Now, let me see,' she said with feigned wonder. 'What mood are we in all of a sudden? Ah, yes—the lustful Duke has retreated. And instead, we have the proud, condescending Duke—pretending to care about my well-being. What a surprise that is.'

'I'm not *pretending* to care,' he stated. He was straightening the lapels of his exquisitely cut riding coat, though his eyes never left her face. 'I hope you'll remember that I have a vested interest in keeping you healthy.'

Deb was finding it difficult to breathe, such was the strength of her emotion. 'Let me assure you,' she answered at last, 'that when all this is over, I shall leave you and all your wealth behind me with a sense of sheer relief, your Grace. I owe you a huge debt for showing me how shallow and obsessive a rich man's life can be.'

'I've told you before to save your melodramatics for the stage.' He was adjusting his cravat now. 'And rest assured, Miss O'Hara. As you've pointed out, I have many faults. But I do keep my promises.'

He strolled closer. He touched her cheek with the tip of one long, lean finger.

Oh, my goodness. She'd been trying to close her mind to the virile power of his body, to the masculine grace of his every gesture. But meeting his blue eyes like this, and seeing the sudden twist of his sensual lips, sent bolts of shock through her all over again. *Just when she'd thought she was safe.* He was all male. He was all animal strength, disturbing and dangerous. The faint burn marks she could see all too clearly now on his raised wrist were a dangerous reminder of their past, and an ominous warning as to their future.

She almost jumped away from him. 'So you keep your promises—your Grace. But your motives for those promises consist solely of revenge and bitterness, it seems to me.'

His blue eyes raked her. 'Perhaps I should tell you,' he said quietly, 'that my brother, Simon, almost drowned while swimming in this very lake several years ago.'

This time she almost staggered. 'I didn't know. How could I know?'

'You couldn't.' His voice was quite calm. 'I wouldn't be surprised, though, if you should find that there are some towels in that chest in the corner—the house-keeper likes to keep them here in the usually misguided assumption that someone else might some day use the lake for recreation. Please get yourself properly dry. As I pointed out, you're of no use to me sick. Oh, and I'd like you to join me for dinner at eight.'

He left without a backward glance, leaving Deb feeling as if he'd kicked her. She found the towels, just as he'd said, then peeled off her wet chemise, and after huddling up in the largest towel, she sat on the *chaise-longue*—hurting, hurting inside.

Never, ever had she felt as she did when he kissed her. She hadn't been acting then, far from it. She wished it *had* all been staged. Most of all, she wished she was far far away with the Lambeth Players, amongst her friends.

The magic of the theatre had entranced her for as long as she could remember. She'd pestered her kind stepfather, Gerald, until she was allowed to act—the young prince in *Richard III* had been her very first part—but the opportunity to play a big role didn't arrive until she was fifteen and the company was doing *Twelfth Night*. The actress who played Viola had suddenly fallen ill, and all of the actors were in despair.

Deb had stolen quietly up to Gerald. 'I can do it,' she'd told him.

Gerald had scratched his head. 'How, lass? We're due to put the play on tonight! You'll never have time to learn it.'

'I don't have to learn it. I know it all. Please let me, please!'

Gerald had looked at his stepdaughter with growing wonder. 'You know it all?'

Staunchly she began to recite the lines.

'Well,' said Gerald. '*Well*. Button my boots…' He'd swung round to the rest of the Players, who had also been listening in amazement. 'The play goes on, ladies and gentlemen—thanks to Deb here!'

It had been a night of triumph. A night when they— and she—realised not only that she had a huge gift for acting, but also that she could remember her lines by just listening to the rehearsals. Though sometimes, re-membering everything was *not* a good idea. She wished she could forget, for example, the spring day that a young actor had come strolling into their midst as they were setting up their makeshift stage on the green out-side Reading a little over five years ago. 'Any chance of a job?' he'd asked casually.

Before anyone could reply, he'd leaped nimbly on to the stage and recited Henry V's famous speech before the battle of Agincourt. After he'd finished, everyone sighed with pleasure and turned expectantly towards Gerald, who said to the newcomer, 'We can't pay you a great deal. But if you want to join us you're more than welcome.'

The new actor—Jack Bentall—had joined the Lam-beth Players and caused not a few mutterings amongst the men, but the women had been delighted because he was so very handsome. Gerald had always been wary of him. 'He thinks too much of himself,' Deb heard Gerald say once to Francis. 'Our Jack won't give a fig for whomever he tramples on, if they get in his way.'

But Jack brought in the audiences all right, and day by day Deb—seventeen years old by then—had grown more entranced by his charm. For the first time ever she wished she was prettier and adept at bewitching men, like Peggy. She began to wear frocks, instead of her usual breeches; she started to tie ribbons in her long curly hair. And during one week of that sun-filled summer, when Gerald was away in London negotiating winter contracts for the Players, Jack suggested to the infatuated Deb that they practise their lines together.

Afterwards, he asked her to take a stroll with him along a country lane in the evening sunshine, and when Jack stopped to kiss her, the innocent Deb responded with artless passion. By the time she'd realised what he intended and tried to break away from him, he grew angry and forced her into intimacy.

It was over very quickly. 'Don't try complaining to anyone that you didn't want this,' he told her afterwards. 'You've been leading me on for days.'

Deb had been devastated. 'Leading you on?' she'd whispered. 'I didn't mean to.'

'With your shy looks and simpering smiles?' he scoffed. 'With those kisses you just offered me? You've only yourself to blame.'

Jack left the Lambeth Players that very night, and Deb never told anyone what happened; she was far too ashamed. Jack was still an actor—she heard his name mentioned from time to time. But her stomach always lurched sickly at the memory of his clumsy, hasty assault.

Thanks to Jack, she'd fiercely resisted any man's approaches ever since. She didn't doubt that true love *did* exist—look at her mother, Emily, and Gerald O'Hara—but she knew that few people were lucky enough to find happiness like theirs. As for the aristocracy, she was aware that emotions played little part in their marriage arrangements. People of wealth were obliged to produce heirs, and their nuptials were usually a carefully planned alliance of status, wealth and title. She wondered if the Duke had a wife in mind and found the thought disturbing, so she turned her sudden agitation into anger and whispered aloud, *I feel sorry for her if he does*. But dear God, he was very hard to resist. She shivered a little.

So his brother, Simon, had almost drowned while swimming in the lake. She was terribly sorry for that, of course, but why should he take out his grief on her? And then, his kiss… The colour rushed to her cheeks. He'd kissed her to prove he was right in his assessment of her, that was all. Just as well she'd *not* tried to deny to him that she was a whore, because she was, at heart—Jack Bentall had told her so, and now the Duke. *You've only yourself to blame*, Jack had scoffed.

And the Duke—the Duke had kissed her to complete his humiliation of her. He'd certainly done that to perfection, because she'd virtually begged him for more.

Slowly picking up her widow's garb, she began to put on the hateful garments one by one. After pulling on the black veiled cap, she went to open the pavilion door and breathed in great lungfuls of fresh air. Once this was over she would have her theatre. And the Duke of Cirencester would be out of her life for good…

Suddenly she remembered that someone was coming

to cut and style her hair—so that she would look more like Paulette, for the Duke. *I hate him*, she vowed aloud. *He is autocratic, and domineering, and…* She shivered suddenly, remembering the delicious feel of his hard body next to hers, his mouth moving lazily over hers.

A water nymph was laughing down at her. *Never again*, Deb vowed. *I swear to God that I won't let him touch me ever again.*

Chapter Twelve

Instead of riding straight on to the house, Beau took a track that led up to open pastureland, where he set his strong horse at a gallop until he'd succeeded—to a point—in getting under control the mixture of heated emotions that seethed in his chest.

When he'd seen that lone figure in the lake, the years had vanished and one of his blackest ever memories had emerged—Simon close to drowning, and Beau plunging in to save him, and Simon fighting him off, whispering, *You always have to be there for me, don't you, big brother? Do I have to be for ever in your debt? Isn't it enough that you're going to inherit a dukedom, and I'll have nothing?*

It was eleven years ago, and Beau had been home from Oxford—clever, ruthless, ambitious, and well placed to succeed his cold-hearted father some day as heir to one of the country's richest titles. Simon had already begun to resent him bitterly. 'Damn you, Beau. Damn you,' he'd whispered as he lay choking on the lake side.

This time the person in the water had been the girl. She, clearly, had been in no danger—except from him.

He had been shocked at how swiftly his anger had turned to equally powerful lust.

Had he really tried to blame her for the kiss? Who was he trying to fool? His own physical need had all but consumed him—good God, his loins still ached from his fierce arousal—but he had to remember that lust must have no part in his relationship with the girl.

He was the fifth Duke of Cirencester, and he had many wrongs to put right. His brother had been lured into marriage with a slut, and Paulette's cousin Deborah must be of the same breed—look at those books of erotic pictures, for heaven's sake. But—and Beau dragged his hand through his hair—why, then, had her kiss been so damned sweet?

Why was it that she'd looked somehow so lost and alone for a brief moment that she'd aroused in him a series of long-buried feelings—tenderness…pity, even—that Beau was hardly aware he still possessed?

Emotion is weakness, he reminded himself fiercely. He reminded himself also she hadn't looked at all lost when she was giving orders in the forest to the pair of vagabonds who'd knocked him from his horse, and trussed him up. Neither had she looked lost when she'd pretended moments later to melt to his kiss, in order to cleverly distract him from the fact that her men were creeping up behind him.

But he'd been watching her these past few days. He'd seen how Miss Deborah O'Hara had taken to slowly walking through the great rooms of the house by herself, often choosing to linger in the sculpture room and gaze at the classical statues that Beau's father had collected. Sometimes, if Beau was passing along the mezzanine gallery to his own rooms, he would pause in the shadows and look down on her, because he found himself thinking in the oddest way that when she was on her own, she became a different person.

Normally she carried herself proudly—defiantly, almost—to the extent that her unusual golden eyes positively flashed fire whenever she caught him studying her. But he'd realised that she looked more vulnerable when she thought that she wasn't being observed. She looked younger than her twenty-two years. Her expression became wistful, her eyes became troubled—more than troubled, she would look almost afraid.

He was having to fight the feeling that she was becoming more and more beautiful every time he saw her. With most women, those widow's weeds would have drained their complexions of vitality, but with her, the sombre clothing seemed to give an extra vibrancy to her extraordinary chestnut hair, and to make her dark-lashed eyes even more stunning, her skin creamier and her rose-red lips fuller.

He remembered with a tug of amusement how furious she'd been over the low necklines he'd ordered the modiste to create—but those very *décolletages* were the finishing touch to her appeal; a breathtaking reminder of the sheer femininity of her curvaceous figure beneath the mourning clothes. Yes, she resembled Paulette. But surely, Deb O'Hara had a hundred times that woman's spirit, character, honesty—

Honesty? Now, he almost laughed aloud at that. How could she be honest, when he'd caught her with a pocketful of books that even some whores would blush to carry?

Yet this afternoon when he'd kissed her in the pavilion, even he, with all his experience of stunningly attractive women, had been overwhelmed by her. He would never forget the sight of her in that wet, clinging chemise, and he'd been completely unable to resist the enticement offered by her small, high breasts and tiny waist and long, slender legs.

He'd wanted to bed her there and then, and was only stopped by the fact that she'd appeared so shocked. In fact, she had been trembling after his advances, he noted; her eyes had been wide and dark, her cheeks white, and she had seemed appalled by what had happened.

Beau grimly urged his willing horse onwards, hoping that a final gallop might drive the last scrap of treacherous lust from his body. She was an *actress*, he reminded himself. She was a rogue, without a doubt, but at least he knew what she was up to. Whereas Paulette Palfreyman had been far more subtle about leading his brother down the path to ruin.

Arriving back at the house, he left his horse with the head groom and strode up the steps through the main door, his mind still furiously working. But he was swiftly dragged back to the present by the appearance of his butler, who held out a letter for him on a silver salver.

'This was delivered from London while you were out, your Grace,' said Delaney. 'The courier said it was urgent.'

Beau went to his study to open it and found that it came from one of his investigators in London; the one appointed by Armitage to keep an eye on the activities of the jewel dealer in London, Newman.

Beau scanned it and folded the letter up again abruptly, realising that Armitage's news in St Alban's today was already out of date. Contrary to the rather leisurely procedure he'd discussed with Armitage earlier, he was going to have to press ahead with his plans rather more quickly than he'd thought.

An hour later Beau was knocking at the door of the girl's room, but when there was no reply, he walked straight in. She was there, of course, but although it was obvious that she must have heard his knock, she made no acknowledgement of his presence. She was just standing in front of the mirror, looking as if she'd seen a ghost.

She was wearing another of the black gowns that had been made for her—he could see her image clearly—and she looked breathtakingly beautiful in it. Beautiful and different—because her long chestnut curls had been cut. The *coiffeuse* had completed her work all too well. The girl's hair was much shorter now, and was tamed into tight little ringlets that cunningly framed her utterly lovely heart-shaped face. Of the vagabond he'd first met in the Ashendale Forest, who'd strode around the clearing with her hands in her breeches pockets, and who'd teased him so boldly with her wicked books, there was no remnant whatsoever, and he found himself profoundly regretting it.

He continued to gaze at her with his face betraying no expression and said, 'If you're having second thoughts, say so, now. After today it will be too late.'

He saw her delicate fingers trembling slightly as she smoothed down the rich fabric of the black satin gown. Again, doubts assailed him. *What a complete bastard he could be*, Beau reflected.

'I want my theatre,' she said. She took a deep breath and repeated more firmly, 'I want my theatre—for my-

self and my friends. I gave you my word that I'd keep
to our bargain—and I keep my promises.'

'Good,' he said. 'Because my plans have changed.
We need to set off for London—tomorrow.'

She sat down—rather shakily, he thought—and he
explained about the letter. How he'd now learned that
Newman—to whom he suspected Paulette might have
temporarily entrusted the jewels—was trying to quietly
sell his business, and might already be making plans to
leave London in the near future.

'Did you get this information from your spies?' she
asked him calmly.

'From my investigators, yes. If Newman *is* moving
out of London, I need to speed up my own plans. Does
it matter very much to you that we go to London tomorrow, rather than next week, say, or the week after?'

'No,' she said. 'No, hardly at all.'

Beau had remained standing—not because he wished
to be aloof, but because he felt safer like this. Yes, *safer.*
He knew that if he sat close—if he was too near to her—
then possibly the scent of her skin, or the memory of
her soft hair against his fingers, might tempt him again.
Emotion is weakness. Emotion is weakness.

He produced the other items he'd been carrying. 'I
have some of Paulette's diaries here. I think that perhaps you ought to read them.'

He saw her react almost with revulsion. 'Read her
private diaries? No!'

Beau's fingers tightened around the little volumes.
'Were you perhaps jealous of her lifestyle and her
money?'

'No!' Suddenly her eyes flashed fire. 'Oh, my God,
no! I have never forgotten the day my mother took me

to Hardgate Hall.' Her voice dropped. 'I had nightmares for weeks afterwards, dreaming that she had left me there for good.'

Beau found himself picturing her, a small, vulnerable child… *Don't*, he told himself fiercely. *Don't start feeling anything like pity for this girl, you fool.* What he was doing simply had to be done, for his family's honour, and she was his instrument. He had to use her, pay her and get her out of his life as quickly as possible. Out of his life, where she had no place.

He picked up one of the small, leather-bound diaries and held it out to her in a manner that allowed no refusal. 'We'll be setting off for London tomorrow afternoon,' he said steadily. 'And I think it would be a good idea if you managed to read at least one of these by then. Paulette left them at my brother's house, and I had a glance at them, but they're full of trivialities— appointments with modistes, the shops where she liked to meet her friends and so on. I don't think you can afford to pretend that you have any honourable feelings about your cousin, but I *do* consider it absolutely essential that you know as much as possible about her, since you're going to have to pretend to be her.'

Wordlessly she took the book from him. Beau found it hard to detect what her mood was, but he sensed a hint of scorn in her voice when she said, at last, 'You've clearly thought it all out, your Grace. But has it occurred to you that the chief problem is that there will be many, many people in London—acquaintances of Paulette and your brother—who will expect me to recognise them when they come to call?'

'I've thought of all that.'

She said softly, 'I rather thought you might.'

He found it easiest to ignore her sarcasm. 'This is how we'll cope, Miss O'Hara. You will offer certain hours for visiting, in the accustomed fashion. I will be with you, so you never receive visitors alone. Any callers will be announced, of course, and that will give me the opportunity to—acquaint you with them.'

'So I'll be living with *you*?'

'In my house in Albemarle Street, yes. You're my sister-in-law, so it's perfectly respectable for you to stay there under my protection. And as you've been very ill, a certain fragility of memory caused by extreme grief would not be unusual—in fact, might almost be expected. Have you any more questions, Miss O'Hara?'

She was silent awhile. Then she said, slowly, 'It appears to me, your Grace, that Newgate almost seems preferable all of a sudden.'

She'd recovered her spirit, Beau realised. Something burned in her eyes as she gazed up at him. Rebellion. Contempt, even.

'Newgate's no longer an option,' he smoothly replied. 'You've come too far for that. You *are* Paulette. Spoiled, vain and selfish as ever, but—temporarily at any rate—quite stricken with grief.' He straightened his coat. 'You'd better start reading those diaries. Oh, and we'll need to find a lady's maid for you.'

'A lady's maid? No!' Deb had found it difficult enough being waited on hand and foot here at Brandon Abbey. But a maid of her own? Just for her? She wouldn't know what to *do* with her!

'Of course you must have one,' Beau emphasised. 'You need a girl who's new to London, and who never knew your cousin or any of her friends. Mrs Martin may have some ideas.'

'Bethany,' Deb said after a moment. 'Bethany is one of your maids here. May I take her? If she's willing, that is?'

'I'll ask Mrs Martin.' He nodded his approval and turned to go, but as he reached the door he stopped again. 'Oh, and by the way,' he said. 'What happened earlier today, in the pavilion, will never happen again. You have my word on that.'

When he'd gone, Deb settled herself carefully on the little sofa by the window and fought for calmness. She tried to remember the breathing exercises Gerald had taught her. She thought she'd sunk about as low as she could—but now she had to read Paulette's *diaries*?

She felt like an intruder, an interloper as she picked up the first volume and tried to read her cousin's scattered writing. Each entry confirmed what she already guessed about Paulette—that she was shallow, silly and vain. All she wrote about were clothes, parties and invariably vicious female gossip. But they were still her private diaries, and Deb knew she had absolutely no right to be reading them. She slammed the little book shut.

He told you to read them. He ordered you to read them.

She forced herself to open the diary again, and realised she was at a page in the midst of June last year—almost exactly a year ago. And Paulette's writing had changed. The words were crammed together and looked as if they were written with speed, with excitement. Deb moved the diary closer to the light.

Two days ago, at the Fairleys' summer ball, I met Lord Simon Beaumaris and he paid me great at-

tention. Lord Simon called on me at home the day afterwards, and yesterday as well. Mama and Father are thrilled, and the other girls are so jealous of me that I think I could die of happiness…

Deb turned the pages one by one.

The wedding is only three weeks away. Three weeks. How will I endure it? I live for the moments when I see him. I love him so much that it hurts…

Deb sat back suddenly, her mind reeling.

So despite what the Duke had claimed, Paulette did love Simon! She loved her husband truly and passionately—so why, then, did the Duke claim that she'd trapped him into marriage to satisfy her own ambitions?

And above all—why had Paulette run away?

Chapter Thirteen

London

The morning sun poured through the windows of the big first-floor drawing room of the house in Albemarle Street where Beau was pacing to and fro. He'd travelled here two days ago with Miss O'Hara—Lady Simon, he corrected himself—and her lady's maid. The girl Bethany had appeared over-awed—frightened, almost—on reaching their new destination, but Deborah had been calm and composed, dignified, even, in her black attire.

He expected no less from her. He'd given her one night and one day only to settle in, and the morning after that he'd told her that her duties must commence.

'My investigators…' he began.

'*Your minions*,' he heard her whisper under her breath.

He carried on. 'My investigators have found further proof that Newman might be on the verge of selling up, quite possibly on account of financial difficulties. So he may leave London at any time, taking with him any assets he can lay his hands on.'

'Including the jewels?' she asked quietly.

'Including the Brandon jewels, if he indeed has them. This is going to be a crucial test of your ability to play the part of your cousin, Miss O'Hara. If my investigators are correct, you left the jewels with him, and so you alone can ask him about them without risk of scandal.'

'Ah, yes. We must avoid scandal at all costs.' Her eyes flashed suddenly. 'What if your investigators are wrong, and Paulette *didn't* leave them with him? Or— what if she did, but this Newman denies it and says he never had them?'

'Use your judgement, Miss O'Hara. Say that you've been ill, and are a little confused. Try to guess, if you can, if he's lying. Armitage will take you there this morning, in a hired carriage. Although it will soon be general knowledge, of course, that you're here in London with me, your visit to Newman must be kept as anonymous as possible.'

He could see that she was listening to him carefully, but when he'd finished she remained very quiet. 'You are expecting a great deal of me,' she said at last.

'I don't think that any of it is beyond your capabilities,' he answered.

After she'd left, all he could do was wait, and remember how he'd discovered that the Brandon jewels had gone only two days after his brother died.

The jewels were kept inside a silk-lined, blue velvet box in a big safe in the study of the Duke's London house. Beau had been searching the safe for some documents needed for Simon's funeral, and he'd had to lift the velvet jewel box out of the way. He'd become very still when he realised how light it was.

It was light because it was empty. And only Simon had known where Beau kept the key. That was when Beau had begun to guess what had happened to the jewels. That was when he'd set Armitage and his men to track down Paulette's movements, during the weeks before she'd fled the country.

And now, it was up to Deborah O'Hara to get them back, as a vital part of his campaign to safeguard his family's honour. Beau had watched the girl leave with Armitage an hour or so ago in the hired carriage, and for the past twenty minutes he'd been listening for their return. He resisted the urge to hurry to the window when he heard the sound of the vehicle pulling up in the street outside, and instead forced himself to wait calmly until Armitage brought her in to him.

She still wore her black cape and veiled bonnet, so he could not read her face.

'You have them?' asked Beau.

She looked almost defiant. 'I'm afraid not,' she said.

Armitage stepped forward. 'Your Grace, there is an explanation—'

Beau cut in. 'And I'd prefer Miss O'Hara to give it to me. Leave us, Armitage.'

Deb had hated arriving in this palatial London house two days ago. After the fresh air of the countryside, she found the heat of the city oppressive. She'd hated the deception of being introduced to all the staff as Lady Simon; and only the necessity of comforting Bethany, who was terrified by London's tall houses and crowded streets, kept her calm.

She'd been introduced to Nathaniel Armitage this morning, for he was to escort her on her visit to Mr

Newman. He at least was polite and kind, and altogether he could not have been less like his master. 'I'm so sorry, Lady Simon,' he'd said earnestly, 'to thrust this task on you in such haste. I know that you've only just arrived in London, and I realise that all this must be a considerable ordeal for you.'

Then he'd gone to tell the driver that they wished to be taken to Gresham Street, and Deb, dressed in a black cloak and veiled bonnet, had turned instantly to the Duke. 'Does Mr Armitage know who I am?'

'He knows,' the Duke said. 'But he's been instructed not to give that knowledge away by the smallest of words or gestures, and I trust his loyalty implicitly. You would be well advised not to try any tricks with him.'

Tricks? Deb had gazed up at the Duke with an odd little smile on her face. 'Oh,' she said lightly, 'were you thinking perhaps that I might try to seduce poor Mr Armitage? It's highly unlikely—for really, you see, he's not rich enough for me.'

The Duke, she recollected, had looked at her pretty much as he was looking at her now, as he waited for her to tell him about her visit to the jeweller's shop. Armitage had left the room, and the Duke's face was oddly blank.

'Perhaps you'd be kind enough,' he was saying, 'to tell me exactly what's happened. Did you get to see Newman? Did he accept that you were Paulette?'

'He never doubted it.' She took off her cloak and put it down carefully. 'Mr Newman expressed his sincerest and deepest condolences for my recent bereavement —your Grace.'

'And what did he say, when you questioned him about the jewels?'

'He reminded me,' she said, meeting his eyes steadily, 'that on the occasion of our last meeting, I told him that I didn't care if I never saw them again.'

A muscle suddenly flickered in Beau's jaw. 'Are you quite sure?'

'That's exactly what he told me, your Grace.'

Beau held himself very still. 'Has he sold them?'

'I don't think so.' Suddenly she sounded weary. 'He said to me, "I'll get them if you really want them, Lady Simon." But he added that it might take a week, possibly more.'

She pushed her veil aside and pressed one hand briefly to her cheek. 'I think Newman thought I was ill. Confused. I explained to him I was still in an acute state of grief over Simon's death, and he promised that he would let me know—he said he would write to me here, at your house—as soon as they were available.'

'Did he make any mention of a fee for looking after them for you? Some kind of redemption charge?'

'No, he didn't. But everything about his manner was very strange somehow.'

Beau walked to the window, frowning. Thinking. 'This could, of course, be some kind of delaying tactic. If Newman's planning to move out of town, then it's possible he was hoping to disappear with them, in which case your appearance will have shaken him. I'll set my investigators—'

'*Minions*,' she whispered.

'I'll set my investigators to continue watching the premises, in case he is indeed about to vanish.'

'Would you be able to stop him?'

'I would prefer this business of the jewels to be kept absolutely quiet, as you know. But, yes, I would take drastic action if necessary.' He leaned his hands momentarily on the windowsill, then turned back to face her, his hard features accentuated by the light. 'Meanwhile, we'll assume that Newman meant what he said when he told you that he would have them for you in a week or so. I'm afraid the bad news is that your stay in London will have to be a little longer than either of us wanted—which will open us up to the likelihood of even more visits from Paulette's former acquaintances than I'd anticipated. Though perhaps that's not too bad a thing; you'll be able to take the opportunity to consolidate your presence here as my brother's widow. I hope you can tolerate staying until Newman contacts you again.'

She held her head high. 'Much as I dislike it, your Grace, we have a bargain.'

He strolled towards her, his face expressionless. He cupped her chin suddenly, forcing her to meet his gaze, and his touch seared her. He couldn't know what his nearness did to her—could he? But she was unable to hide the way the warmth flooded her cheeks at his merest touch, nor could she hide the fluttering of her pulse that left her shaking and breathless.

'You cannot possibly dislike all this as much as I do, Miss O'Hara,' he told her softly.

As soon as he'd left the room, Deb let out her breath in a small, shuddering sigh and sank into a chair, feeling utterly distraught.

Beau went to his library, where he sat at his desk, pushing the day's mail aside, trying to gather his thoughts. He felt relief that Newman still appeared to have the jewels, somewhere, but he didn't understand the delay. He had expected the man to hurry to retrieve them for Lady Simon. To be anxious to please, and eager for a monetary reward.

What troubled Beau even more, though, was that he just couldn't stop thinking about Deborah O'Hara, Couldn't stop hearing her voice as she said, *Much as I dislike it, your Grace, we have a bargain.*

He ran his hands through his hair, then pressed his palms to his eyes. He *had* to do this, for his family's sake. He had to get the jewels back quietly, for his family's honour; though sometimes, if the truth be told, he wished the damned things at the bottom of the ocean. Or the lake at Brandon Abbey. He pictured Miss O'Hara's lovely eyes opening very wide indeed if she were to learn that.

She would end up hating him, and he couldn't blame her. It shouldn't matter, that she hated him—but it did. Too much.

Over the next few days Deb became as familiar with the routine at the Duke's London house as she'd been with that at Brandon Abbey. But she still made mistakes, and the Duke never failed to notice them.

'You are proud,' the Duke reminded her whenever he caught her putting away an item that should have been left for a housemaid, or thanking a footman for some small service he'd performed. 'You are haughty, and conscious always of your own importance. Tidying up after yourself is a servant's work. Paulette would never do it.'

She saw too much of him, she thought distractedly. As his sister-in-law, she had to eat with him, of course, at meal-times in the vast dining room, and she was expected to sit with him in the evenings in the drawing room, where she would pretend to read a novel—he had reminded her that Paulette had liked romantic fiction, in a tone that indicated what he thought of her tastes.

His presence disturbed her. She could not help being aware of his physical charisma—he was, after all, the Dangerous Duke, who left beauteous mistresses with broken hearts scattered in his wake—although these days he showed nothing but apparent indifference to her. Often she retreated early to her room, where she continued to study Paulette's diaries.

She'd skimmed them rapidly the day before they left St Alban's, but now she read them more thoroughly, absorbing Paulette's breathless accounts of her London Season last year; her descriptions of the daily parties she'd attended, the clothes she wore, and the people she met. But nothing else affected Deb quite as much as that single, moving sentence: *I love him so much that it hurts.*

She gazed out of her bedroom window, seeing how the summer-flowering shrubs in the back garden shimmered slightly in the twilight.

Why had Paulette left her husband? How had it all gone so terribly wrong?

The fact that Bethany knew nothing of Paulette or her past made the little maid the only person in that vast house with whom Deb felt in any way comfortable. Indeed, Deb found a kind of solace in the daily routines Bethany was so eager to organise, and grew to enjoy the warm baths, the luxury of having her hair washed and brushed, even the unchanging predictability of the clothes that Bethany laid out for her.

The clothes were, of course, all in relentless black. There were gowns for the morning, gowns for the afternoon, gowns for dinner and gowns for visiting hours, because the Duke had been quite right about the attention she would attract. Indeed, as news of her arrival spread, people came to call every afternoon, one after the other, although at first the Duke would not let them meet her.

'Lady Simon is extremely tired,' she would hear him say calmly out in the hallway while the visitors—mostly female—expressed their regrets.

'Your Grace,' she heard them say, 'if there is anything at all we can do for your poor sister-in-law…'

'She will be glad of your company soon, though not just at present. I'm sure you will understand, and sympathise.'

But he showed no sympathy to her. If anything, he appeared to distance himself from her more each day. One evening after dinner, when she'd endured an almost silent meal while the footmen served course after course, she told him calmly that she was going to her room.

He told her, equally calmly, that she was not, but she was coming with him to the drawing room, so he could remind her how she was supposed to behave.

'How I'm—' she'd exploded.

'Please don't give way to your emotions in front of the servants. Come with me.'

She followed him, and wished she hadn't.

'Sometimes you clump around,' he told her after closing the door sharply, 'as if you're still wearing the scruffy breeches and jacket you wore when I first laid eyes on you. You're meant to be wealthy and elegant, even if you are in mourning. You must remember that rich people live differently.'

'In which case, I'm very glad that I'm poor,' Deb murmured fervently.

'Did you say something, Miss O'Hara?' His voice was icily, dangerously polite.

'Nothing of any importance whatsoever, your Grace,' she replied.

His eyes raked her slowly. He was wearing a formal tailcoat that hugged his muscular frame, and a white cravat in which sat a single diamond pin. No wonder women almost fell at his feet, Deb thought helplessly, turning her attention instead to the small glass of port he'd handed her. She hated port even more than sherry, but that was the least of her troubles—the main problem was that the Duke was, quite simply, the most compelling person she'd ever met. There was a brooding, intensely masculine quality to him which set him apart from any other man, and he knew it.

She sipped the port, finding it rich and sickly, and for some reason her hand was so unsteady that the glass rattled against her teeth.

He took the glass from her, put it to one side and leaned closer. 'You know, of course, that in general, you're learning to play Paulette very well.'

She caught her breath. 'I'm glad to hear it—your Grace.'

'Are you?' he asked softly. 'Is—*this* intentional?' And calmly he reached out to adjust the black stole she wore to hide the low neckline of her gown. It had slipped, she realised in utter dismay. It had slipped—and he thought she'd done it deliberately.

She jumped away from his touch as if it burned her. She wanted then, more than anything, to tell him the truth about those hateful books. She even moistened her throat and opened her mouth to say, *They weren't mine. They were Palfreyman's*. But the words died on her lips.

Now it seemed so very late to tell him the truth. Too late. Would he even believe her? And…wasn't he right, to think her weak and sluttish? Wasn't she a whore at heart, to react as she did to his kisses?

'Was there something you wanted to say, Miss O'Hara?'

She shook her head. 'Nothing,' she whispered. 'Absolutely nothing.'

He turned and left the room, leaving her standing there. He was maddening, he was hateful—and she was trapped. *Trapped.*

Time and time again he did that to her, winding up her emotions to breaking point; then, when she'd finally had enough and was about to erupt, he would walk away, leaving her shaking, and filled with the longing to run after him, and—what? *What, Deb, you fool*?

Insult him? Slap him? No. She didn't want to do *any* of those.

What she really wanted, what she longed for, was for this man to pull her into his arms and kiss her.

She had to be losing her mind. She was spending too much time alone, she told herself, and she hated being alone; she was used to being amongst her friends, the Lambeth Players, sharing fun and hardships with them. She hadn't realised until now how truly rich her life was. She wished she could be with them again if only for a short while, but she had given the Duke her word, and his power over her was complete.

Her helplessness was, Deb told herself urgently, the only reason why everything around her seemed to suddenly *change* whenever the Duke came in. His overbearing manner had to be the sole reason why she awaited his visits with a kind of tension that made her pulse pound and her heart beat so painfully against her chest that it almost hurt. And when he was with her, she wasn't in the slightest bit happier. His dark, brooding maleness dominated her senses almost unbearably, and much as she fought against it, she was only too aware, whenever he was near, of her blood rushing to her head, and her breath coming shallowly.

At night, once Bethany had left her, she would walk around her room and recite some lines from her favourite plays, and even do her breathing exercises, but it was no good.

It was as if the Duke was in the room there watching her. Sometimes, she even imagined she heard his mocking applause, but of course when she whirled round he wasn't there. Often, when she'd put on one of the extravagant silk nightdresses Madame Celine had made for her—*oh, how she'd rather sleep in cotton*—she would look in her mirror before she climbed into bed, and see—Paulette.

Paulette, with her carefully tended hair and her mischievous dark-lashed eyes. Paulette—her eyes shadowed now—whispering, *I love him so much that it hurts*.

Soon the dealer, Newman, would contact her. She would get the jewels back, she would perform her role as Simon's grieving widow for just a little while longer, and then it would be over, she told herself. *Over.*

Meanwhile more and more visitors called, and a fresh set of challenges faced her.

'Dear, poor Lady Simon!' her visitors would exclaim. 'We heard from the Duke that you have been extremely ill. And there we were, thinking…' They glanced at one another, eyes glinting. 'You see, my dear, there really have been some very *odd* stories about you.'

Deb sheltered behind her black veil and her fan, and murmured, 'I fear that people are always ready to spread cruel gossip, are they not?'

The Duke was constantly at her side during these visits, and she was aware of his steady eyes on her as her visitors talked, learning to quickly adjust her own behaviour to his subtle shifts of mood. Some of their guests he welcomed quite warmly, whereas with others he was almost frigid.

When a particular gentleman called one day—his name was Lord Featherstone—the sun was as hot as ever outside, but Deb instantly sensed that the atmosphere in the room was frigid. Featherstone was younger than the Duke and could probably have been his brother Simon's age, Deb guessed. Well dressed and handsome, Featherstone's manners towards Deb—*Paulette*—were faultless.

'Lady Simon,' Featherstone said fervently, bowing low over her hand. 'How we have missed you.' He turned round to address the Duke. 'Your sister-in-law's absence has compounded our grief for your deeply lamented brother, your Grace, has it not? Your brother, who was such a fine upholder of all the traditional Beaumaris values—honour, integrity, family duty…'

Featherstone talked on a little longer, but Deb noticed how abrupt the Duke was with him, and how, after a few more moments, he was virtually showing him the door. Deb confronted him as soon as he returned to her.

'You were very rude, I think, to Lord Featherstone,' she said, a little shaken.

He answered curtly. 'That's because he treats his young wife abominably by parading his mistresses around in public. He's also a notorious gambler.'

'I see.' Deb spoke very quietly. 'And does knowing all this entitle you to…to sit in judgement on him—your Grace?'

He cast her a short, sharp glance. 'That's not all I know about Featherstone,' he answered flatly, 'believe me.'

Most of the visits were more relaxed, and easier for her to handle. She would sit quietly, protected by her veil, while the ladies would sip tea and the gentlemen wine. 'Dear Lady Simon,' one of the ladies said as they at last turned to go, 'I cannot quite put it into words, but you seem different, somehow.'

'Perhaps I did not know what true grief was,' Deb murmured, 'until now.'

The gentlemen were quite awed, and the women glanced at one another with feeling. 'So we see.'

And so the whispers began to spread around London that summer, about the overwhelming grief of the enchanting young widow who was the Duke of Cirencester's sister-in-law. 'Don't overdo it,' Beau said to her afterwards. 'But—well done.'

He approved of her? He wasn't criticising her? Deb felt pure relief—it *was* relief, wasn't it, and nothing else?—flowing through her veins, warming her.

And so it was that the next stage in the reclamation of the Brandon jewels came as an utter and mind-numbing shock.

Chapter Fourteen

It was a little under two weeks later that the Duke brought Deb Mr Newman's sealed letter. She opened it quickly, conscious of his watchful eye. Briefly, Newman told her that he would welcome a visit from her regarding the items she required, at her earliest convenience. Wordlessly she handed the letter to the Duke, who scanned it and said, 'Armitage will escort you to Gresham Street, later today.'

Mr Armitage did indeed take her, in a hired carriage again; Deb entered the jewel-dealer's premises as before, and Newman greeted her politely, but still, she felt, a little oddly.

'Here are the items you left in my safekeeping, Lady Simon,' he said, putting a black satin box on the table in front of her. 'You will want to inspect them, of course.'

He was already opening the box for her, and she looked carefully at the ornate necklace and earrings, made of rubies and diamonds. She found herself frowning a little. Yes, they looked *exactly* like the ones Paulette had worn in that portrait, but she'd expected to be dazzled by them. She'd expected to be *stunned* by them.

She touched the necklace with her gloved fingertip and said to the jeweller, 'Thank you. You will have to remind me, Mr Newman, if we agreed on any fee for you to take care of the Brandon jewels during my convalescence. They are such valuable items—you can imagine my joy at seeing them safe once more...'

Her voice trailed away as she saw the expression on Newman's face. He looked startled. He looked utterly bewildered.

'My dear Lady Simon,' he said, 'surely you cannot have forgotten?'

Deb felt her throat go dry. 'Forgotten what?'

'Why, that these jewels are fakes! I had to tell you so when you brought them to me, back in March, to have them valued. It was a great shock to you, naturally, and you were extremely angry. You *must* remember!'

Deb's mind reeled. *Remember to breathe deeply and speak calmly. Remember you are playing a part.*

'Of course I remember,' she said quickly. 'I was speaking of the value of these jewels to me personally, of course, and I would like to offer you a reward for your discretion, Mr Newman.' She was already reaching for some coins from her purse, and handing them across the table to him.

'My thanks, Lady Simon. That is generous of you, in the circumstances.' He took the coins, and dabbed at his brow a little with his handkerchief. 'I did in fact try to find out what happened to the originals, as you asked me at the time. But I made little progress, I fear, apart from learning that my suspicions were unfortunately true—that your husband secretly gambled them away.'

Deb need all her acting skills to hide her shock at

that. Somehow she managed to nod. 'So you haven't succeeded in discovering who has them now?'

'All I know,' Newman said heavily, 'is that your sadly departed husband lost the jewels at cards one February night—not in a club, but at someone's private residence. As is sometimes the case, the person who won them allowed him a respite of a few days in order to have replicas made. I happen to know the jeweller who made the copies—one of my less conscientious colleagues, I fear. These, of course—' he pointed to the jewels '—are the replicas.'

'And they are exactly what I wanted. Thank you so much, Mr Newman.' She picked up the box and rose to her feet. 'I trust I can continue to rely on your absolute discretion?'

'Of course. Of course, Lady Simon.'

Deb tucked the black jewel box beneath her cloak and went out into the cobbled street, still stunned by what she'd just learned. Armitage was waiting outside the hired carriage, a little distance away, and he came swiftly towards her. 'Is there a problem?' he asked anxiously. 'My dear Lady Simon, you look pale. Let me offer you my arm...'

'There is a slight problem.' She was feeling very tired suddenly. 'But I would rather tell the Duke himself, Mr Armitage.'

'Of course,' he said. 'Of course.'

All the way back to the Duke's house, she was thinking, *How can I tell him that his dead brother gambled away part of his family's heritage*? Always, the Duke spoke of family honour; family duty; family loyalty. Always, he blamed Paulette for the disaster of his brother's marriage. But Simon had lost the jewels at cards. Even worse, he had tried to cover his deception by having counterfeits made.

Desperately she tried to imagine how she would tell the Duke all this. Should she hand over the counterfeit jewels after she told him, or before? *I'm afraid I have bad news, your Grace. Your brother Simon was a cheat, and a liar.*

As soon as they reached the big house in Albemarle Street, Mr Delaney, the butler, told her that his Grace the Duke wished to see her in his study. Bethany was already in Deb's room, waiting to help her remove her cloak and gloves; to assist her in putting on a black cap and veil, instead of her bonnet. *I must tell him*, Deb kept thinking. *I must tell him.*

She hid the box of jewels deep in a drawer. *I can bring them downstairs later.* It was going to be difficult, she knew. But she hadn't realised quite how difficult until she entered his study half an hour later, and saw what was laid out on the big desk in there. The medals that Beau had shown her at Brandon Abbey. The officer's sash. The sabre, and the pistols; the portrait of his brother in uniform…

When he was a boy, Beau had said, *he always dreamed of being a soldier.*

'You've had Simon's things brought here,' she blurted out.

He looked at her steadily and nodded. 'I told you, I think, that I was hoping to organise some kind of memorial service—a thanksgiving, if you like—for Simon's life. To have them here seemed appropriate. Please—' he gestured to a chair '—sit down.'

She sat, and he lowered himself into a chair also.

'I've postponed dealing with Simon's possessions for too long,' he went on. 'But as with everything else relating to my brother, I must proceed to draw as much as I can of his life to a fitting conclusion. I hope you didn't find your outing this morning too tiring, Miss O'Hara?'

She could hardly speak. In his portrait, Simon was smiling and carefree; a younger, happier version of Beau…

'The housekeeper brought in some cordial,' he said, pointing to a jug and glasses on a tray. 'Shall I pour you some? Armitage told me that there appeared to be a slight problem with the jewels.' His voice was very steady. 'Newman hasn't sold them, has he?'

Deborah drew a deep breath. She couldn't tell him. Not yet. Not with what she recognised as deep-seated grief still shadowing his eyes.

She sipped at the half-glass he'd poured for her. 'There's no problem,' she lied. 'But Mr Newman told me that he has lent the jewels to a colleague of his, a goldsmith who—who wished to make a study of the jewels on account of their craftsmanship….' *Oh, God. She hated herself, for doing this.*

He watched her for a long time—so long that her heart began to thud slowly. Did he know? Did he suspect? She almost jumped when he spoke at long last.

'Did he tell you when you may have them back?'

'Very soon,' she whispered.

'Then I must thank you for visiting him.' His voice was very calm. 'It was clearly an ordeal for you. And I'm afraid there is another ordeal I must put you through, Miss O'Hara. You see, you and I have been invited to a private party in Grosvenor Square tonight. I fear I failed to calculate that your arrival in London would cause something of a sensation, and set tongues wagging all around town.'

He was starting to put away some of the medals, very carefully. Deb found that her throat had gone quite dry. 'They aren't—beginning to guess?'

'There are one or two malicious whispers.' He looked at her steadily. 'That's why your attendance at this party is essential to convince people that you really are my brother's widow. We'll stay there for an hour, that's all; you may rest assured that I won't leave your side.' He looked at his watch. 'You'll no doubt have much to do to prepare yourself. I'll let you go.'

She nodded mutely and hurried upstairs. Beau waited till she'd gone then put the lid down, heavily, on the case of his brother's medals.

And he felt like hurling it to the floor.

One year, his brother had lasted in the army. One year, then Simon had left—after gambling and drinking his way through a small fortune and making his fellow officers glad to see the back of him.

Simon had next turned his thoughts to a rich marriage. Paulette Palfreyman had been the sensation of the Season, and Simon perhaps thought to recover some of his lost pride by marrying her. When Simon learned in March that his wife had run off abroad with the latest of her lovers, he had turned to Beau with a bitter smile on his face and said, *Well, big brother. It turns out that you were right all the time about my beauteous bride. But then, you always were right, about almost bloody everything, weren't you?*

Beau picked up Simon's sabre and gazed bleakly at the gleaming hilt. He was normally a good judge of character. Of whether people were telling the truth

or not, and he was sure—he was absolutely sure—
that Deborah O'Hara had been lying her head off to
him just now. He was pretty sure what had happened
to the jewels, for her visits to Newman had not gone
unnoticed, nor had his agents' enquiries been fruit-
less. Over the last few days, certain developments—
developments he'd almost expected—had ensued. For
it had been part of his overall plan that bringing Paulette to London would set the cat amongst the pigeons,
so to speak—and force out the murky truth.

During the past couple of weeks he'd had Newman
followed more closely than ever. Newman had been
careless in whom he spoke to and what he said, no doubt
startled out of caution by Lady Simon's sudden return.
Armitage had broken the news to Beau two days ago.

'I'm afraid it's my belief that your brother lost the
Brandon jewels at cards, your Grace,' Armitage had
said in his level voice. 'Back in February. He had counterfeits made, and he gave the counterfeits as a gift, to
Paulette.'

In some last-ditch attempt to save his marriage?
wondered Beau. If so, Simon was a fool not to antici-
pate that the greedy Paulette would immediately go to
have them valued—and after discovering the truth, she
had walked out on him entirely.

Miss O'Hara must have learnt all this today. And
Beau was filled with anger and bleak disappointment
that she hadn't told him.

At eight o'clock that evening, Beau's carriage was
waiting at the front of the house. His driver William
was ready and so was Beau, dressed in full black evening attire as befitted mourning for a brother whose

untimely death had shocked London. Whose untimely death continued to send ripple after ripple of speculation and vicious gossip throughout so-called polite society.

Well, Beau was prepared, especially since Armitage had come to him less than an hour ago with fresh news. He had the name of the man who had, in all likelihood, won the Brandon jewels off Simon.

'I'm surprised he's managed to keep quiet for so long, your Grace.'

'He'll be biding his time,' answered Beau curtly. 'Wondering exactly how high a price he can demand for returning the jewels to me, and for thereafter keeping silent over the whole affair.' Beau remembered the tightness he'd felt in his chest when he'd discovered, soon after Simon's death, that the jewel box in the safe was empty.

Armitage offered up one final piece of information: that the man to whom Simon had lost the jewels was quite likely to be at the party tonight. Beau was prepared. But he was never prepared for the effect that Miss Deborah O'Hara had on him. He had never been able to forget what she had felt like, in his arms.

He was becoming obsessed by her—yes, *obsessed* was the word. It had to be a kind of madness, surely, for him to wake in the night because *she* had been drifting in and out of his dreams.

In his dreams she would sometimes be wearing black—did she realise how damned alluring that half-veil was? Or she'd be dressed in the rough boy's attire he'd first seen her in, when she'd teased him with those wicked books of hers. *Which one do you find most interesting, Mr Beaumaris?* she'd said, letting her tongue flick over her lips while that mischievous gleam glinted in her golden eyes. Oh, she'd enjoyed making him squirm in his bonds. She must, she *must* have realised how his pulse was pounding and he was growing hard with desire.

In his dreams he also imagined her rather too often with nothing on at all—except perhaps the jewels. The damned Brandon jewels.

He fought down his fantasies. He fought down the constant, simmering need to take her in his arms. He told himself he was able to resist her. At least, he'd *thought* he was, until at five past eight that evening Miss O'Hara came gliding down the broad staircase.

She was in black as usual, with a gauze veil covering half her face, and Beau caught his breath. She was the perfect epitome of an elegant, grief-stricken widow about to embark on a social outing on the arm of her brother-in-law. She really was Paulette, except that she had a quiet dignity and courage to which Paulette could never aspire.

As she came slowly towards him, he glimpsed her eyes through the gauze of the veil, and they looked—haunted. 'Am I suitably dressed, your Grace?' she whispered.

He said to her, 'You look perfect.'

She glanced up at him, wary as ever, and Beau saw the lost child in her again, despite her fine clothes. The knowledge that she was accustomed to selling herself smote him bitterly, time and time again. And once more he wondered, with equal intensity: Why hadn't she told him what she must surely have discovered that afternoon from Newman? That the jewels were fakes?

He lifted her hand to his arm, to guide her to the doorway, then stopped. 'By the way, Miss O'Hara, I mentioned to you a while ago that I intend to organise a memorial service, in honour of my brother. And I would very much like you to attend, before you officially retire to the countryside again.'

She bowed her head, but was silent.

'I've decided,' he went on, 'that it would be fitting to hold a ceremony at St Margaret's church in Westminster, which is where he and Paulette were married. Your presence there should put paid to any lingering whispers about Paulette's treachery.'

She looked—tormented. Might she tell him the truth *now* about the counterfeit jewels?

She raised her head, and this time the look on her face reminded him of a wild creature in captivity. 'Very well,' she whispered. 'I will attend the memorial service…'

And those were her only words. She rested her small, black-gloved hand on his arm once more and he led her in silence out to his waiting carriage.

The merest touch of her hand on his arm. That was all it took—and his resolve to guard himself against her, which should only have been strengthened by her duplicity today, was once more almost fatally wrecked. Beau agonised anew over his inexplicable reaction to her. She was no virgin, by her own admission. She had lived a hard life, she must be accustomed to intrigue and lies. But something about her challenged him in a way he'd never experienced. And when she'd come down those stairs, and looked up at him almost uncertainly, whispering, *'Am I suitably dressed, your Grace?'*—he'd felt desire for her burning hard and dangerous.

Soon—one way or another—he would retrieve the jewels. His brother's memory would be duly honoured, and the girl would be paid off, with the lease of some lowly theatre for her friends. They had an agreement, didn't they? But, as the Duke had been finding out to his cost lately, things did not always work out according to his plans.

As soon as they arrived at the big house in Grosvenor Square, their hostess, Lady Rebecca Tansley, pushed her way through the crowds of guests to greet them. 'Your Grace. Lady Simon! It's so very good to see you in town again. Even though the circumstances are *extremely* sad. My dear Lady Simon, I trust that you are feeling a little—stronger?'

'The peace of the Norfolk countryside,' said Deborah with a slight catch in her voice, 'has helped to heal my grief a little. And I am almost resigned to my loss—if indeed such a loss can ever be borne.'

Lady Rebecca blinked. 'But of *course*. And to think that some wicked people have been whispering—'

'Yes,' the Duke interrupted. 'I do believe there have been certain rumours about my widowed sister-in-law's whereabouts. But Lady Simon and I thought it beneath her dignity to even try to refute them.'

'I quite understand!' said Lady Rebecca, flushing a little. 'Dear me, these gossips.'

'These gossips.' Beau knew that Lady Rebecca herself was the biggest tattler in town. Leading Deb away, he introduced her to all those who eagerly awaited her, and they greeted her like a long-lost friend, even though Beau knew many of them had scarcely been on speaking terms with Paulette. He stood close as one by one they expressed their condolences. Those who'd already visited Beau's house took a special pride in reminding her of their calls.

They are liars and she is superb, the Duke thought in wonder. She was calm, and radiant. She was Paulette, but not the Paulette he'd known, who was an excitable little flirt unable to rest at any social gathering until she had every man in the room grovelling at her dainty and expensively clad feet.

He himself was the subject of much attention, of course; but he was skilled in making polite talk while his mind was elsewhere. In fact, his eyes too were often elsewhere, because he was following his protégée always, watching her, guarding her with his presence. Several of the younger men had not met her before, and were clearly entranced.

If only they knew, he thought, *how she gained her skill in casting her spell over you all*. He remembered vividly that day in Oxford, when he'd seen her climb on to a makeshift stage outside the Angel Inn, and how all the rough men in the crowd there, young and old, had listened to her spellbound. She was having pretty much the same effect on them all tonight. Some young gallant had brought her a glass of lemonade, while another had fetched her a chair, and she sat there with her eyes hidden beneath that veil, demurely responding to their questions, while she plied her fan.

And then Beau saw someone else watching her—Lord Featherstone.

Beau walked slowly towards him—Featherstone now had his back to him—and touched his shoulder.

Lord Featherstone was badly startled. 'Beaumaris,' he said with false heartiness. 'Good to see you again.

I enjoyed visiting you and poor Lady Simon the other day…'

'Did you?' asked Beau. 'But I believe you were intending to make a private visit to me—alone—some time soon. Weren't you, Featherstone?' Featherstone opened his mouth, then closed it again.

'About something…confidential?' went on Beau. 'You know, I truly was surprised to learn that you're so friendly with a second-hand dealer in shoddy jewellery called Newman. He came to visit you in rather a hurry recently, didn't he?'

Featherstone paled, and Beau was certain. Absolutely certain. 'Shall we go somewhere quiet,' said Beau, 'and discuss the business of the Brandon jewels *now*?'

Chapter Fifteen

'Why, Miss O'Hara, didn't you tell me? If you knew—as clearly you *did*—then why did you not inform me *straight away*?'

'I—I couldn't quite take it in.' For the first time Beau could remember, Deb looked visibly cowed by him. 'I could hardly believe that your brother Simon had gambled the jewels away. And above all, I could not think how to break the news to you…'

Her voice trailed away.

Beau stared at her. 'What, exactly, did you think I'd do? Collapse with grief, because my brother had been so wicked?'

'No!' She shook her head, looking terribly distressed. 'No, of *course* I didn't! But I needed just a little time to think. I was trying to find some solution…'

'Were you really imagining,' said Beau grimly, 'that *you* could get the jewels back for me? Didn't you think that I could have done something myself about the situation, if you'd told me?'

They were in the Duke's study. He'd brought her home early from the party, taking his leave of their hostess with icy politeness, but Deb could see that he was turbulent with inner rage. The summer heat had been transformed by a sudden rainstorm; hurrying her from Lady Rebecca's house, he'd ushered her into his waiting carriage without a word, and the journey had passed in utter silence, broken only by the thudding of rain on the roof.

When he *did* start speaking, once he'd led her into his study and firmly shut the door, his anger was all the more frightening.

She clasped her hands together. 'I—I thought you would be upset beyond belief to know that your brother had gambled them away.'

'You were right. I was even more upset to learn that you knew of it but hadn't told me. And as it happened, the news wasn't as much as a shock to me as you appear to imagine.'

'You'd guessed?' Her lips were white.

'Yes. Perhaps I should have been more honest with *you*.' Beau's jaw was clenched. 'You see, I always knew that my brother was a reckless gambler. He was thrown out of the army for drinking, brawling and—gambling.'

She continued to listen, speechless.

'After your first visit to Newman,' Beau went on, 'it was apparent that the jeweller was disturbed by your reappearance. That same day, soon after you'd left him, Newman shut up shop and went to see Lord Featherstone. Yes, the very man who came here the other day to pay you his respects. You wondered why I didn't like him. There were several reasons, one of them being that he was a gambling crony of Simon's—though you thought him rather charming, I remember. Anyway, Newman went to see Featherstone straight after your first visit to him, and of course I guessed that it might be to warn him that Paulette was back in London, and was now under my protection.'

'So you're saying that your men continued to watch Newman? Even after I'd reported back to you?'

'I'd have been a fool *not* to have him watched. And I knew Featherstone would be at the party tonight. So I tackled him about the jewels, and he has them.'

'But you said—you told me you would know for certain, if someone else had them…'

'I said I would know if someone else had *purchased* them, on the open market. Featherstone won them at cards. I forced it out of him this evening that one night late in February, he and my brother played privately, just the two of them, till three in the morning. The Brandon jewels were Simon's last stake—and he lost them. Simon begged two favours of Featherstone—one, that he be allowed to keep them for long enough to make copies of them, and two, that Featherstone keep quiet about his winnings. Simon gave the fakes to Paulette. She found out the truth, of course, when she took them to Newman to get them valued. By then it was early March, and Simon's deception prompted her to leave her husband—and the country—for good, with her new lover. Simon's last chance to win her back had gone.'

A sudden burst of rain rattled against the window; Beau waited for it to subside, then began again. 'In April, my brother died. I got out of Featherstone tonight that he was intending to come to me and request an exorbitant sum, in return for him handing back the jewels and keeping quiet about how they were lost. But he hadn't quite summoned up the courage, it appears.

Nor had Featherstone grasped the reality that the jewels were in fact stolen. My brother was a thief.'

Deb let out a low gasp, but Beau carried on relentlessly. 'The Brandon jewels belong to whoever is the current Duke of Cirencester, and cannot ever be sold or gifted away. Unknown to me, Simon took them from the family safe on the day before his gambling spree with Featherstone. I didn't realise it until shortly after his death, and then I guessed he'd either gambled them away, or given them to Paulette. As it happened, I was right about both.'

His eyes, if anything, grew bleaker. 'Featherstone will return the jewels. But I still don't understand why you didn't tell me that you learned today the jewels were counterfeit. What you hoped to *achieve*, by lying to me.'

She was very pale. 'I—I was trying to think of some way to break the news to you. I thought, you see, that you loved your brother so much.'

'Well, now you know the truth.' Beau dragged his hand across his temples. 'I'd still like you to stay till the memorial service, if you feel you can manage it. Then you can go.'

And that was it? thought Deb, panicking. A half-hearted request and a dismissal? For good? She felt as if—as if he'd pounded her and hung her upside down like a piece of laundry. He'd walked over to the drinks table, to pour himself one of his sparse brandies, and she turned on him, heaving air into her lungs. She whispered, 'Do you think all this has been easy, playing the part of Paulette under your scornful gaze?'

He poured her a small sherry and held it out. 'Drink this. You look as though you need it. And you'd have found everything a great deal easier if you'd told me the truth,' he rapped out.

She was tired. She was overwrought. She was emotionally exhausted from living in this new and strange world that she didn't even like. 'Perhaps I *didn't* tell you the truth,' she breathed, 'because I guessed you would fly into a cold rage and blame me for everything! Just as you are doing now, your Grace! I have no fondness whatsoever for my cousin Paulette. But I feel as if I've been selling my soul during my time with you. And I could tell you that you're selling *yours*—but of course you haven't got one!' She slammed down the tiny glass of sherry without drinking it, then went to pour herself some brandy and swallowed it in one.

Oh! She shuddered a little. *My goodness. That was— strong. That was…*

He'd knocked back his own brandy and was pacing towards her, but she held her ground—he admired her for that. He suddenly realised that he admired a whole lot of things about this young woman—which was unfortunate, since she was nothing but trouble.

'You think you know a good deal about me, don't you?' he said in a voice that was icy with menace. 'But you know nothing. Absolutely *nothing.*'

She clenched her fists. 'I've realised that you're ruthless and heartless. And sometimes, I almost feel sorry for Paulette—'

'Why?' he answered harshly. 'Why feel sorry for *her*? Her family was hateful to your mother and to you.'

'And you think that revenge is the answer?' she exclaimed. 'I don't! I despise the very notion of revenge—it's pitiful and it's life-wasting. I'm only doing this—being Paulette—because you forced me into it!

You have got so very much, and yet you're wasting days—no, weeks—of your life trying to honour Simon's memory, or so you say. And yet a large part of that time has been taken up with your efforts to claw back a few jewels, that with your vast wealth, you shouldn't care tuppence for! Although I suppose that one day some predatory woman might beguile you into giving them to her…'

Oh, no. She shouldn't have said that—big mistake, Deb.

'Some predatory woman?' he echoed silkily.

Her heart thumped. He was towering over her, in a way that made her lungs suddenly ache and her pulse pound. The memory of how his lips had felt against hers sent a disturbing tremor straight to her heart.

'Why not?' she shrugged. 'There were enough of them after you at that party—Lady Rebecca, for one.'

He drew closer. 'Lady Rebecca,' he said softly, 'is a brainless fool with a squawk like a parrot's.'

Somehow, Deb realised, his hand had slipped round her waist and was sending warm flickers of sensation to all her nerve-endings. Or was it the brandy? Oh, Lord, she shouldn't have had that brandy…

'Leave me alone,' she whispered. 'You make it quite impossible for me to defend myself against you.'

His blue eyes were hooded suddenly. 'You think that I'd harm you, Miss O'Hara?'

'Oh, no.' Deb twisted out of his grasp and faced him scornfully. 'Apart from threatening to throw me in Newgate. And making me watch, while you surround yourself with the kind of empty-brained society beauties who were flocking around you tonight…'

'They *did* make an impression on you,' he murmured. 'But as I think I've told you before—I don't have to buy women.'

She tilted her chin. 'They throw themselves into your arms, of course?'

'Well, yes,' he admitted. 'As a matter of fact, quite often, they do.'

She began to laugh. A rather hollow laugh. Because something was happening. Beau had put his strong, lean hands on her shoulders and was pulling her slowly towards him—no, was that right? *Was* he pulling her, or was she leaning into him? Oh, that brandy…

Beau gazed down at her and watched the emotions flickering across her piquant and expressive face. She was right about him, of course; he was, in so many ways, proud and arrogant. And she, with her outspokenness and downright honesty, was troubling him more and more each day. But—*why didn't she tell him she knew the jewels had been gambled away*?

He reminded himself that he too had been far from honest. He hadn't told her yet that Simon had always hated his older brother, ever since they were small. God knew, Beau had tried to make his brother's life easier. But he'd failed, just as he'd failed to make this girl confide in him, or even like him. And what she was doing to his own peace of mind just terrified him.

Deborah O'Hara was turning his previously well-ordered life upside down. At this precise moment, she was demolishing his self-control as well, for his body pounded with the primeval urge to take her in his arms. He could see her small breasts rapidly rising and falling as if she was struggling for breath; he could see her golden eyes grow shadowy, and her lips flutter, and all he could think was that he wanted to kiss her, very badly.

He bent his head and breathed in her scent. She smelled sweet, of soap and lemons. He wanted to kiss her, to challenge her damned obstinacy, and teach her a lesson for her insults. He wanted to kiss her because— damn it, he'd been wanting to remind himself of the taste of her lips for days. He wanted to kiss her and a whole lot more. He angled his head, to possess her sweet mouth, and he found with a rush of fierce arousal that she was as delicious as he remembered...

He drew back, realising that she was trembling.

'Why won't you leave me alone?' he heard her whisper.

He cupped her face in his hands. 'I keep trying to,' he answered softly. 'I'm finding it rather difficult.'

She was struggling to pull herself away. 'Don't do this. Please.'

He answered the only way he knew—with another kiss. A deeper kiss. Her mouth opened sweetly, but he felt her low moan of protest, almost of despair, through every fibre of his body.

He thought he'd lost her. But then her slender arms suddenly encircled his neck, and she pressed herself against him almost with a shudder, the sensual movement sending the blood pounding to his loins. There was an old sofa in the corner and, remembering its position more by luck than judgement, he steadily guided her back towards it, his mouth bestowing gentle kisses all the time to her cheeks, her throat.

I'm sorry, he wanted to say. *I'm sorry, for using you...* Her warm hands clasped the back of his neck as if she felt that if she let him go she would fall.

Unless she let him go, Beau knew there was only one way this would end.

He lowered her carefully to the sofa, nibbling at her throat, probing at the delicate pulse there with his tongue. Her tiny gasp—was it an expression of denial, or was it encouragement?—drove him wild. That dress drove him wild. He'd never realised till he met Deborah O'Hara that black could be so damned alluring. He acknowledged that those gowns, with their daring necklines, had been filling him with desperate desire for her for weeks now. She had one of her flimsy shawls draped over her shoulders, but that was no protection—already it was slipping aside to expose the exquisite curves of her breasts, and the sight of her creamy rounded flesh made his pulse thud thickly.

Dragging his thumb over the silk that barely covered those rigid peaks, he stroked his other hand down over the flat planes of her stomach, feeling her shiver and tremble—she *must* feel the power of his arousal, dear God, he was so hard and heavy for her. But he must be steady, he must be gentle, and…

In the distance he heard the sound of the heavy knocker on the front door being banged repeatedly. *It was gone eleven. What the hell*…? Beau heard servants' footsteps hurrying; heard the great front door being unlocked and opened. There were voices: the butler Delaney's hearty greeting, and a girl's glad reply. Deborah had heard the sound too by now, for she was pulling herself dazedly away from him, her face still warmly flushed, her hair awry. Dear God, thought Beau, she looked delicious. Another few moments and he'd have had trouble exercising any kind of self-control at all.

'What is it?' she whispered. 'That noise—what's

happening?' She was pushing her hair back from her face, and gazing at him with wide, dazed eyes.

Beau was rising steadily to his feet, smoothing down his coat, straightening his cravat and running his hands over his thick dark hair. 'It sounds,' he said heavily, 'as if my little sister, Laura, has arrived.'

'Your sister!' Deb's hands flew to her shawl to drag it over her breasts.

'Beau. Where are you?' The high-pitched voice was coming nearer. 'Are you hiding in your study as usual?' There was a merry laugh; the door to the study flew open, and a girl with light blonde curls and a mischievous, pretty face stood there. She was dressed in a cherry-pink pelisse, and her beribboned bonnet dangled from her fingers. 'Darling Beau!' she cried. 'So you are in here! And Paulette— Oh, I *heard* that you're back at last!'

There followed a few moments of frantic activity as the seventeen-year-old Lady Laura Beaumaris hugged her much bigger brother over and over again, then handed her pelisse to a hovering footman and flung herself on the sofa that had been so recently vacated. She patted the place beside her for Deb to sit there, and turned to her supposed sister-in-law with sheer wonder in her blue eyes.

'Paulette. You look different, somehow!'

Deb's heart was beating hard. *That kiss. His caresses.* She had been frighteningly near to surrendering. She was horrified by how near she'd been to surrendering…

'You may well say that she appears different,' broke in the Duke steadily. 'You need to remember that Paulette has endured a great deal since you last saw her in January, Laura.'

'Of course. Poor, poor Simon—we all miss him, so badly.' Laura's eyes misted with tears, but then she dashed them away. 'Beau, darling, do go and see that Delaney tips the carriage driver handsomely, will you? I made him bring me all the way from Brighton, and he was so kind, even to poor Miss Champion, who was disastrously travel-sick.'

'I'll be back in one moment,' Beau said, after shooting a meaningful glance at Deb. *Be careful*, that look said. *Say as little as possible*.

In fact, Deb didn't get a chance to say anything, for the minute Beau left the room, Laura turned on her again. 'Miss Champion used to be my governess, but now she's my companion, even though Beau thinks she's no use at all,' she explained in her bubbly way. 'Though of course, you know that. When I first met you, I wasn't sure that I liked you awfully. It seems a dreadful thing to say. You see, I worried that poor Simon was perhaps making a dreadful mistake. After that you and I didn't meet terribly often, did we? But last week, in Brighton—I've been staying there with my friend Helen, and we had *such* a time, what with the theatre, and the shopping, and everything—last week in Brighton, I heard you were back! We met people from London, who said everybody was talking about how sad and how beautiful you were, and so I just *had* to return to London to see you—'

She broke off as Beau came back in, and Deb watched in a daze as pretty Laura sprang up to hug her older brother again with great affection. He'd told Deb, of course, that he had a sister. But she wasn't supposed to be here, and this changed everything.

There was a smile on Beau's face as he touched his little sister's cheek, but his eyes were sombre. 'I hope you haven't been wearying Paulette with your chatter, Laura.'

'Oh, no, it's just that I'm so pleased to see her! And I wish to see a great deal more of her, and of you. I can stay here, can't I, darling Beau? I could be a companion for Paulette!'

'I'm not sure that's a good idea.' Beau's rigid stance told Deb that he thought it a terrible idea. 'I do hope, Laura,' he went on, 'that you've not forgotten Paulette is in mourning.'

'Of course not, and I'm sorry.' Laura sat on the sofa beside Deb and pressed her hand, then looked up at her brother once more. 'But it must be so lonely for Paulette in this great big house, just with you. You can be such a cantankerous bore, Beau darling. Please let me stay!'

Deb didn't have time to see Beau's reaction, because Laura had turned to take her hand and say, 'Dear Paulette. We are going to be such friends!'

And then Laura was on her feet again, almost dancing towards her brother and saying, 'I'll have my usual rooms, I suppose! And now I'd better see that poor Miss Champion has recovered from the journey. Mr Delaney has promised to send me up some supper, then I shall go to bed. I'll see you tomorrow, dearest brother!'

Chapter Sixteen

After Laura had gone, Deb said very quietly to Beau, 'I thought you told me that your sister was staying with a friend in Brighton for the whole summer. And that I was unlikely to meet her.'

She also remembered him adding, *At least, I hope you don't meet her.*

'She wasn't meant to come to London.' Beau looked agitated. 'Not yet. I just wanted to keep Laura out of this damned mess…'

This damned mess being her, presumably. Deb felt very tired suddenly.

'I do *not* want her to stay,' he emphasised. He'd started pacing the room in that way he had when he was sorely troubled.

She planted herself in front of him and said, 'I think there is every reason for your sister to stay.'

He stared at her in astonishment.

'Don't you see?' Deb went on urgently. 'You've already told me that I have to remain here with you until the memorial service. If your sister stays as well, it will look as if we are living here as a family, and that will put an end to any gossip about you and me…'

Her voice trailed away, because the Duke's eyes had become shards of blue ice. 'You've heard gossip?'

She hadn't been going to tell him. 'I—I heard someone whispering, at that party, that I was a very pretty widow for you to have under your protection.'

Beau uttered a quiet oath. He'd loosened his coat, because it was warm in here, and had gone to fling open the French windows that led out to the garden, with its cascading roses and trickling fountain. The rain had stopped, and the fresh scents of flowers invaded the room. He turned round, his eyes shadowed—and she knew then what was coming. 'I can send *you* away,' he said.

With those few words, Deb realised that this man had come to mean so much to her that her world—yes, even her beloved, familiar world of the Players—would be nothing without him.

She'd seen the public façade he put on for outsiders, and tonight she'd seen the tenderness in his eyes for his little sister. She also knew that beneath the iron control he exerted over himself, there was something primitive raging. The passionate need to see justice done, for his brother and for his family; whatever the method, whomever he had to use and destroy.

It would be safer to hate him. Instead a bone-deep longing for this proud man infected every part of her being. Seeing him so tender with his sister, Laura, had reminded her that he could be so kind that it took her breath away. Yet he despised her, and thought her nothing but a cheap little actress. He thought that she could be bought.

And she'd done little to dispel his illusions tonight,

she thought wearily. That kiss just now. Another few moments, and…

Deb had spent the past few years having to guard her emotions, and she would continue to do so. But—if only she'd never met him. If only he hadn't been travelling to hateful Hugh Palfreyman's on the day she'd decided to burgle Hardgate Hall. If only…

He loosened his cravat and went to sit on a chair, resting his forehead in one hand.

'You don't have to send me away,' she said steadily.

He rose again, forcing his limbs to work. He forced his *mind* to work, which made a change from the last few days, he thought bitterly. Laura's arrival had made him see sense. He'd been living in a world of ridiculous delusion, thinking that he could have her. Could have the lovely young woman who was looking at him now with her clear golden eyes.

Deborah. He said the name to himself softly, gazing down at her, drinking in everything about her, because he knew that his little sister's arrival was a timely warning, and this had to be the end.

But even now, she drew out from the recesses of his heart some fathomless emotions he didn't realise he possessed. She looked bewildered. She also looked utterly beautiful. She shone like a candle flame on a dark, dark night. She was bright, brave and honest. And he was using her.

Yes, she'd hesitated over telling him the truth, about the jewels being counterfeit. But he, Beau, had lied to her from the very beginning. Because he'd already guessed that Simon might well have gambled the jewels away, and so he'd sent her forth, the unknowing and innocent bait in the trap, to draw out the truth. *He* was the one who was despicable.

And she looked as if his talk of dismissal had stunned her. He raked his hand through his dark hair. 'I *must* send you away,' he said. 'Back to your actor friends. I've decided that I cannot go on with this.'

She hadn't realised she could hurt so much. 'But what about the memorial service for your brother? And—people have seen me, Beau.' That was the first time she'd called him that. She was still gazing up at him, her vulnerability for once laid utterly bare. 'How are you going to make me just disappear again?'

'I'll say that you found appearing in public too much of a strain.'

'But it's important for me to be at this memorial service—you told me so. It would have been important to Simon…'

He shook his head. 'I can't ask you to go through with it.'

She said steadily, 'And don't *I* get any say in the matter? What if I *want* to do this, for Simon's sake?'

He looked incredulous. 'You didn't even know him.'

She faced him stubbornly. 'Does that matter? I owe nothing to Paulette and her family, that's for sure. But you must have loved your brother so much, just as you love and care for Laura—'

'No,' he said, suddenly urgent. 'I let Simon down. *Always.*'

'I don't think so,' she said steadily. 'I don't think you would willingly let *anyone* down.'

She spoke with such sincerity, and with such belief in him, that he was shaken to the foundations of his being. Nobody had spoken to him like that, ever. No one had looked at him with such complete and utter trust.

Emotion is weakness. That was what his father had taught him, over and over again. But suddenly, for Beau, only she existed; only she and the wild surge of wanting that he'd never experienced in his life before. He'd known plenty of women, all of them eager and willing, but this one *was different*.

Her golden eyes, like a cat's, were full of fathomless depths that he wanted to explore. He felt that in taking her he'd be trying to catch the whispering breeze, or the pure scent of some rare forest flower...

Pure? Who the hell was he fooling? '*Damn it,*' he muttered aloud, only then he saw her flinch at his oath, at his cynicism; she was backing away as if he'd physically hurt her, and he recognised something almost like despair in her dark-lashed eyes. He reached out to catch her small hands, which were still sheathed in black mourning gloves.

'Don't go,' Beau said. His voice was almost hoarse with desire.

Deborah lifted her eyes steadfastly to his hard blue gaze. In that moment, she saw the longing there, and a kind of hollow despair that matched her own. She realised, with a great leap of her heart, that he was suffering as intensely, perhaps, as she was. And suddenly, she reached up to touch his cheek.

He shivered slightly, and for a heartbeat she wondered if she'd made an appalling mistake. Then he was dragging her into his arms, pressing kisses to the top of her head. 'Don't leave me tonight,' he whispered. 'Please.'

She rose up on tiptoe, and her lips met his. Moments

later, they were upstairs. In his bedroom. With the door locked, and no time now for regrets.

Beau acknowledged that his sister's arrival had given them their one opportunity to leave each other alone, and they'd have been wise to take it. But now it was too late. *No time for regrets*.

He never stopped kissing her as he eased her on to the quilted silk coverlet of his big, lonely bed. He didn't stop kissing her as he pulled away her shawl, revealing the upper curves of her smooth breasts. Just for a moment she tried to cover them with her hands, but he grasped her wrists very gently and eased his hips over hers, pressing her down against the bed, allowing her to feel how very much he wanted her.

Her black skirt was already splayed out, and he was able to slide his hand beneath it up to the top of her thigh; he felt the tiny movements of her hips as her body instinctively begged for his possession. Kissing her again, cherishing her mouth with deep, slow strokes of his tongue, he encountered the soft curls of her maidenhair with his forefinger, and as he continued to explore gently, he felt her gasp against his mouth, a gasp that turned to a moan of longing as he stroked her, roused her. She clasped her hands around his shoulders and quivered, her trembling body acutely sensitised.

He couldn't control his own desire for much longer. He reached to unfasten himself, then he shifted down on to the bed beside her again, sliding his hands under the luscious curve of her bottom, lifting her until he could feel the warmth and passion of her silken body in his arms. Pressing kisses to her throat, he unfastened her damned dress at last—*where were the buttons? The side, you fool, down the side*—then the petticoat, and the corset. And exultation surged at last through his veins, along with despair, as he gazed down at her luscious naked form and bent his head to take first one sweet nipple in his mouth, then the other.

They leaped to his touch. She cried out his name—*Beau*—and tangled her fingers jerkily in his hair as her legs moved for him, opened for him. *This had been inevitable*, he thought almost viciously as he eased his hips between her thighs. He had known this was going to happen from the moment he met her. And he should have damned well stopped it, before it was too late—but it was already too late.

Lifting his head, he moved his hands down her ribs, across the quivering flatness of her stomach. Taking his weight on to his elbows, he arranged himself so that his erection was nudging at her silken folds, and he heard her gasp. Surely—surely she couldn't be nervous of this? Of pregnancy, perhaps. That must be it.

'It's all right,' he breathed. 'It's all right.'

Trying to keep some sort of control, he reached to guide her legs around his. Then he began his rhythmic thrusts, and her breathing grew jagged, her words incoherent.

He put his mouth to her breast again. He reached with his hand to finger her at that most sensitive of places where her desire centred, and he knew when she was almost there, because the frantic tightening of her body around him told him so. Engulfing need raged through him as he continued to pleasure her with deep, deliberate strokes, and she was crying out her ecstasy, arching her back and crying for more, climbing to her extremity.

How could this sweet girl be a whore? Dear God,

it was almost as if this was her very first time! But there, rational thought ended. He plunged deep inside her, again and again, while she called out his name. Her climax all but engulfed her. When she'd finished, he kissed her lips—his last moment of restraint—then he pulled out and spent himself, hungrily, almost viciously. She kissed him afterwards, pressing tiny, hot kisses all over his chest and his face, while he soothed her and tried not to think of the consequences of what he'd just done.

Tangled in one another's arms, they slept.

When Deborah woke, the full moon was casting its light through the filmy curtains, and the gilded clock on the marble fireplace told her that it was a little past two. Beau was asleep beside her, and she was curled in his arms. She eased herself away, careful not to wake him, shocked beyond words by the enormity of what had just happened. By what she'd *allowed* to happen.

Her eyes swept the moonlit room, taking in the opulence of it—the grandeur of its hand-painted wallpaper, the extravagance of the beautiful walnut furniture and priceless gilded ornaments. The man who'd just made love to her was a peer of the realm—a Duke—and she was nobody. Very carefully she moved from beneath the smooth sheets and went to sit by the window, pulling back the curtains just a little so she could gaze out into the moon-bright garden.

She knew that for rich, powerful men like the Duke of Cirencester there were three categories of women. The first kind were the ones they married, and, oh, God, she was as far from that as she was from the moon and the stars. Then there were the women they took as their public mistresses—women who were often wealthy in their own right, and were of a high enough status to mean there was no shame attached to being seen with them in public. Indeed, these elegant *chère-amies* were often set up in pleasant town houses, and attended social engagements at their lovers' sides without any censure from society.

That censure was saved for the females the rich men visited in secret. The trollops. The ones they were ashamed of.

That was all she could be. In her past, she'd had only one brief and hateful experience of intimacy, with Jack Bentall—but that was enough to make her damaged goods. She had hated Bentall's lovemaking, and had thought that no man could ever cure her of her revulsion. But now she gazed across at the Duke's sleeping figure and remembered what it had been like to be in his arms, and to share that extremity of passion with him. She felt her lips still burning where he had kissed her.

Then he stirred. She watched, her heart pounding, as he stretched himself, and opened his eyes, and—

'Deborah?' he murmured huskily. '*Deborah*?'

More abruptly, he raised himself on one elbow and saw her by the window. 'I thought you'd gone,' he said, very quietly. 'Stay with me. Please.'

She tried to be strong. 'The servants might find out I'm here. Your sister, Laura, might find out…'

'They won't,' he said. 'Only Delaney ever comes to my rooms, and he, along with Armitage and my coachman, are the only three people in the world whom I would trust with my life. Come here.'

He held out his arms, and she let him enfold her once more in his embrace. He made love to her again, worshipping every inch of her body with his mouth, his lips, his virile power, and she responded with equal urgency, revelling in the glorious male strength of him. For a while she slept in his arms, but at dawn she was wide awake, and he was too. 'I'd better go to my own room,' she whispered. 'Before Bethany arrives.'

He held her tightly. 'I don't want you to go. But you're right.'

So she crept from his bed before even the servants were up. *Just as well she was going back to her own rooms*, she thought dizzily. She would at least be able to catch up a little on her sleep.

At nine, Bethany brought in her morning tea and toast, and soon after that Beau's sister arrived, full of plans.

'I know that you're in mourning, Paulette,' Laura declared, settling herself on her bed. 'But you are allowed to go out a little, aren't you? You *must* be, because last night I know you went to that party with Beau. Will you come for a carriage ride with me in the park later today? Beau said it would be all right, if you wore your veil and if I behaved myself. And I'd *far* rather go with you than with Miss Champion, who can be so dreary. Oh, and at four, Madame Lisette, who makes the most divine bonnets, is coming to show me some of the newest designs from Paris, so will you look at them with me, please?'

Thus was set the pattern of the next few days. Morning and afternoon, Laura was with Deb almost constantly, and sometimes they went for drives in the park. But at night, when the house was quiet, Beau would come to Deborah's bedroom, and their need for each other would be overwhelming, shocking even in its intensity. Time and time again he would bring her to a shuddering release, and she would almost beg for mercy; but he would kiss her, he would kiss her *everywhere* and begin all over again until even he was sated.

I am in love, she realised dazedly as he slept at last. She gazed at his strong, perfect profile, which was dusky with stubble; his eyes were closed; she was lying in his arms, her cheek against his chest, her legs still tangled with his. She loved him. And it couldn't last. It mustn't, for her sake as well as his.

Laura had a passion for the theatre, Deb soon realised, and to visit a London play, especially in the company of her big brother, was to her the height of pleasure. She told Deb about the productions she'd seen in Brighton with her friend Helen and her mother.

'Will you come to the theatre with me, Paulette?' Laura asked. 'When your mourning is over?'

Deb hesitated. When her mourning was over, she would have no place in this family's life. But she said evasively, 'I should like that very much.'

'I'm glad. Though you used to dislike the theatre excessively, you know, and sometimes Simon or Beau would take me instead!'

A bad mistake there, Deb. 'Well,' she said quickly, 'perhaps I meant that even if the play doesn't particularly appeal to me, it would still be a pleasure to keep you company.'

'Oh, good! Paulette, do you know anything about a play by William Shakespeare where brave King Harry fights the French?'

'Do you mean *Henry V*? Yes, a little.'

'I don't suppose you remember the speech that King Harry made before the battle of Agincourt, do you? I saw it performed in Brighton, and it was wonderful!'

Deb actually knew the whole scene by heart, but she said, 'I'll go and fetch it for you, shall I, Laura? I know your brother has a volume of Shakespeare in his library. I'm sure he won't mind if we borrow it.'

She hurried down the stairs, thinking that in fact, Beau might even be pleased. He'd said to her that he feared his sister's mind was too filled with frivolity and gossip—so surely a little Shakespeare was to be encouraged?

She burst into his study, and stopped.

She'd thought he was out—a business meeting, he'd said—but she hadn't realised that the business meeting was *here*, with Mr Armitage. She felt the colour warm her cheeks. *Be careful, you fool, or Armitage will see how much Beau means to you…* 'I'm so sorry, your Grace,' she blurted out. 'I was hoping to borrow a volume of Shakespeare, if possible. There is a play that Laura wishes to study.'

'By all means.' Beau's demeanour, unlike hers, was perfectly cool as he pulled the book down and put it on his desk for her. 'And, while you are here, you might like to look at these.'

He pointed to an open, silk-lined box on his desk, wherein lay the most exquisite pieces of jewellery she had ever seen—a superb necklace and matching earrings, made of rubies and diamonds that almost set the room ablaze.

The Brandon jewels. And they were as different from

the counterfeits Mr Newman had shown her as silk from sackcloth. 'So you got them from Lord Featherstone?'

'Armitage—' Beau gestured to his secretary '—*negotiated* for them. But your help was invaluable in ascertaining what had happened to them.'

She gazed at them again, nestling in their box. 'You were always most welcome, your Grace,' she said quietly, 'to any help I could offer. What will happen to the jewels now?'

He looked surprised. 'They'll go back in the safe, of course. Where else?'

'It just seems a pity,' she blurted out. 'To go to so much trouble, for something that will be locked away again, for ever...'

She broke off, conscious of Armitage staring at her in astonishment, and the Duke—Beau—tightening his jaw in that way he had when she'd said too much. 'I'm sorry,' she whispered. 'It wasn't my place to say that.'

She took the book and hurried out quickly, closing the door. He had the jewels he wanted so very badly. There was only the memorial service to be got through now. And then—that would be it, wouldn't it? That would be—the end.

She would have her theatre, she told herself desperately, climbing the stairs again. She would have her memories, and she still had a few days—a few nights— of him in her arms...

Up in Deb's parlour, Laura was impatiently waiting for her. 'You've been simply ages, Paulette. I thought you'd forgotten me. Have you got the book?'

'I have.' Deb forced a calm smile, but her thoughts were still clearly awry, because once seated she turned without thinking straight to the very speech Laura had spoken of, and was already murmuring to herself,

'Once more unto the breach, dear friends, once more;

'Or close the wall up with our English dead—'

She broke off abruptly when she realised that Laura was gazing at her in a mixture of awe and bewilderment.

'You know all the words, Paulette!' Laura breathed. 'You weren't even looking at the book when you began that speech! I thought you found plays boring. But— you know it all by heart!'

She would have to be more careful, Deb realised. Fortunately Laura was already enthusing again about the actor who'd played Henry V in Brighton; how handsome he was, and how the crowd had cheered. Deb tried hard to concentrate on her chatter. But…

The memorial service, she kept thinking. She had promised Beau she would stay for the memorial service. But after that, she had to go. Before she was truly, badly hurt.

That night Beau took Laura to the ballet, and Deb, restless, went out into the garden, where the roses perfumed the warm evening air. She could see this garden from her bedroom window, and she'd been astonished when she first stepped into it. Who would have guessed that such a leafy retreat lay here in the heart of London? There were small but elegant trees, there were lavender beds, there was even a tiny fountain trickling merrily from a lion's head set in the high stone wall that gave the place such privacy.

But now she was oblivious to its beauty. Now, for

the first time ever, she felt as if she didn't care whether she got her theatre or not.

Scarcely a breath of wind stirred the air, and moths danced in the light cast by the windows of Beau's mansion. She walked slowly along one of the lavender-edged paths, away from the vast house into the darkness of the shrubbery.

This is where I belong, she thought. *Out in the shadows. Far, far away from the dazzling, aristocratic circles in which Beau moves.* She had been incredibly, recklessly stupid to have let all this happen. To have fallen in love.

And then—she was aware of a wooden door, slowly opening at the far end of the high wall, and someone was there, dressed in a familiar, shabby old red coat. It was Francis, and he was whispering, 'Deborah? Deborah? Is it safe for me to come in and talk? You see— we need you.'

Chapter Seventeen

Deb led Francis swiftly to the rose-clad arbour, where they couldn't be seen from the house, and he told her how Luke had caught sight of her driving in the park with a young lady—Laura. He told her that Luke had followed her back here. 'We had no idea you were in London,' Francis exclaimed. 'And as for this fine house…' He looked around in fresh astonishment. 'You told us you were visiting relatives, Deborah.'

Francis must have seen the look of consternation on her face, because he went on hurriedly, 'Well. We know, of course, that your poor mother came from a wealthy home. And it's no business of ours who you stay with, or who you visit. But we worry about you. You are all right, aren't you?

'I am, Francis,' she told him earnestly. 'Really I am. But—there was something I needed to do for someone, you see. How are you? How are the Players?'

And it all poured out. Francis told her that they'd been delighted to be offered—at short notice—a two-week booking at the Dragon Theatre in Southwark. 'We're staying in lodgings by the river,' he explained, 'and we're preparing our usual bill of fare—songs, dancing, a bit of tragedy, a bit of comedy. But some of the younger Players didn't want to come to London, so they went their own way.'

'You mean they just left you?'

Francis nodded. 'They did. It wouldn't have happened in Gerald's time. I don't think it would have happened if *you'd* been with us, Deborah.'

'I'm sorry,' she whispered.

'Oh, I know it can't be helped. I know you had to do your duty. We've just about got enough actors left, but everyone's arguing about who's to play which part, and we badly need to get some new actors. The truth is, we need *you*, Deborah. The others will listen to you. Please can you visit us? It doesn't matter how briefly.'

I should have been there for them, she thought. *I should not have left them so suddenly.*

'I'll come now, Francis,' she told him without hesitation.

Ten minutes later Deb, wrapped in a cape and bonnet, had joined Francis at the back of the house to find that he'd already hailed a hackney carriage, and during the journey to Southwark he told her what had been happening, and who was causing the problems. 'We're hoping to perform some acts from *Twelfth Night*, you see, Deb. But Joseph is really getting too old to play Duke Orsino, and he keeps forgetting his lines. Peggy's playing Viola, and she's for ever complaining about him.'

'Can't *you* play Orsino, Francis?'

'I'm Malvolio,' he said. 'I'm *always* Malvolio.'

That was true. Swiftly they discussed all the parts and all the actors, and by the time they'd crossed the river and reached the Dragon Theatre, she knew that she had a difficult task ahead. All the same, she was over-whelmed by the welcome the Players gave her.

It was difficult, yes, but not impossible to smooth ruffled feelings and to make dextrous changes to the casting by use of flattery—just as Gerald would have done. Joseph would have to be Orsino—she could see no way around it—and Peggy sulked, but Deb promised her she would look out for someone new to take on the leading male roles, just as soon as she returned to them.

'So you are returning, then, Deb?' Peggy gave her a quizzical look. 'Some of us wondered, you see.'

'Of course I'll be back.'

She was aware of little sighs of relief, from all those gathered round, and Francis was full of gratitude af-terwards. 'Your visit's been just what we needed,' he said, 'and now I'll get another hackney carriage and take you back to where you're staying. But—Mayfair! My, Deborah, that's a grand place. And—you *are* all right, aren't you? You look—different.'

'I miss you all,' she answered quietly. *And I've been stupid enough to fall in love. Hopelessly in love.*

Once the carriage reached Albemarle Street, Francis came with her along the lane to the little door that led into the garden, then he said a brief farewell and hur-ried off. She really did miss her old life, she thought with a sudden rush of emotion as she slowly climbed the stairs. With the Lambeth Players, she'd been so sure of everything, and acting had been all she cared about…

She pulled to an abrupt halt as she approached her room, because the door was open, a candle was burning in there—and Laura was sitting on Deb's bed.

Deb froze in the doorway. The window looked out on the garden. *If Laura had seen her stealing back in there…* 'Laura. I thought you would still be at the ballet!' she tried to say lightly as she walked into the room and took off her cape.

'No. No… Oh, I'm so unhappy, Paulette!'

Deb saw that the girl's pretty face was blotched with tears. Quickly she sat at her side. 'Why, my dear? Whatever's the matter?'

'It's Beau!' Laura was sobbing again. 'At the ballet I asked him if he would take me to Vauxhall Gardens one evening, but he said no. He wouldn't even discuss it. So I sulked, and he was so cross that he brought me home in the interval. And then he went off again—to his club, I think—and, oh, Paulette, he can be unbearable! He orders me about, he lays down stuffy rules…'

'Dear Laura.' Deb took the girl's hand. 'It's only because he cares for you, so much.' She also guessed that Laura would be heiress to a considerable fortune when she was older, and needed the firm protection of her brother.

'But Beau's always stopping me from having fun! A few days ago I ordered a dress in sheer muslin, like my friend Georgina wears, but when Beau saw me in it, he said—he said that if I tried to go out in it, he would follow me and bring me home. *Carry* me home, if necessary, he said. Paulette, I'm so tired of being treated like a child!'

Deb put her arm around her shoulder. 'Oh, Laura. You're very lucky, to have someone who cares for you so much. And you should remember, perhaps, that like you, Beau will still be feeling great grief for your brother. To lose him so tragically must have been very hard for him, especially when they were so devoted—'

'But they *weren't* devoted!' Laura's eyes had widened in surprise. Slowly she pulled herself away from Deb's embrace. 'And you must have known that better than anyone, since you were Simon's wife!'

Deb's pulse was racing. *Be careful. Be careful.* 'Of course,' she said lightly, 'all brothers fall out from time to time. So do sisters and brothers too, I believe...'

Laura was frowning at her. 'You surely realise that Simon was always terribly jealous of Beau? And I'm afraid I didn't help. You see, I worshipped Beau, because he was wise, and funny, and brave. I never knew my mother, of course, and I remember very little of my father—he was always so remote somehow. But Beau was a lovely brother. I loved Simon too, of course I did, but he wasn't the same. I think Simon was so envious of Beau that he grew almost to hate him... You *must* know that, though. Anyone who knew anything at all about Simon knew that. Poor, poor, Simon...'

Deb touched her hand again. 'You're very tired, Laura,' she said gently. 'Time for bed. And remember how lucky you are to have a brother like Beau on your side, always.'

Once she'd seen Laura to her bedroom, Deb returned to her own room and put her palm to her forehead. Simon *hated* his brother?

Beau had told her not to expect him that night, since he would most likely be late; but she heard him come into the house and head for his own rooms soon after midnight, and she was awake for long after that. When she did at last get to sleep, she dreamed vividly of a shipwreck, and in her dream she was floundering in a wild, storm-tossed sea. Then suddenly Beau was there, and she was safe in his strong grasp; he held her tightly and struck out for the shore, but at the last minute he let her go, and though she cried out his name he was swimming away from her. She sank down and down into the icy depths, and when she awoke she was filled with a kind of raw and aching dread.

When Bethany brought in her tea tray the next morning and began as usual to lay out her clothes, Deborah felt as though she'd scarcely slept. Beau had told her he wanted her to stay, and with the morning light, she was beginning to hope. He would find some way for them to be together, surely? And she would make a new start also, by telling him that those dreadful books—yes, she still had them with her, pushed out of sight in her old valise—were not hers, but Palfreyman's. She would tell him that she'd stolen them to save her friends, and that the longer she was with him, the harder it had been to reveal her lie…

Suddenly she realised that Bethany had asked her at least twice which gown she wished to wear.

'I'll wear anything,' Deb said swiftly. 'You decide.' *Anything as long as it's black.* Bethany helped her into a satin gown, and when Deb examined herself afterwards in the looking glass, she realised she wasn't as pale as she'd feared.

But the colour fled from her cheeks swiftly enough when Bethany selected a shawl for her and said, 'His Grace has had an early visitor, my lady. A man who seems really cross. He just stormed in past the footman, and was ever so rude to Mr Delaney.'

Deb turned slowly from the looking glass to face her. 'Do you know who this visitor is?'

'I thought I heard the footmen say his name when I was coming up the stairs with your tea tray, my lady. It was something like—Palfreyman. That was it, Palfreyman.'

Without saying a word, Deb pulled on the shawl and made for the door.

'But your tea, my lady!' called Bethany anxiously. 'And the toast—'

'It doesn't matter. I'm really not hungry.'

She hurried down the stairs. Her uncle had a house in London, she knew, but Beau had assured her that Palfreyman would stay well away while she was here...

Already she could hear his voice coming from Beau's study and she quickly made her way there, almost pushing past a startled footman—only to freeze outside the door, because she could hear her uncle's hateful voice, raised in anger.

'I know,' Palfreyman was saying in staccato bursts of fury. 'I know now, why your brother died. It was because my daughter was madly in love with *you*. Simon was riding north to Brandon Abbey to challenge you— to punish you—when he fell from his horse, and he died that very night, his neck broken!'

Beau's voice next. 'How do you know this?'

Deb stepped backwards at that, her hand to her throat. No denial from Beau. No angry rebuttal. Just— *How do you know*?

'Your brother,' Palfreyman was stating, 'called on my wife in early April, a few days before he died. Simon informed Vera of his suspicions, and told her that he intended to fight a duel with you. Vera didn't tell me at the time, the foolish, foolish woman—I got the story from her only last night, when I found her crying over some old letters from Paulette. She confessed that she didn't dare say anything of it, because she was so afraid of *you*. Of course, by then Paulette had already left your brother, and run off abroad for good, with her new lover. But that was because you'd rejected her—you'd broken her heart, and she could not bear the sight of Simon, because he reminded her too much of *you*…'

Deborah found herself somehow back in her room. Bethany had gone. She sat on the edge of the bed, feeling quite sick. Those words in Paulette's diary kept going round and round in her head. *I live for the moments when I see him. I love him so much that it hurts*…

Paulette had been writing, not about Simon, but about Beau. Paulette had loved Beau. And had Beau, however briefly, loved her back?

She got up and walked to and fro, clasping her arms tightly across her chest and wondering how to stop her own heart from *hurting* so much. And then another horrifying thought struck her. Had Beau perhaps been pretending, every time he made love to her, that she was Paulette, whom he'd cursed himself for loving? Was he purging himself of Paulette?

No. *No*. He would not do that to her, would he? She couldn't think he would do that…

Somehow the time must have passed, because it was gone eleven when Laura called at her room, to see if she wanted to come shopping with her to Bond Street. Deb declined, saying she had a slight headache, and Laura gave her a swift, sympathetic hug. 'Of course.

Poor you. I'm sorry to have complained so bitterly about darling Beau last night. And you won't leave us, will you—*please*?'

After Laura had gone Deb sat down suddenly by the window, remembering the first time she'd met Beau in the Ashendale Forest, and recalling the way his eyes had widened with astonishment when he'd taken his blindfold off, and seen her. He must have laid his plans straight away. And how bitter he had been, she recalled, whenever he mentioned Paulette's name—had he fallen for her, however briefly, as Paulette implied?

A little after noon, Bethany came to ask hesitantly if she was going downstairs for lunch, and Deb declined. It had started to rain outside, and she was sitting in the shadows when Beau knocked and entered.

He said, 'Do you mind if I come in and talk?'

She jumped up. 'Of course not. Please sit.'

Beau remained standing. 'I'm afraid,' he said, 'that there is going to be a little trouble over the next few days. Your uncle has unwisely taken up residence in his house in Curzon Street, and he's just paid me a visit.'

She looked very tense, he realised, and her cheeks were pale. 'I know,' she said. 'I came downstairs to find you, and—I heard.'

And he knew straight away what she'd heard, without her telling him. He said evenly, 'You didn't believe a word of what Palfreyman said, did you? You didn't think that your uncle's vile accusations were true?'

'But—you didn't deny it straight away…'

'That's because Palfreyman was right,' Beau said sharply, 'to say that Simon was riding north to challenge me to a duel when he died. He was right to say that Paulette considered herself in love with me. But I never touched Paulette. *Never.*'

He thought he saw her tremble a little, and the colour rushed to her cheeks once more. Beau had to fight hard the instinct to catch her in his arms, *now*, and hold her and kiss her. He'd always thought of himself as a supremely rational man, ruled by his head rather than his heart—but this girl, who used her pride to mask her vulnerability, made him lose all reason.

He remembered how he'd thought her brash and tough in the forest, when she'd defied him with her hands on her hips and a jaunty smile on her face. Now, he realised she'd been terrified out of her wits, most likely, but still she was possessed of endless resourcefulness, endless courage.

Ironic that now *he* was the one who was terrified.

Terrified at the thought of losing her. Terrified at the thought of not possessing her sweet lips again, or seeing the wonder in her eyes, or the joy in them as he made love to her.

Now she said, in her quiet, calm way, 'Please, will you tell me the truth? About Paulette?'

And he did so. At last.

Chapter Eighteen

Deborah listened very carefully, knowing that what Beau said to her, and her understanding of it, might affect the rest of her life.

'Paulette made advances to me,' Beau said. 'Both before her betrothal to Simon, and after it. I made it plain from the very start that I wasn't interested in her, but unfortunately she wasn't deterred. If anything, she became even more determined—for example, she planted herself in my bedroom one night, shortly before her marriage.'

Deb let out a low exclamation of horror. He took her hand. 'Believe me, I made my disgust all too apparent, and she didn't try again. But she made my brother endure a few months of what I'd guess was a hellish marriage. First, she retreated to Norfolk—and then in March she ran away for good, as you know, with an extremely rich Italian admirer of hers. From Venice, she wrote to Simon to say that she and I had been lovers, both before and after his marriage. A final, bitter act—and it all but destroyed my brother.

'Simon wrote to me at Brandon Abbey, as soon as he received Paulette's poisonous letter, and he accused me of seducing his wife. I wrote back immediately, to say that it was all a terrible lie. But by then he'd set off to ride to Brandon Abbey overnight. He told his friends in London that he had an affair of honour to settle.'

Deb hardly dared move. She could hardly breathe, even, for the terrible intensity of his emotions.

'So he rode in the dark,' Beau went on, 'in a drunken rage, to challenge me to a duel—though I'm pretty sure that at that point, he would have much preferred to kill me without the fuss of pistols at dawn. He never reached Brandon Abbey. He fell from his horse on the turnpike road just north of London, and broke his neck. He was found in the ditch the next morning.'

Deb said very quietly, 'Couldn't you have warned him before his marriage, about Paulette's approaches to you?'

'I tried. He didn't listen to me.' He dragged his hand through his hair. 'He never would listen to me. You see, he always thought that he was second best to me. I think that he hated me.'

She sat down. She was shivering deep inside. 'But Beau, from everything you've said, I've always formed the impression that you loved him. You wanted to protect him. Why should he hate you?'

'There's one word for that, I'm afraid. Jealousy.' He was standing before her now, his blue eyes dark with intensity and his hands thrust deep into the pockets of his beautiful dark grey tailcoat. 'Simon was weak. Oh, he was charming, he was handsome, but all in all he felt he could never best me. He could not forgive me for the fact that I would be the one to get the title and the estate. I was twenty-five when I inherited the dukedom, and though I gave Simon a London house and lands in

Bedfordshire, he accepted it all as surlily as if I was throwing scraps to a dog. I told you how he attempted a career in the army. But they threw him out in less than a year, because of his gambling and drinking.'

He realised that all the time she was listening to him with a burning intensity. Self-rebuke slammed into him like an iron fist. How could he ever have thought that she was anything like Paulette? Physically, yes— enough for them to be briefly mistaken for one another. But Deborah O'Hara was beautiful. Undeniably, heart-wrenchingly beautiful, and he had no idea how this was going to end, but he didn't want to lose her. He couldn't bear to lose her.

She was gazing at him with her clear, lovely eyes. 'So you guessed from the beginning, that he might have gambled away the Brandon jewels?'

'Indeed. From the moment I saw that the jewel case was empty, it was my biggest fear. Simon's gambling made my family vulnerable. Even worse, it made Simon vulnerable. When I first met you, I thought that you might be able to uncover, far more subtly than I could, what had happened to the jewels. I was almost relieved to find out that Simon had apparently given them to Paulette. But then it turned out that my brother *had* gambled them away, after all.'

He paused and looked directly at her. 'Do you remember that day at the lake, when I was so hateful to you? And I told you that I'd rescued Simon from swimming there? I didn't tell you everything. I didn't tell you that the night before I'd saved him, I told him I'd paid off an enormous gaming debt of his, and that it was the very last time I would do so. The next day he drank himself into a stupor, then tried to drown himself in the lake. I followed him. I rescued him.

'Afterwards, Simon said, "Damn you, Beau. You always have to be there for me, don't you?"'

'I'm sorry. So sorry,' she whispered.

'I begged Simon not to marry Paulette Palfreyman,' he went on. 'He was furious with me for interfering. "Still trying to belittle me," he said. And I wish to hell I hadn't been, as always, the one to be proved right.' His voice was very low now. 'I find it hard to live with the fact that my brother died wishing he could hold a duelling pistol at my head. And what is impossible to bear is the threat of Palfreyman spreading that very fact all around the town.'

'And falsely blackening your name,' Deb whispered, horrified. 'This is dreadful for you. But surely there's something you can do?'

'I'll stop Palfreyman from talking, of course. In the heat of his so-called "discovery" about Paulette and me, he's quite forgotten why he agreed to participate in my plan in the first place. He's forgotten how terrified he is, of the shame he'd face, if it became known how his daughter cheated and lied and ran from her marriage.'

He smiled at Deb tiredly. 'I'll remind him once more that we both have a vested interest in keeping all this quiet. There's absolutely no need for you to worry.'

'Beau,' she breathed, 'this is so unfair. It sounds to me as if you've done your best for your family, always, and you've been repaid with all *this*. With a brother who hated you. And a sister-in-law whose family are intent on ruining your reputation.'

'Life has its—surprises,' he acknowledged, 'even when you're a Duke. For example, only the other month

I was waylaid in a forest, by a bunch of quite shameless vagabonds…'

She'd risen to her feet and was walking towards him. 'I can't tell you how much I regret that. If there's anything I can do, about my uncle…'

He'd caught her hand and was gazing at her intently. 'I'll tell you what you can do,' he said. 'You can believe in me. You can *trust* me. I have to go now, I'm afraid. I have a longstanding business appointment, but as soon as that's over, I shall take steps to ensure that Palfreyman's slanders are cut off at the root.' His eyes searched her face gravely. 'You will be here for me tonight, won't you?'

'I'll be here,' she said steadily.

He cupped her face in his hands and kissed her forehead, but as soon as he was gone, she went to her valise and pulled out one of the books she'd hidden, because there was something she really had to do. Hugh Palfreyman had done his best to destroy her mother, and to try to ruin her Players. Now he was attempting to ruin the reputation of a man who was brave and self-sacrificing and honourable—and she wasn't going to let him.

Somehow she felt that her anger was steadying her as she hurried through the rain, swathed in her black cloak and veiled bonnet, to Hugh Palfreyman's house in nearby Curzon Street. So much had happened since Beau had told her that she, a travelling actress, was about to play her biggest part yet. And she'd played it well. She'd actually become Paulette in the eyes of society, and in doing so she'd come to know who Beau really was. She'd seen the strength and the honour beneath the chilly mask he wore—was *forced* to wear—for a so-

ciety that was all too ready to pounce on the least sign
of weakness in any member of such a prominent family.

She'd experienced a tenderness and passion she
didn't know existed in his arms, and now she was trying her hardest not to imagine her future; because she
could not see any way out except hurt—unimaginable
hurt—for herself. But she felt instinctive, rebellious rage
welling up as she waited in the Palfreymans' reception
room for her uncle to receive her. Looking around, she
realised that once she would have been intimidated by
its grandeur, but now Palfreyman's attempts at over-
ornate luxury looked as contemptible as he was. Yes,
she thought, he *was* contemptible, for threatening to expose Simon's sad end. To try to contaminate the Duke's
reputation with his lies.

*Remember to control your anger and it will make
you strong*, Gerald O'Hara used to tell her. And perhaps it was true, for when Hugh Palfreyman came in
at last and she rose to face him, Palfreyman looked just
a little afraid.

'Now—what's this?' he blustered. 'We weren't expecting you.'

'I though I'd pay you a visit, Uncle.' Deb was smiling sweetly, but something in her voice made him take
a step backwards.

'Well, well,' he said. 'You *are* giving yourself airs
and graces, aren't you?'

Without saying anything, she walked slowly over
to a table full of curios, on which stood various gilded
ornaments and a portrait of Paulette. She gazed at the
portrait, then at him. 'I've saved your daughter's reputation, Uncle,' she reminded him softly. 'If everyone
were to know what she'd *really* done—that she'd run

off into exile with her Italian lover, and caused her own husband's death with her vicious lies about the Duke—then you would never dare to set foot in society again.'

He muttered, 'A pity the Duke could not have improved your manners, slut.'

She stepped towards him. 'What did you just say—*Uncle*?'

He flushed and looked furious. 'Nothing. Absolutely nothing.'

'Good,' she said. 'Because now, you're going to listen to *me* for a change.'

And she told him.

She told him that she had his books of erotica, with his name inscribed in the front of each one. She told him that if he didn't immediately retract his threat to expose the fact that Simon Beaumaris died while riding to challenge his brother to a duel, she would make sure that all of London society knew about Palfreyman's secret library.

She patted her pocket. 'I have one of your books in here, Uncle. And two others, very safely hidden, believe me.'

For a moment he was speechless, but then a torrent of abuse began to spill from his mouth. 'You must have got the books from those travelling thieves, the Lambeth Players,' he spluttered. 'The rogues must have sold them on to you!'

'Wrong on two counts, Uncle. Firstly, the Lambeth Players are *not* thieves and rogues. Secondly, they didn't sell them to me. I stole them from you myself—because *I'm* one of the Lambeth Players.'

Palfreyman was backing away from her, stunned. 'You're one of *them*?'

'I'm one of them, yes. As my mother was. You tried to have the Players prosecuted, but you underestimated us. I know about your secret room; I know about the hypocrisy of your life as a Justice of the Peace. So here's my plan. You will contact the Duke as soon as possible—tonight would be ideal—and you will *apologise* for threatening to reveal the fact that the Duke's sadly misguided brother was about to challenge him to a duel. You will *grovel* to his Grace for daring to make the false claim that the Duke had an affair with your daughter. For you know, and I know, that his Grace the Duke of Cirencester has always acted with integrity and with complete honour.'

Palfreyman looked as grey as death.

'Well? Do you agree?' she persisted calmly. 'Will you apologise to the Duke for your vile slanders?'

'Yes.' He wiped the perspiration from his forehead. 'Yes, I will, very soon…'

Suddenly the big door flew open and Palfreyman swung round to see a familiar figure standing in the doorway. 'I've got an even better idea,' said his Grace the Duke of Cirencester. 'You can apologise to me right now, Palfreyman.'

When Beau had returned from seeing his lawyers and found her room empty, his first emotion had been bewilderment, followed by temporary relief, for he could see straight away that she hadn't left. All her belongings were still here. But where was she?

She was always so reckless. Whatever she was about to do, she should have consulted him. She should have trusted him…

He stopped, closing his eyes briefly. Why in God's name *should* she trust him?

Utterly selfishly, he'd dragged her to London to solve the mystery of the jewels, and to let society see that she was paying her dues to his dead brother. And his plan had actually worked.

But he'd gone further than that. He'd seduced her.

She'd never pretended to be an innocent—with those books of hers, she'd even made out that she was a professional courtesan. But it hadn't seemed to him, when she was lying in his arms, as if she was used to being paid. She made love to him as if she was giving him something she wasn't prepared to give to anyone else.

He stood in the centre of her room, breathing in the faint and delicious perfume of her soap, wondering where she'd gone, and why. And then, suddenly, he caught sight of that old brown valise lying open in the corner of the room. He'd guessed long ago that she kept those books in there, and swiftly he went to search it—to find that there were only two left. Wherever she'd gone, she'd taken the other one with her. But why?

Distractedly he flicked open the cover of the book in his hand. With dawning incredulity, he saw the name inscribed in the front.

And suddenly he knew *exactly* where she'd gone.

Arriving at Palfreyman's house, Beau swept in past the bewildered butler towards the drawing room. Already he could hear a familiar voice—Palfreyman's—and her defiant one.

Those books. By God, they weren't even hers. They were dratted Palfreyman's.

He felt something clench inside him; something that

made him want to punch the hell out of Palfreyman
for his insults and clasp Deborah O'Hara tightly in his
arms. Except that he realised she could take on Palfreyman by herself, and had clearly been doing so, prior to
his arrival, because as they both swung round to face
him, Palfreyman looked furious.

'Come here, Deborah,' Beau said. As well as her bewitching beauty, he silently acknowledged that he was
astounded by her strength, her resilience, her courage.
'Come here,' he repeated, this time more gently. 'Please
stand by my side.'

Slowly she did so, her eyes never leaving his face,
and he felt, somehow, as if those few steps she took towards him represented the most important moments
of his life. He turned back to Palfreyman. 'Well? I'm
waiting for you to apologise, for your insinuation that
I seduced your daughter.'

'I'm sorry, your Grace,' Palfreyman stuttered. 'I was
wrong.'

'You were *very* wrong—and listen to me carefully.
If you should even *think* of trying your sordid trickery
again in the future—if you should ever try to repeat the
obnoxious lie that I slept with your daughter, or encouraged her infatuation with me in the slightest—then just
remember this. Not only can I tell the world the entire
truth about your daughter—but I know about your reading habits, Palfreyman.'

Hugh Palfreyman lost colour then took a step forward. 'She told you. That lying little bitch told you—'

'Any more talk like that,' said Beau through clenched
teeth, 'and I'll take the greatest pleasure in giving you a
hiding here and now, before revealing your filthy secret
to the world. Miss O'Hara *didn't* tell me, as a matter of

fact. She didn't breathe a word of it, though it would have been to her advantage to do so.'

He glanced at her and saw that she was holding herself very still. 'Miss O'Hara,' he went on, 'has something called integrity—I don't think you even know the meaning of the word. Our game is almost at an end, Palfreyman.'

Palfreyman looked like a whipped dog.

'For your information,' Beau said levelly, 'there's to be a memorial service for my brother at St Margaret's church very soon. Miss O'Hara will be there, as Paulette.' Beau raked him contemptuously with his eyes. 'If you and your wife should decide to attend, then please ensure that you keep as far out of my sight as possible.'

Palfreyman's mouth worked furiously. The Duke turned his back on him and said calmly, 'Are you ready to go, Miss O'Hara?' He escorted her outside.

Beau had brought his carriage, and William Barry was already holding the door open. Once inside, Deb sank back against the velvet seat.

The Duke sat close to her, so close she was sure he must hear her pounding heart. He'd looked so angry at Palfreyman's. Angry with her uncle. Angry with her, for going there.

He sat opposite her as the carriage moved off and leaned forward. 'Oh, Deborah,' he said quietly. 'Why on earth didn't you tell me everything from the beginning?'

She drew a deep breath. 'You mean the books, I suppose. I didn't want to have to tell you that I'd broken into Palfreyman's house, and stolen them—since burglary is a hanging offence. And at first, I thought you were Palfreyman's friend.'

'But surely you learned soon enough that I *detested* Palfreyman?'

'I also thought you detested me,' she answered quietly.

He leaned back abruptly against the padded seat. 'Go on. Please.'

'I thought you despised me,' she repeated. 'And as time went on, I found it harder and harder to tell you that I'd lied so much, about those books.'

'But to let me think, all this time, that you were for sale…'

She bowed her head. 'I felt it was safer for *me*, to let you think that I was the kind of woman you judged me to be. That I was…experienced.'

'*Why*?'

A faint flush tinged her pale cheeks. 'I thought I could perhaps protect myself from my emotions. By reminding myself that you could never feel anything but contempt for someone like me.'

'*Someone like*—' He broke off and drew in a harsh breath. 'Deborah. You've not once uttered a single word of blame against me. But all this is my fault too. My fault, for never giving you the chance to explain. Very much my fault, for not realising much, much earlier that your story about the books *had* to be a false one. For not letting myself acknowledge what I'd guessed all along—that you were sweet and innocent and honourable—'

She interrupted him with something like anguish in her eyes. 'I could not claim to be innocent,' she whispered.

And she told him, about the actor, Jack Bentall, whom she'd allowed to seduce her five years ago. She told him how after her experience with Bentall she had gone out of her way to deter any other possible suitors, and instead put all her passionate heart into her acting.

He listened, and when they were almost at his house he called out to his driver. 'Ten more minutes, please, William.'

William took the carriage around the streets again, slowly, so Deb could tell him the rest: about Palfreyman trying to prosecute the Players; about breaking into Hardgate Hall, because it was the only way to save her friends from a fine or gaol, even; and how horrified she had been, to return and find Beau trussed up in the forest.

'I'm so sorry,' Beau said. He drew her into his arms and lifted one of her hands to kiss it. 'You were forced into an impossible situation, I can see that. Even when you realised I was Palfreyman's enemy—as *you* were— I gave you not the slightest reason to trust me, or confide in me. Let me make it up to you, Deborah. Let me come to your room tonight. Please.'

Chapter Nineteen

That night Beau undressed her with great tenderness, unbuttoning her gown and slipping her undergarments from her body one by one until she stood there in her nakedness. He'd lit only one candle, so the light didn't daunt her, but instead made subtle play over the planes and curves of her body. He'd already taken off his coat, and now steadily began to remove his shirt and his boots, while Deb stood gazing at him, at this man who'd come so unexpectedly into her life and altered it, for ever.

Hope warred with terrifying doubt. She thought she'd made herself immune to him, but of course she hadn't. Instead she'd let herself fall in love with him. What would she do, if he asked her to stay in London and be his mistress? Since her station in life was so lowly, that meant he would have to hide her away somewhere, visit her in secret; then she really would be a whore. But how could she say no?

She loved him. She loved him because she'd seen the honesty and courage and true compassion beneath his iron-hard façade of power and wealth.

He walked steadily towards her, picked her up in his

strong arms and gently laid her on the bed. 'Stop thinking,' he breathed, kissing the lobe of her ear with light
brushes of his lips that set her blood on fire. 'Or if you
have to think of something, think of me. Because *I'm*
thinking that you are the most beautiful sight I've ever
seen—Miss O'Hara.'

He stood back from the bed and began to strip off
his breeches while Deb feasted her eyes, and he was
completely unselfconscious as he exposed the rest of his
muscular body. *Oh, my.* Her breath caught in her throat.
His extremely *aroused* muscular body...

He walked to the bed, and with the palm of his hand
he pushed her gently back against the pillows and came
to join her. But there was nothing gentle about the pres-
sure of his chest against her sensitised breasts, as he
eased himself beside her and gathered her in his arms.
Nothing gentle about the ferocity of his erection, burning against her soft abdomen.

'I want you,' he breathed. 'You want me. This is about
us and only us, do you understand?' He took her hand
and drew it down against his pulsing arousal. 'You are
exquisite, Miss O'Hara. And I've wanted to make you
mine ever since that day in the forest when I was tied
up and you wore those damned breeches and flaunted
yourself in front of me. I want you. Forget about the jewels, forget about Palfreyman—all I want to think of at
this precise moment is you. Are you listening to me?'

His hands slid under her hips. While she was struggling for a reply beneath his fierce gaze, he parted her
thighs and entered her, thrusting deep; and Deb aban-
doned any hope of answering him with words. She was
his. Whether it was for days, or for weeks, she was *his*.
As he pleasured her, her body responded with a will of

its own, and then everything inside her began to break apart; until she was convulsed by the beginnings of an explosion of delight so impossibly intense that she thought her heart might stop beating. Sensations that were almost too exquisite to bear rolled through her as he kissed her breasts and lips. She was dazedly aware afterwards of him pulling out and spilling his seed on her belly as he breathed her name, then he gathered her in his arms and kissed her again.

Beau realised, after a few moments, that she was asleep.

Deborah O'Hara. He gazed at her with tenderness and wonder. She'd actually broken into Hardgate Hall, to save her friends. And today, he'd seen her stand up to Palfreyman with all the determination of a feisty little warrior. He looked at her in fresh astonishment. She was tough. She'd *had* to be tough, to survive everything that fate had cast her way. He was determined to keep her in his life —*somehow.*

And with that resolve dominating his thoughts, he slept too.

Beau woke up in the night to find that she was no longer in his arms, and realised how cold the bed felt without her. How empty his arms and his heart felt without her. He got up and pulled on his dressing gown, then he saw her in the small parlour that adjoined his bedchamber, sitting on the window seat. She'd parted the curtains and was gazing outside.

'What are you looking at?' he asked her gently.

She turned to him. 'The moon. It's so low and full tonight. Do you see it?'

He sat beside her and drew her into his arms, real-

ising she wore only her nightgown, and was cold. He
held her very close, so her back was snug against his
chest. Breathing in the scent of her hair, he gazed over
her head at the moon, but hardly registered it, because
all his thoughts were concentrated on her.

He remembered the hurt in her eyes when she'd told
him about the wretch of an actor who'd seduced her,
and his anger boiled again, but then he felt a different
if equally urgent emotion; the need to protect and cher-
ish her—yes, for ever.

He kissed the top of her head and said, 'You were
rash to visit Palfreyman. Rash and brave.'

She laughed softly. 'Not really. He was the one who
was horrified to see *me*. He wanted to know what I
planned to do, after my arrangement with you was over.
I think he was worried I would come back and haunt
him.'

He stroked her hair and the soft nape of her beautiful
neck. 'What did you say? About what you'd do next?'

She turned a little, so he could see her sweet profile. 'I let him assume I'll do what I've always done, of
course. I'll carry on being an actress.'

He nuzzled her hair. 'You're very good at it.'

'Oh, yes,' she said tonelessly. He couldn't see her
expression. 'I've always been good at it.'

He turned her round properly to face him. 'Deborah. These times we've spent together. The nights. Were
you acting then?'

She couldn't lie to him; not now. In his powerful
arms, with his wonderful blue eyes scorching her soul,
she couldn't lie. 'No,' she breathed. 'Oh, no.'

'Then stay,' he urged her. 'It's the memorial service
for Simon, in a week—please stay for that, and then…'

He stroked her hair back from her cheek. 'I cannot bear the thought of not seeing you again.'

Her eyes were full of emotion. 'I would be no good for you. No good at all.'

Beau said softly, 'Let me be the judge of that. I'm inclined at the moment to feel that I've never met anyone who's *better* for me.'

'You must *not* feel like this.' Her voice was a little desperate. 'You thought I was for sale, and I wasn't—but I'd done something almost as bad! I burgled Palfreyman's house...'

'To get those books—how truly wicked.' He twined a lock of her hair around his finger.

'But there's something else you need to remember.' Her eyes were full of anguish. 'If I were your mistress, Beau, you would have to hide me away. From all your friends, from society...'

'Paulette would have to vanish to the countryside again, that's true.' His voice was serious now.

And you would have to keep me in a small house somewhere, in secret... 'Beau,' she reminded him, 'I don't even know who my father was.'

'Does it matter?'

'Of *course* it does. You must let me tell you. After my mother ran away from Hardgate Hall, she went to London and found a job as chambermaid at an inn—Gerald told me her story, when he felt I was old enough to understand. She—she was seduced by a rich traveller, and when her pregnancy began to show, she lost her job and had nowhere to live. But then she met the Lambeth Players, and began a new life with them. When I was born, the Lambeth Players became my family too—especially when she and Gerald married.'

Beau was listening intently. 'You loved your stepfather, didn't you?'

'Oh, yes. Gerald couldn't have looked after me better if I'd been his own daughter. But I cannot hide the fact, Beau, that I am illegitimate. That I have no idea at all who my father was. And what's more, I've spent years as an actress, a travelling actress...'

He was laughing. Her heart suddenly lifted. 'Do you know,' Beau said, 'I believe it's considered quite the thing to be in love with an actress.'

In love with. Her heart bumped and her breathing almost stopped.

'And,' he went on, 'I might come and meet your actor friends some day—after all, I'm providing them with a new theatre, remember?'

She was still speechless.

'I mean it, Deborah,' Beau went on quietly. 'I don't want to lose you. I will make this work, somehow. You don't have to give me your answer this very minute. But please think about staying in my life, will you?'

Over the next few days, she never stopped thinking about it. He had to marry, he had to have heirs; she knew that. But...if he *did* set the Lambeth Players up with their own theatre, as he'd promised, she would be able to live in London from now on, and continue with her acting. They could still meet, if they were discreet. She wouldn't have to give him up.

By day, Beau was occupied with the final plans for the memorial service, so she tended to see him at mealtimes only, with Laura in attendance, and the footmen and butler hovering nearby. By night, though, he came to her room, always, and their lovemaking was almost frighteningly intense. As she lay in his arms afterwards, he would tell her more about his own secrets: about his father's harshness, his mother's infidelities and his brother's gambling.

'I tried my best to help Simon,' he said, lying on his back with her curled against his chest. 'But he seemed to find a refuge in his gambling. And gamblers are always their own worst enemies.'

'It was cruel of Paulette to marry him,' said Deb.

'She was certainly calculating. Once she realised that she wasn't going to succeed in entrapping me, I think she resolved to be happy with Simon at first—if only, perhaps, to say to me, *You'll be sorry you didn't marry me!*'

Deb pulled herself away from him just a little, to draw her finger across his naked chest. *Beau*, she wrote. *I love you, Beau.* 'I feel sorry for anyone,' she whispered, 'who doesn't have *this*.'

She kissed him, trying not to think about the future, and soon she was lost in his lovemaking, and he in hers once more.

Because of her overwhelming need for Beau, she didn't notice as swiftly as she should have done that Laura was becoming unusually secretive in the next day or two, not only spending more time by herself in her room, but also declining Deb's offers to accompany her when she went shopping, and taking only Miss Champion.

Up till then Laura had been a lively and welcome distraction in the big house, what with her extravagant shopping expeditions, and her many friends who came to call. Often Deb looked on in amusement as Laura

showed all her latest purchases to her distinctly unim-
pressed big brother.

'You see this pink bonnet, darling Beau? It's quite
delightful, isn't it? And it only cost ten guineas! But I
do need a gown to go with it, in the latest style from
Paris. And I also think that I should have a horse and
gig of my own, to go out driving in the Park, so that all
the gentlemen fall in love with me. You do want me to
make a wealthy match, don't you?'

'My dear Laura,' answered her brother, 'I can't think
of a single gentleman in London who could afford to
keep you.'

Deb was always touched to see how kind and humor-
ous Beau was with his little sister. *What a lovely father
he would make...*

To think like that was lethal, and she knew it. And
then, suddenly, Laura seemed to change, and Deb saw
less and less of her. At first she worried in case Laura
suspected something, about her and Beau's relationship;
then one afternoon she came upon Miss Champion on
the steps outside the front door, talking in a hurried
voice to William, the coachman.

'Miss Champion?' Deb was puzzled. 'Miss Champion, I thought you'd gone shopping with Laura.'

Miss Champion, always nervous, looked almost
frightened. 'Lady Laura went to the theatre, Lady
Simon. There was an afternoon performance—a comedy, I believe...'

'She's gone on her own?'

'No—she went with her friend Helen, my lady, in a
hired coach. She didn't want me with her, she said she'd
be quite all right—'

Deb could see William looking grave. 'A *hired*

coach?' Deb exclaimed. 'You let Laura go out without you, in a hired coach?' What would Beau say? He would be livid.

Miss Champion flushed. 'I'm sorry, my lady. And since she's a little late back, I was asking William to go and find her.'

'I'll go straight away,' said William. From his expression, the Duke's coachman clearly regarded the situation as seriously as Deb did.

'Which theatre was it, Miss Champion?' Deb asked with sharpness in her voice. *Oh, the foolish woman. To let Laura run rings around her like this…*

'It's one of the small theatres over the river, I believe.' She looked even more frightened. 'Lady Laura told me the name, and I was trying to remember it for William, but I can't. Though I *can* remember the name of the entertainment. I've seen it on a poster. It's called *All For Love.*'

Deb uttered an exclamation. *All For Love* was a miscellany of songs and theatrical scenes put on by the Lambeth Players—they always staged a light afternoon show in advance of their main production. And *Twelfth Night*, she remembered, would begin later in the week.

'I know where to find Laura,' she told William swiftly. 'She'll have gone to the Dragon Theatre in Southwark. Wait for me, please. I'll get my hat and cloak, and I'll come with you.'

Beau was out, she knew, on business; and it was as well. He would be so very angry.

When they got to the Dragon, it was clear that the performance of *All For Love* had just ended, for dozens of people were spilling out into the street, laughing and talking eagerly to one another. *Always a good sign they've enjoyed it*, she registered automatically. And then—there amongst them was Laura, arm in arm with her friend Helen, chattering excitedly; but when Laura saw Deb her smile vanished.

Laura was the kind of girl, though, who could not be daunted for long, and she gave Deb a wave and hurried towards her. 'What are *you* doing here, Paulette?'

'I've come to take you home, Laura.' Deb forced herself to sound calm. 'Before your brother discovers that you've been out without Miss Champion. Do you realise that if he knew, he might forbid you to leave the house for a week or more?'

Laura's face fell. 'But he wouldn't…'

'I rather think he would. And I can't say that I blame him. I've tried to explain to you before that he makes these rules only because he cares about you very much.'

Laura looked rather pale. 'And I love him too, but… Oh, Paulette. You won't tell him, will you? *Please*?'

'I won't, no,' Deb said more gently. 'But you must go home, *now*, before Beau returns and finds out you aren't there. William's here to take you—he'll take Helen home too.'

Laura's friend Helen was looking anxious as well by now, and she gave a little sigh of relief. 'Thank you so much, Lady Simon.'

'Yes,' said Laura, 'thank you, dear Paulette. You're always so calm and understanding. I wish you lived with us *all* the time! And I'm sure Beau wishes that as well. You know, he's been *different* since you came to stay. Less sombre. Happier. And he likes you so much!'

Deb's heart was thudding. *Please. Please don't let this innocent girl ever guess about their nights together…*

'Hush now, Laura. In you get, into the carriage with Helen, and leave room for me. Look, William's up on the driver's seat, all ready to go. I'll just explain to him that he's to take Helen home first…'

But then she saw it. The gaudy playbill, posted to the wall of the Dragon Theatre.

Twelfth Night
by the Lambeth Players.
Starring Francis Calladine, Peggy Daniels and
all your favourites,
with Jack Bentall as Duke Orsino.

Her head swam. Jack. *Jack*?

She heard her name called and whirled round, to see Luke hurrying eagerly towards her along the crowded pavement. He was in a jester's costume; he must have just left the stage. Swiftly she turned back to William. 'Will you take the two girls home for me, please? There's someone I must speak to.'

'But, my lady, how will you…?'

'I'll take a hired carriage, William. Trust me, please—and say nothing of all this to his Grace, do you understand?'

William nodded. Slowly the big carriage moved off and Deb turned back to Luke, who had pulled up, uncertain, when he realised that she wasn't alone. But as soon as the carriage had departed, he spoke up again eagerly.

'Miss Deb, you've just missed our afternoon show—the theatre was packed! Francis guessed that you might be back to see us, with news of that theatre you were saying we might get—'

Deb cut in. 'Luke, listen to me…'

'We've got a new Orsino,' Luke said proudly, bubbling over with excitement. 'Old Joseph just couldn't remember his lines, so he and Peggy had an almighty row, and we've got Jack Bentall as Orsino instead! Do you remember him, Miss Deb?'

Luke had no idea—no one did—that Deb had reason to remember Jack Bentall all too well. 'I do,' she said. 'Luke, is Francis nearby? I need to speak to him, about Jack…'

'Deborah,' said Jack Bentall.

He'd strolled up behind her and now he stood there, smiling and arrogant; the same as ever. But she didn't think him handsome now. She didn't know how she ever could have found him handsome.

She turned to Luke. 'Will you leave Mr Bentall and me together, Luke, just for a few minutes?'

'Very well. But, Miss Deb, why don't you come to the performance next week, if you can? You'll be proud of us—won't she, Jack?'

'She certainly will,' said Jack, still smiling. 'Though Peg's not nearly as good a Viola as Deb would be.' His eyes roved her figure salaciously. 'But—all in black, Deb? *Expensive* black? What game are you playing now?'

She ignored him. 'Luke. *Go*,' she repeated more forcefully.

Luke left. She turned slowly back to Jack. *Hateful, hateful man*. Then—'What are you doing here, Jack?' she breathed.

'Me? Oh, I was booked for a run at the Haymarket, but the manager turned out to be a fool. So I decided to look around. Then I heard that the Lambeth Players needed an Orsino, and I've got rather fond memories of the Lambeth Players. I even heard that *you* were in charge of them, Deb. Sadly, you weren't around, but I decided to rejoin them anyway—for the time being.' He gave her his sleek grin. 'So here I am.'

She felt her heart drumming. 'I *am* still in charge of the Lambeth Players,' she breathed. 'And I would not have hired you if you were the last man on earth.'

'Such flattery,' he murmured. 'Don't worry, I haven't told a soul, sweet little Deb, about you and me. But, you know, you're looking really well. If you fancy a secret meeting one day, to relive old times...'

She was backing away. 'No. Never.'

He was watching her, one eyebrow raised. 'Now, you're not going to send me packing, I hope? I'm afraid it's a bit late for that—your play would be ruined, besides which I bring quite a few female admirers with me.' He was smiling now at some young women who'd stopped to gaze at him with interest. 'And you needn't worry that I'm pining for you, Deb. I'm after richer pickings these days, believe me. Though you can help me keep my bed warm any night you fancy—I've got a snug little room at the Red Lion Inn, only a short way from here—'

Deb slapped him.

He took a step backwards, rubbed his reddened cheek and laughed. 'I like a woman who has a bit of spirit,' he said, and strolled away, back towards the theatre.

Deb found a carriage to take her home, and as it rattled along over the bridge and towards Mayfair, she closed her eyes and pressed her hands to her cheeks. *Jack Bentall—lowering himself to act with her company.* Why?

He must have been dismissed from the Haymarket—

for his arrogance, perhaps. But soon enough even Jack Bentall was dashed from her mind. She'd entered the house and was about to climb the staircase to her room, when she heard footsteps behind her and realised Laura was there.

'I knew!' cried Laura. 'I *knew* you weren't Paulette! Helen told me that she saw you last year, on stage with the Lambeth Players. You're an actress, aren't you? But why…?'

Swiftly Deb led her into the nearest room, away from the servants. 'Laura, listen to me. It's really vital that you don't tell *anyone* that I'm not Paulette.'

'But Beau knows, of course?'

'Yes, Beau knows, but no one else. There are good reasons for all this, reasons that are very important to Beau and to the memory of Simon. Also, Laura—I'd be really grateful if you didn't tell Beau that I was talking to my friends from the Lambeth Players this afternoon.'

'All right. I promise,' said Laura obediently. 'But it's so exciting. You're an actress, a real actress…'

'Laura?'

'Yes?'

'Please don't go out without Miss Champion again, will you? You know that your brother wouldn't like it in the slightest.'

Laura gave her a lovely, dimply smile. 'We've both got secrets.' She nodded eagerly. 'And you and Beau—you like each other very much, don't you? It's all *so* romantic—but I won't say a thing! I *adore* secrets.'

Chapter Twenty

'My brother,' said Beau, his voice ringing clearly around the lofty pillars and stained glass windows of the crowded church, 'was taken from us too early. Many of you knew Simon when he was a boy. You will remember how kind he was—how generous, and full of life.'

Deborah sat on the front pew, with her black mourning veil pulled low. Laura, in black also, sat beside her. The church was full for Simon's memorial service. The congregation listened as one to Beau's words.

He holds them in the palm of his hand, she thought, just as a gifted actor would. Without apparent effort, his clear tones rang with warm resonance around St Margaret's church. He spoke with a calm and moving dignity, reminding them of everything that was good and kind about his younger brother—though God knew, thought Deb, there was another Simon, a Simon who'd resented and almost hated Beau. Who'd married Paulette because he thought that in doing so, he would be spiting his older brother.

But this was Simon's day. All that was good about Simon was being honoured, and that was why Deb was here, next to Laura, who had tears trickling down her cheeks. Deb reached out silently to hold her hand while gazing up at Beau, knowing the heartache that underlay his calm words.

Last night, the night before the service, he had come to her and he was in low spirits, she could tell. He'd stood there in her bedroom, loosening his black cravat, raking down his hair and looking so tired, and she'd gone over to him. The soft candlelight highlighted the frown that furrowed his brow and she raised her hands to cup his face.

'You did everything you could for Simon,' she said softly. '*Everything*.'

He said in a bleak voice, 'That still doesn't alter the fact that he's dead.'

'It was a tragedy, I agree. But it was not your fault—do you hear me? Not your fault.'

He held her almost fiercely, kissing the top of her hair, then breathing, 'I want you. I need you, Deborah, so badly. Stay in my life, please.'

They had talked till long after midnight. 'We can keep to our original plan,' he urged her. 'As Paulette, you can retreat to the countryside again, and vanish from society. But then—' and his grip on her tightened '—you can come back as Deb O'Hara of the Lambeth Players. And we can be together.'

'But people might guess...'

'Guess what?' he demanded. 'That you were Paulette for a few weeks?' He stroked her cheek. 'No. You're far lovelier than she was. You can let your hair grow long again, and swagger around in breeches and boots, and no one will know. No one.'

She was smiling—she couldn't help but smile and grow warm inside because of the sheer need for her that she saw in his eyes. 'But Beau—just *think*,' she pleaded. 'How can His Grace the Duke of Cirencester be seen around town with an actress?' Beneath her smile, her heart ached. *It's impossible. Impossible…*

He said steadily, 'I can think of no one I'd rather have at my side. I'm already going to provide your friends with a theatre. I will provide you with a house also, and I won't be ashamed of you, ever. Don't leave me.'

Her feelings for this man were overwhelming. *Beau, you must marry*, she thought to herself. *Some day you and I will have to part.* But then he was kissing her, and when he broke briefly away to begin to unbutton her gown, all she could say, rather breathlessly, was: 'We'll talk again. After the service, tomorrow. Shall we?'

They'd made love, and afterwards—after she'd sighed out his name and caressed him passionately until he lost his iron self-control and joined her in an extremity of pleasure—afterwards she thought, *I cannot bear to give him up yet. Please, God, not yet.*

Deb knew, of course, that he would not be able to come to her on the evening after the memorial service. He was hosting a reception for countless friends and relatives, which she attended for less than an hour, still veiled, accepting all their expressions of sympathy with murmured thanks. After that she retreated to her room, where Bethany helped her to undress, and she lay awake, reading by candlelight.

It was after midnight. Beau's guests were still below, she could hear their distant voices. They were all at the front of the house, in the first-floor reception rooms, but suddenly she heard another sound, from the rear of the house—from the garden. Guessing instantly that it was the sound of the gate in the far wall being carefully opened, she rose from her bed and tiptoed over to the window, to see in the moonlight that the gate was closing again.

Someone had just left. But she guessed also that someone had just come in.

Her heart filling with sudden, unnamed dread, she waited a few minutes, then pulled on a dressing robe and hurried along the passageway to knock softly at Laura's door. There was no answer, but she went in regardless, and saw Laura, still in a dark cloak, taking off her bonnet.

Laura backed away defensively when she realised Deb had come in. Deb closed the door and said, 'Laura. Please tell me you've not been out on your own.'

It was as if she'd unleashed a torrent of pent-up emotion in the younger girl. 'Yes,' Laura cried, 'I've been out to meet a friend, who's so kind to me, and so respectful! But Beau wouldn't understand. He just wouldn't!' Tears sparkled in the young girl's eyes.

Deb felt sick and panicky inside. 'Is your friend a man?'

Laura didn't reply. 'Listen,' Deb went on. 'Listen, Laura. You must see, surely, that no one—no man— who really cared for you would ask you to come out at night to meet him. No man would ask you to keep this a secret from your brother. You surely realise that Beau loves you so much; he only wants what's best for you.'

'But Jack loves me, and I love him! He's so handsome, he could have anyone—but it's *me* he wants, he's told me so! And Beau would only be stuffy and strict, about Jack being an actor…'

This time Deb was not only feeling sick, but the room was whirling about her. 'Laura. Don't tell me you've been seeing—Jack Bentall?'

'Why not?' The younger girl tilted her chin defiantly. 'My friend Helen took me to the theatre in Brighton to see him; she was wild about him, and so were all her friends. Then Helen and I realised that he was acting at the Dragon Theatre, and we went there together. The next day I went again on my own, and he came to talk to me. Since then I've met him several times. He's the most wonderful and talented actor in all of London!'

Deb fought to stay calm. 'Where have you been to-night?'

'Jack took me to the Vauxhall Gardens,' Laura said defiantly.

Deb closed her eyes. 'What about Miss Champion?'

'Oh, she's always sick, or has a headache. Tonight, she came in the carriage with me as far as the river; but then I told her to go home, and I went to meet Jack at the place we'd arranged.'

'So Miss Champion knew?'

'She guessed I was meeting someone, but I told her I was going *whatever* she said. And she's too scared of losing her position to report me to Beau.'

Foolish, foolish Miss Champion, thought Deb tiredly. Beau had been right to think her of no use at all.

'Besides,' went on Laura, 'Beau is so busy tonight, with all his guests.' She dashed some more tears from her eyes—the girl was overwrought, Deb realised, and her fragile, youthful emotions were dangerously stretched. 'You *must* understand,' Laura was emphasising. 'Jack loves me, and I love him, so much!'

'Laura,' Deb managed at last. 'With Jack—you've not let him…'

'Oh, no! He—well, he kissed me tonight, just once.' Laura blushed furiously, then continued fervently, 'But he says that he respects me far too much to want any more. And he *means* it, I'm sure, although he loves me wildly!'

Keep calm, Deb reminded herself over and over. *Don't frighten her, or she'll hate you.* 'Laura, you know very well, I think, that this is wrong. You know that your brother would not approve…'

'But this is *true love*. Nothing can stand in our way, Jack said! And he has asked me to marry him. Oh, I know that Beau would be aghast, but he will get used to it, he'll have to. Beau is *always* saying that he wants me to be happy—and, you see, I'm only happy when I'm with Jack!'

'Laura. Laura, please listen to me. You know you're not of age, so your brother would have to give his consent to your betrothal. And he's unlikely to, but that's only because he's thinking of your future, your happiness…'

Deb's voice trailed off as she saw the stubborn tilt to Laura's mouth. *She's just a child*, she thought despairingly. *Damn you, Jack Bentall*. A sudden, horrifying thought struck her. 'Laura, Jack hasn't suggested anything like elopement, has he?'

'And what if he has? We *love* each other, Deb, don't you see?'

If Deb's spirits could have sunk any lower, they did so there and then. *You needn't worry that I'm pining for you, Deb. I'm after richer pickings these days, believe me*. 'Laura,' she implored. 'You're very young. There are so many fine young men out there who will fall in love with you—but the best of them will proceed honourably. They won't court you in secret. They'll come to your brother, and ask his permission to meet with you, because they truly care for you…'

'Are you saying that Jack is *not* honourable?' Laura was crying bitterly now. 'Just because he's not rich? You cannot stop me seeing him. Beau cannot stop me seeing him. Jack is a wonderful, wonderful actor, and I'll never meet anyone else like him, never! Haven't you ever realised what it's like to be in love?'

She threw herself into Deb's arms and Deb comforted her, while Laura wept, 'I cannot stop seeing him. I cannot.'

'Darling,' said Deb gently, 'I'll go and make you a warm drink. I'll be back in a moment.'

Deb went downstairs. The big house was very silent. Beau would be sleeping upstairs, all his guests gone at last. He would turn perhaps in his dreams and reach out for her, murmuring her name.

A tremendous pain clutched at Deb's heart. She'd grown to love him, so very much. Yes, he was proud and powerful; but he was deeply honourable as well. He'd tortured himself over the sad course of his younger brother's life, and he'd taken upon himself all the burden of Simon's weaknesses. He'd shown nothing but protective, generous love to Laura. And he would be appalled at this latest turn of events.

She paced the cold kitchen and shuddered. What was Bentall hoping for? Did he really think he could elope with Laura to Gretna, or was he planning on perhaps blackmailing the Duke by asking for money to stay away from the girl? Bentall had underestimated the

Duke badly, if he thought he could succeed with *that*. But even if Beau managed to curtail this—even if Deb went to Beau now, and told him all this—Laura's heart would still be broken, and Laura would hate her brother for ruining her imagined happiness with Bentall.

Deb heated a little milk over the still-warm range, then took it upstairs. Laura had already changed into her nightgown, but was shivering; Deb made her wrap a shawl round her shoulders then sat her down, gave her the milk, and began to talk to her.

Better she suffers this now than later, she told herself inwardly, again and again. *Better for her now than later.*

Deb told Laura that Jack Bentall was her first lover. 'He seduced me,' she said calmly. 'When I was about your age. I was foolish, and innocent.'

She saw the growing disbelief and shock in the girl's face. 'Jack and you? No. No…'

'I'm afraid it's true, Laura. Though he tired of me quickly enough. He makes a habit of finding impressionable girls, but they don't last long with him unless they're rich.'

'Are you trying to say,' Laura whispered, 'that he picked on me because I'm the sister of a Duke?'

The heartbreak in her eyes was pitiful to see; Deb had to force herself to go on. 'I'm afraid so, yes. Jack is very ambitious. He has the talent to get to the top of his trade, but he could make even more money by enticing a Duke's sister to fall in love with him.'

'And by marrying me? But why not? Why *shouldn't* he marry me, when we love one another so much?'

Beau would never let his sister marry Jack Bentall. Never. 'I'm afraid—' Deb shrugged '—that it's more than likely Jack will be planning on demanding a large sum of money from your brother, to stay away from you. He'll know marriage to you is impossible—and neither will Jack want it, Laura. He's not one to be faithful to any woman for long.'

Laura's face was very white. 'You're jealous. You're jealous, because he didn't love you, but he loves me!'

'You'd better listen to me, then,' said Deb calmly. 'I'm afraid it's only a matter of days since Jack asked me to spend the night with him.'

Laura was trembling. 'No. *No.* You're lying.'

'I wish I were, but it really is true. I'm sorry, Laura.' *More sorry than you will ever know, to have to tell you this.*

Laura was silent a moment, then she sprang to her feet. 'I hate you. I hate you! I shall tell my brother that you've been meeting with your friends the Lambeth Players, and with Jack Bentall too! I shall tell him you ordered me not to say a word about it—but I shall tell him now!'

'I know you will,' whispered Deb, rising also. 'And I'm sure that your brother will still love you and care for you, Laura, as he always has done. As for me—I'm leaving.' She felt terribly cold all of a sudden.

Laura stared at her, hostility still blatant in her eyes, tears still trickling down her cheeks. 'Leaving to rejoin your actor friends? To be with Jack?'

'I've no desire to be with Jack again, as you put it,' Deb said quietly. 'But I'm going to deal with him. Believe me, I'm going to deal with him.'

Back in her own room, Deb changed into her old clothes—her breeches and shirt, her boy's jacket—and packed the few things that were hers. Then she just stood there.

She'd always known that it would have to end some time. She just hadn't realised that it was going to end like this. That her past and her present would collide so disastrously, in the shape of Jack Bentall and poor, heartbroken Laura. At least she hoped she had saved her from the wretch, for good. But what a stark reminder this was for her, of the impossible gulf that separated her world and Beau's.

She felt as if all hope, all feeling, had been brutally extinguished, leaving her hollow and icy-cold. Laura would blurt out everything to Beau—about the girl's youthful passion for Bentall, and Deb's part in destroying her dream. Laura would tell her brother that Deb was still meeting with the Players, and that Deb had asked Laura to keep quiet about her contact with them.

She would tell Beau not only that Deb and Jack had a past—which Beau already knew—but that Jack had, within the past few days, invited Deb to start their liaison anew. Beau would be appalled with her, and appalled to find that his own little sister had found her way into such hazardous company

Deb slipped outside with her old valise in her hand and made for the gate at the far end of the garden. As she carefully opened it, she gazed back once at the now-dark house. She could picture only too well Laura tearfully telling Beau—*I was so in love. But she's spoiled everything for me, and I hate her…*

Beau would be devastated, to realise the risks his little sister had run; but he would calmly offer the comfort that Laura so badly needed, with words of love and reassurance. He would hold his sister tightly, and help her to face her future, and show her that it would be full, some day, of love and happiness.

Thanks to Deb's confession, Laura was safe. This was Deb's last gift to Laura; and to the man she knew she would always love. He had burst into her life that day in the Ashendale Forest so unexpectedly, and he'd altered her life for ever. He'd made her irretrievably his.

But—their love for one another was always impossible, wasn't it?

Chapter Twenty-One

'Deb? Deborah, is it really *you*?'

She'd arrived amongst the Lambeth Players at nine the next morning. Her friends had gathered over their breakfast in the public room of the inn next door to the theatre, and it was Francis who saw her first, jumping up to greet her with a cry of welcome.

She'd spent the night at a cheap lodging house nearby, sleeping very little, and when she did she dreamed of Beau, imagining the utter contempt on his face when Laura told him her news. Now, Deb's friends surrounded her; but their faces were anxious.

'It was meant to be our first performance of *Twelfth Night* this evening, Deborah,' Francis was telling her. 'But Peggy has quite lost her voice.'

'Oh, Francis! So you've no Viola?'

'No Viola. And it's worse than that. Jack Bentall's upped and disappeared in the night. His landlady from the Red Lion down the road was here first thing, complaining that he's gone in the night. Vanished completely—without paying his bill. I never did trust him, and this means we've no one to play Duke Orsino either.'

'We've got *you*, Francis,' Deb said steadily.

'But I told you—I'm Malvolio. I'm *always* Malvolio.'

Deb looked around and saw Luke standing listening. 'Luke can play Malvolio for a change. Can't you, Luke?' Luke almost jumped for joy. 'There we are, then,' Deb concluded. 'And I'm sure you know Orsino's part, Francis.'

'But I'm a little old…'

'Nonsense. You'll be a *wonderful* Orsino.'

Francis's face brightened, then sank again. 'But what's the use of me being Orsino, if we've no Viola?'

Deb looked around them all, thinking, *These are my friends. I owe them so much.* 'I'll play Viola,' she said. They gave cries of delight. 'But we need to rehearse,' she went on. 'We need to get started, right now. The show has to go on.' She took a deep breath and smiled. 'We are the Lambeth Players, after all.'

Jack Bentall wouldn't be back. As she organised them and encouraged them in their final rehearsal, she remembered how last night, after leaving Beau's house, she'd gone straight to the Red Lion and found Jack Bentall in the tap room with a plump barmaid on his lap.

'Deb!' He'd looked startled, then slowly began to smile and eased the protesting barmaid away. 'Little Deb, come to see me for old times' sake.'

She walked steadily up to him. 'I'm going to make this brief. I've come to tell you that the Lambeth Players don't want you any more, Jack. Not *ever*. Do you understand?'

His face darkened. 'But the play starts tomorrow. And I have a contract—'

'Not any longer,' she interrupted. 'I'm in charge. Remember?'

After that she'd turned and left him there, openmouthed.

Beau could not believe it. He *would* not believe it. His little sister had come to him late last night almost incoherent with grief, sobbing through her tears about some wretched actor and how she loved him.

'But Deb knows him too!' she wept. 'And she said such dreadful things about him!'

The first thing that slammed into his mind was that Laura knew Deb wasn't Paulette. The second was that Deborah had gone. That was made plain enough the instant he pushed open her bedroom door and saw everything so tidy; the bed unslept in, her few things—including that old brown valise—gone.

He turned to his sister, who had followed him. 'What was this actor's name, Laura?'

'Jack,' she whispered. She started crying again. 'Jack Bentall. She said—she said she knew him a long time ago. And he's been after her *again*, Beau. She said she didn't care for him, but she must have been lying—she's most likely gone to him, tonight...'

No, thought Beau, a fierce rage gripping him. No. He remembered Deborah's expression when she described to him her one and only encounter with Jack Bentall years ago. She'd said she detested the man, and he believed her. He believed her when she told him she'd let no man touch her since Bentall, until the day he, Beau, kissed her in the forest...

After that Beau comforted his little sister and saw her to bed, and only when she was settled and half-asleep did he say very quietly, 'Laura. This Jack. I think you know what I'm going to ask. He didn't do anything to you, did he, my dear, that you wouldn't want me to know about?'

'He kissed me, Beau,' Laura whispered. 'That was all.' A single tear ran down her cheek.

And that, swore Beau as he finally left her, was the only reason the wretched Jack Bentall would be allowed to live. He returned to his own room, where he tried to settle down to sleep but couldn't, and dawn found him pacing the floor, dressed and restless.

Deborah. Why had she told Laura about what had happened between her and Jack Bentall?

The only reason he could think of was that she'd done it in order to *save* his sister from the wretch. She detested Bentall. Even if Laura was right, and Bentall had made fresh approaches to Deb recently, she would have rejected them—because she loved him, Beau. He was utterly sure of it, and he was going to take appropriate action.

He stopped by his window as a cool dawn mist stole over London's rooftops. Beau's life as an aristocrat had confirmed for him that very few men could be trusted, let alone women, and he'd long ago decided that his own best course was to build an iron wall around his own heart. His mask of cynicism had become a integral part of him, until one day—he'd been lying tied up in the forest, for God's sake—a certain Miss Deborah O'Hara had come into his life. She'd struck him as clever, and daring and beautiful, and...

And brave. Searingly, honestly brave.

He didn't believe for one moment that she would

willingly associate with Bentall again. And he couldn't live without her. That was the truth of it.

Before taking his breakfast, he'd summoned Armitage and told him to send out his investigators—*his minions*, Deb had called them—to track down Bentall. Now, they were back. He went downstairs to talk with them in his study, and they told him that Jack Bentall had, last night, left the Red Lion inn in Southwark quite unexpectedly.

'He hurried off without paying his bill, your Grace. We hunted around and found that he spent the night in a cheap lodging house nearby. It appears that he's no longer one of the Lambeth Players.'

'You're sure?'

'As sure as we can be, yes. They started rehearsals at nine this morning—they're putting on a play at the Dragon Theatre tonight—but this Bentall was still abed.'

Beau glanced at his pocket watch. 'Then we'll give him a morning surprise that he won't forget,' he said.

It was a warm summer evening and dusk was enfolding London. The dome of St Paul's gleamed in the fading light, and the boatmen were busy ferrying people across the Thames from Westminster to Vauxhall, to the gardens and the busy inns and the theatres clustered along the south bank.

The stage of the Dragon Theatre was open to the sky, and Deb could see some early bright stars twinkling overhead as she stood and clasped her hands together. *'She never told her love, But let concealment, like a worm i'the bud, feed on her damask cheek. She sat like patience on a monument, smiling at grief.'*

Shakespeare's beautiful words about forlorn love had never seemed so apt. She *was* the broken-hearted Viola. Deb poured out her emotions to the people crammed on the tiered benches that were arranged on three sides of the stage. She didn't have to raise her voice to be heard, because although all the seats were full, the audience was completely lost in the magic of the play.

And Deb was thinking of Beau. Always of Beau. *She never told her love…*

She was even wearing the kind of clothes she'd been in when she first met him—breeches, a shirt and a boy's jacket, because of course Viola was dressed as a man for most of the play and was secretly, heartbreakingly in love with her Duke Orsino, just as Deb was with Beau.

There never could be anyone but Beau. As they reached the end of the play, there was a moment of stillness—of utter silence. And then the applause began to ring out, and the cheers; Deb bowed low, and realised some were getting to their feet; they were throwing flowers to her, and calling out her name. They'd adored the play. She should be happy. But how could she go on, without Beau in her life?

She loved him so much, but she could never see him again, and of course she knew that he would never have the slightest wish to see *her*. Laura would have told him about Jack Bentall; how Laura had entered into a dangerous liaison with him; how Deb herself had seen him again, only recently, without telling Beau…

She almost shivered as she pictured the ferocity of his emotions. As she imagined the contempt he must feel for her, for keeping something so vital from him.

Oh, Beau.

By now the entire audience was on its feet, whistling and clapping, begging for an encore. 'Viola!' they were calling. 'Viola!' And suddenly she couldn't keep this fixed smile on her face a second longer. She began to go; Francis moved to stop her. 'Deborah? Is everything all right?'

'Everything's fine, Francis.' But then she *wasn't* fine. Something—no, someone—had caught her eye: a tall man with black hair, who was shouldering his way through the cheering audience, his face set with determination. And Deb was frozen to the spot.

Beau.

Breathe, Deb, you idiot. Remember to breathe…

His eyes not once leaving her, Beau climbed the stairs to the stage two at a time. And while the rest of the actors were taking yet another bow, he strode towards her, he caught her in his arms, and he kissed her, hard.

She glimpsed Francis's face, and the faces of the other actors. They were astounded, and the audience went wild, thinking it was part of the entertainment. Beau kissed her so thoroughly that she could scarcely stand, and so Beau picked her up in his arms very tenderly, and carried her from the stage—to the greatest chorus of bravos and huzzahs that Deb had ever heard in her life.

Beau wanted to kiss her again the instant they'd left the stage, but instead he said, 'You're coming with me now. Aren't you?'

'Yes,' she whispered. *'Yes*. But I'll just have to tell my friends…'

'I'll wait for you outside,' Beau warned. 'And if you don't join me in five minutes, I'm coming for you again. Do you understand?'

'Yes,' she said again. She stood on tiptoe to kiss his lips softly. 'I understand.'

Of course, before she left she had to placate a horrified Francis.

'But it's Mr Beaumaris, Deb,' Francis objected. 'You know what we did to *him*!'

'Of course,' she answered calmly. 'We tied him up in the forest and kept him prisoner for the night.' *And he's come for me. He doesn't hate me. He's come here for me.*

Francis's mouth opened and closed. 'But you can't go off with him! Surely he'll have us clapped in irons—'

Deb touched his hand to stop him. 'He won't, Francis.' This time she couldn't suppress her dazzling smile. 'It's all right, believe me. Everything's going to be all right.'

'You mean—you trust him?'

'I do,' she said quietly. 'With my life.'

She could see now that Beau was waiting for her by the door. 'Oh, and by the way, Francis,' she said, turning back to him, 'he's *not* Mr Beaumaris. He's actually the Duke of Cirencester.'

Francis's face was a picture.

They travelled back to Albemarle Street in Beau's coach. And scarcely had the carriage—driven by William—moved off, when Beau gathered her once more in his arms and said, 'I know everything. About the despicable Bentall and my sister. Laura told me. She also told me that you'd seen him recently—she suspected there was something between you, but I didn't believe you would tolerate the rogue's presence for a second longer than you had to. So I paid a visit myself on Jack Bentall.'

She looked dazed. 'You...'

He put his finger gently on her lips. 'Apparently, last night he left a local inn called the Red Lion because someone—a rather spirited young woman—had come to give him a mighty tongue-lashing.' His eyes gleamed with humour. '*You*, I believe, Miss O'Hara. Bentall spent the rest of the night in a cheap lodging house—where my men found him this morning.'

'You set your minions to work?' she breathed.

'My minions.' He nodded. 'I went first thing this morning to speak to Jack Bentall—about my sister, and about *you*. Bentall made the mistake of trying to tell me that Laura had lured him on.'

Deb's eyes were anguished. 'Beau. I'm sure she didn't. It's just that she's so innocent. So trusting...'

'As you were, I imagine,' he said, 'when Bentall seduced you.'

She nodded. 'And please believe me. I only met him by chance in Southwark the other day. And I was horrified to learn that he was with the Lambeth Players. I hated having to see him again, and to speak with him.'

'I do believe you.' His gaze was steady; he'd wrapped one of her hands in his. 'You must have hated having to tell Laura about your past with the rogue. But you were thinking of *her* all the time, weren't you? Ensuring that she would realise what a despicable creature he was. And then, I gather, you went straight away to see Bentall at the inn and told him he was no longer part of your theatre troupe. He's had an uncomfortable time, since I also visited Bentall at his latest abode this morning, and I gave him a few home truths that should ensure he won't be showing his face in London for quite some time. Especially,' he added thoughtfully, 'as his features are now rather bruised.'

'Oh, Beau.' She gazed at him, wide-eyed. 'You didn't…'

'He was foolish enough to try to throw a punch at me,' he answered calmly. 'But he'd got the wrong man. His face won't be quite so pretty for a while, but he'll recover. And I think we can be quite sure that he won't, ever, dare to breathe a word of all this.'

She thought to herself, *Beau believed her. He trusted her.* Whatever happened now, she could bear it. Almost. *Almost…*

Beau was still talking. 'I realise, of course, that your actors had to cope at very short notice tonight without Bentall. Though that companion of yours—Francis, I believe his name was—did a good job of replacing him. I must say he's better at acting than he was at keeping me prisoner in the forest.'

Deb's heart stopped. *He recognised Francis.* Of course he did…

'We'll have to go about finding a new theatre for your friends soon,' Beau was saying steadily. 'They deserve it. They were good. And *you* were breathtaking.' He took her face in his hands and turned it up to his. 'I don't want to be apart from you again, Deborah O'Hara. Ever. Do you understand me? Not ever.'

Beau ordered supper to be brought up to his rooms— cold chicken and bread and wine—and Deb suddenly realised that she'd not eaten all day. Beau ate very little, but watched her and filled her glass, and when she was replete he drew her on to his bed; not so they could make love, but just so he could talk to her, while holding her in his arms. To make sure this time that she could not escape.

'I don't want to be parted from you again,' he told her. 'When Laura confessed to me last night about her meeting with Jack Bentall, and I realised what it must have cost you to tell her what you did, I could have torn Bentall into pieces—especially when I found you'd gone. By then, of course, I was starting to realise the whole story. How brave you'd been. How self-sacrificing.' He took her hand to kiss it. 'As for me, I've done nothing in my dealings with you of which I can be particularly proud. In fact, a great deal of the time my conduct has been despicable.'

'No. Never,' she breathed. 'I've misled *you*, remember!' She blushed, remembering the forest, and the books.

'Well—a little,' he admitted, touching her cheek tenderly. 'But only, I'd guess, because I was so impossibly overbearing and arrogant. I just want you to know—that I love you, Deborah O'Hara. And I cannot imagine my life without you.'

'But you're a Duke. I'm—*nothing.*'

'Listen,' he said. 'I've thought it all out. You, as Paulette, will retreat to the countryside again, for good—and we know already that the real Paulette will never return.' He took her hand again. 'So you can continue to be who you've always been—Deb O'Hara, a wonderful actress. And I shall court you, ardently. After all, it's only a few years since the Earl of Derby swept Elizabeth Farren from the stage of the Haymarket Theatre and made her his wife. Why shouldn't I marry Miss O'Hara?'

'But…'

He put his finger to his lips to silence her. 'You're going to mention your illegitimacy. But do you think I care? That's one advantage of wealth—I don't need to take any heed whatsoever of the gossip and whispering that might arise. Yes, some tongues will wag for a Season or two, but we're going to ride this out together. The men of the *ton*, at least, will adore you. You will be a sensation.'

She was silent. He watched the emotions playing across her beautiful, expressive face, and he began to feel cold fingers of fear at his heart. *To lose her. To lose her, now...*

She was gazing up at him. 'But, Beau, have you thought about this? Really *thought* about it? Surely, you could marry anyone in the world.'

'But I don't want to marry anyone in the world,' he pointed out. 'I want to marry *you*. I love you, very much. And if you can find it in you to love me back...'

'Oh, Beau,' she whispered. 'Oh, Beau.'

He watched her, hardly daring to hope. 'Does this mean that...?'

She flung herself into his arms and kissed him, revelling in the roughness of his jaw against her sensitive skin. 'Darling, foolish man. Don't you realise that I fell in love with you the very first moment I saw you?'

He was laughing now, a beautiful, husky chuckle that melted her soul. 'Even though I was tied up? Muddy? Furious with you?'

'Oh, yes,' she said, putting her finger to his cheek thoughtfully. 'I saw your...*potential*, you see. Though I was a little taken aback to discover you were the Duke of Cirencester.'

'But do you think you can tolerate being my Duchess?'

She gazed at him, this man she loved, thinking of his strength and his tenderness, and the way he made love to her… *Oh, the way he made love to her.*

She wrapped her arms around his neck and softly said, 'I think, darling Beau, that I can indeed tolerate being by your side and loving you night after night for the rest of my life. Is that the right answer?'

'It's exactly the right answer,' Beau breathed. 'Wait. I have something for you.'

Deb watched in wonder as he went to a chest of drawers and took out—a blue-velvet jewel box. *The Brandon jewels.* Easing himself back beside her on the bed, he drew them out, and the diamonds and rubies blazed like fire in his strong hands.

'Once,' he said steadily, 'you rebuked me for going to such trouble to get these back—only to lock them away again. *Never to be seen*, you said. Well, now they are most definitely going to be seen.'

Very carefully, very tenderly, he fastened the heavy, priceless necklace around the slender column of her throat. 'You're going to wear them, my darling. For me.'

She touched the jewels with fingers that trembled slightly. 'Beau. I cannot. They're so very valuable…'

'You think so?' he responded. 'They're nothing to me, compared to you. All my wealth is nothing, compared to you.'

She flung her arms around his neck, pressing her face to his chest as she strove to control her emotion. 'Oh, Beau. I misjudged you, so much…'

That made his eyes glint wickedly. 'I thought you said that you fell in love with me straight away?'

She drew back from him a little and pouted. 'Well,

I did, of course! How could I help it? But then everything went so wrong, and…'

'And now,' said Beau huskily, 'everything is going to be perfect. Especially as you are, I hope, about to kiss me.'

He wrapped his arms around her and she lifted her mouth to his with a blissful sigh.

* * * * *

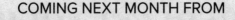

REQUEST YOUR FREE BOOKS!

 HARLEQUIN® HISTORICAL:
Where love is timeless

2 FREE NOVELS PLUS 2 FREE GIFTS!

YES! Please send me 2 FREE Harlequin® Historical novels and my 2 FREE gifts (gifts are worth about $10). After receiving them, if I don't wish to receive any more books, I can return the shipping statement marked "cancel." If I don't cancel, I will receive 6 brand-new novels every month and be billed just $5.44 per book in the U.S. or $5.74 per book in Canada. That's a savings of at least 16% off the cover price! It's quite a bargain! Shipping and handling is just 50¢ per book in the U.S. and 75¢ per book in Canada.* I understand that accepting the 2 free books and gifts places me under no obligation to buy anything. I can always return a shipment and cancel at any time. Even if I never buy another book, the two free books and gifts are mine to keep forever.

246/349 HDN F4ZY

Name	(PLEASE PRINT)
Address	Apt. #
City	State/Prov.	Zip/Postal Code

Signature (if under 18, a parent or guardian must sign)

Mail to the **Harlequin® Reader Service:**
IN U.S.A.: P.O. Box 1867, Buffalo, NY 14240-1867
IN CANADA: P.O. Box 609, Fort Erie, Ontario L2A 5X3

Want to try two free books from another line?
Call 1-800-873-8635 or visit www.ReaderService.com.

* Terms and prices subject to change without notice. Prices do not include applicable taxes. Sales tax applicable in N.Y. Canadian residents will be charged applicable taxes. Offer not valid in Quebec. This offer is limited to one order per household. Not valid for current subscribers to Harlequin Historical books. All orders subject to credit approval. Credit or debit balances in a customer's account(s) may be offset by any other outstanding balance owed by or to the customer. Please allow 4 to 6 weeks for delivery. Offer available while quantities last.

Your Privacy—The Harlequin® Reader Service is committed to protecting your privacy. Our Privacy Policy is available online at www.ReaderService.com or upon request from the Harlequin Reader Service.

We make a portion of our mailing list available to reputable third parties that offer products we believe may interest you. If you prefer that we not exchange your name with third parties, or if you wish to clarify or modify your communication preferences, please visit us at www.ReaderService.com/consumerschoice or write to us at Harlequin Reader Service Preference Service, P.O. Box 9062, Buffalo, NY 14269. Include your complete name and address.

HHI3R

"Welcome to Strone Bridge."

Ainsley smiled weakly, clutching tight to Innes, her legs
trembling on the wooden planking. "I'm sorry, I think my
legs have turned to jelly."

"You don't mean your heart? I'm not sure what you've
let yourself in for here, but I am pretty certain things are in
a bad way. I'll understand if you want to go back to Edin-
burgh."

"Your people are expecting you to arrive with a wife. A
fine impression it would make if she turned tail before she'd
even stepped off the pier—or more accurately, judging by
the state of it, stepped through it. Besides, we made a bargain, and I plan to stick to my part of it." Ainsley tilted her
head up at him, her eyes narrowed, though she was smiling.
"Are you having cold feet?"

"Not about you." He hadn't meant it to sound the way
it did, like the words of a lover, but it was too late to retract. He pulled her roughly against him, and he kissed her,
forgetting all about his resolution to do no such thing. Her
lips were freezing. She tasted of salt. The thump of luggage

being tossed with no regard for its contents from the boat to the pier made them spring apart.

Ainsley flushed. "It is a shame we don't have more of an audience, for I feel sure that was quite convincing."

Innes laughed. "I won't pretend that had anything to do with acting the part of your husband. The truth is, you have a very kissable mouth, and I've been thinking about kissing you again since the first time all those weeks ago. And before you say it, it's got nothing to do with my needing an emotional safety valve either and everything to do with the fact that I thoroughly enjoyed it, though I know perfectly well it's not part of our bargain."

"Save that it can do no harm to put on a show now and then," Ainsley said with a teasing smile.

"Does that mean you'll only kiss me in public? I know there are men who like that sort of thing, but I confess I prefer to do my lovemaking in private."

"Innes! I am sure we can persuade the people of Strone Bridge we are husband and wife without resorting to—to engaging in public marital relations."

Don't miss
STRANGERS AT THE ALTAR!

Available December 2014, wherever
Harlequin® Historical books and ebooks are sold.

HHEXP1114

HARLEQUIN®

HISTORICAL

Where love is timeless

COMING IN DECEMBER 2014

Outlaw Hunter
by Carol Arens

An outlaw's wife...

With her home burned down, her outlaw husband believed
dead and five children entrusted to her care, Melody Dawson
must leave the ashes of her past behind to start afresh...

And an outlaw hunter...

Atoning for a youthful mistake, US marshal Reeve Prentis has
made tracking down criminals his life's work. His dangerous
job has always demanded a solitary existence, yet escorting
Melody across the Wild West has Reeve longing for change,
and a family of his own!

Available wherever books and ebooks are sold.

HH29811

3750

HARLEQUIN®

HISTORICAL

Where love is timeless

COMING IN DECEMBER 2014

Captured Countess
by Ann Lethbridge

Never trust a spy!

Nicoletta, the Countess Vilandry, is on a dangerous
mission—to lure fellow spy Gabriel D'Arcy into bed and
into revealing his true loyalties. With such sensual games at
play and such strong sensations awakened, suddenly Nicky's
dangerously close to exposing her real identity.

Gabe knows that the countess has been sent to seduce him.
The only question is to what end? He's never met such a
captivating woman—and he's determined to enjoy every
seductive second she spends as his very *willing* captive!

Available wherever books and ebooks are sold.